≈

RIPPLES

≈

≈

RIPPLES

≈

R. J. SUNDEAN

RJSUNDEAN.COM

Dedicated to my parents, Alan and Elaine,
for always believing in me.

CHAPTER 1

THE ENDING THAT BEGINS

Orchard Lake.

The typical American small town. The perfect small town you always read about in books. The one always portrayed on the random postcards you can find in every single gift shop.

A total of three traffic lights run the length of town, part of a three-for-one deal with the County when the town originally purchased the lights, and all of them are located on the single main street that runs through the center of town. Bell's Supermarket, located at the southernmost intersection with the first traffic light, is the only grocery store in town and handles the shopping needs of the whopping two hundred people who populate Orchard Lake at any given time. Sam's Sundries & Gas Station is located at the intersection with the middle traffic light, and Sam is extremely proud of that light. He makes sure to point out to every customer who walks through the door how the light helps everyone in town make it to his store safely.

Sometimes it's the little things in life you have to hold on to. The third and northernmost traffic light merely ensures that tourists who are passing through don't speed out of town as fast as they can. Beyond that, the town has two schools, a fire department, a post office, a car wash depot, a small walk-in clinic with a single doctor, and a police station, but each are located slightly off the beaten path and not visible from the main thoroughfare. There is also one solitary restaurant, Ellie's, which doubles as a bar in the evenings. Or in the mornings, if a little hair of the dog is your kind of thing.

However, unlike the postcards you always see, this quaint, classic, small town isn't always sunshine and blue skies. More often than not, it's raining on this happy little town. It was raining yesterday.

It's supposed to be rain again today.

Then again, it's always raining when you work at the car wash. It's never as exciting as the movies and songs make it out to be. With time, every car and truck begins to look the same. Dirty. Scratched. Unloved by the owner. The loved cars are never brought to the car wash. Probably because the protective owners hand wash those cars at home. Colin thinks about the cars as they come to the car wash again and again, always in the same condition, realizing it soon begins to become the mantra for your life. Dirty. Scratched. Definitely unloved by the owner.

Colin checks the level of the cleaning chemicals in the pumping system and watches the next car drive up to the stop block so the automated treadmill can carry the car through the cleaning brushes. He nods at the driver, who is focused on their cell phone and not paying any attention to him. He wonders when he became an outcast, although he already knows the answer. He thinks back to what he likes to call his glory days: his high school days, as stereotypical as it sounds. The days when he was the star, the popular one, the one who everyone wanted to hang out with and who everyone secretly wanted to be. . The person who was never ignored by anyone. Star quarterback for the Orchard Lake Mustangs. Undefeated state champions for his entire four years of high school. A fiercely loyal girlfriend, an amazing best friend, free beer even though he was underage, no rules, and no consequences. He smiles as he reminisces; now paying as much attention to the latest customer as he is to him, and once again the incessant spray of water from the car wash jets fall around Colin.

"My life was like a real-life version of every perfect teen movie you could think of," he tells the falling droplets around him. "Except the fairy tale I was living didn't have the perfect little ending you would expect from the movie."

Reality snaps back into place with the loud honk of an impatient customer waiting their turn in the line.

"Yeah, yeah, I'm coming," he mutters as he waves and nods at the elderly woman scowling behind the wheel of her oversized Lincoln. It never ceases to amaze him how so few people can comprehend the simple concept of inserting the correct amount of money into the automated machine to start the washing process. It's a small town, and almost all of the cars in line today are repeat business. You would think practically everyone would have learned to understand the concept by now. *Then again,* Colin realizes, *it's always the elderly coming through the line who need help with the payment machine. Maybe they want me to feel needed, since all I really do is to make sure nothing stops working in the automated line and if it does stop, a quick call to the corporate office up north in Shelton takes care of the issue.* Shelton is a large metropolitan city about ninety miles north of Orchard Lake, and it is the commercial hub for just about every town within one hundred miles in each direction. It has a large mall, just about every chain restaurant and store you could think of, and boasts a population of several million people. Colin makes a trip up there once a month to pick up supplies for the car wash that are unavailable for him to pick up here in town.

The elderly woman honks her horn again, waving frantically with a handful of ones at Colin.

He frowns. The honking irritates him, and he wishes they would just insert the money on their own, leaving him to his thoughts.

Just another day in the rain, he surmises.

Eight o'clock comes around quickly though, and Colin is happy to shut down all the equipment. Time to head home, enjoy a cold beer, and see the only reason he keeps going every day: his daughter, Penny. Eighteen going on twenty-five, too smart and too pretty for her own good, and nothing like her father. Which is good, Colin ponders, since she seems to have no interest in dating even with the incessant stream of random guys calling the house asking for her. By the time he was sixteen, he had already dated or slept with half the girls at school and had his fair share of pregnancy scares. He didn't want to think about how he would react if his little girl came home and told him she was pregnant. Every father's worst nightmare, he guesses, even if he may have caused a few of those same nightmares for other fathers while he was a young buck himself. But Penny, she's too smart for that. A straight-A student and adamant about going on to college to become a doctor, most of her time is split between her studies and her internship at the local walk-in clinic. Her evenings, though, are usually reserved for time with her dad. And Colin is thankful for their time together. If anything good has come from his dead-end life, it's Penny. His little hummingbird.

The neon of the CLOSED sign hums as it lights up. Bugs begin to flock to the bright light as if it is a red, glowing lighthouse offering guidance in the dark. Colin locks up the door to the room with the cleaning chemicals and walks over to his beat-up truck. He sighs. *What happened to me*, he wonders. *How did my life, at thirty five, end up like this? At what point did everything start going wrong?* It could have been when his high school best friend Nick was killed overseas while serving in the military. It could have been when he dropped out of college to work full-time. It could have been when Alicia, the mother of his little girl and the love of his life, left him without any explanation at all. Then again, it could have been any number of mistakes he made in the last ten years that slowly snowballed and finally turned into the reality he now lives in. Either way, Colin doesn't see a way to escape this situation without making life harder on him and on Penny. Maybe when she goes away to college, he will try to find a new job in a new city, far away from the memories that haunt him every day here. Especially the memory of Alicia. One day, everything was perfect; he was working up in Shelton as a construction supervisor and had the pleasure of coming home to a beautiful, smiling wife and an adorable baby daughter, who would laugh at everything. The next day, Alicia was gone without taking anything at all; and Colin was left with their daughter, confused and terrified on how he could still maintain his job out of town while still supporting and caring for Penny. Shortly after Alicia left, the people of Orchard Lake—people who Colin had known his entire life—began to avoid him. Shy away from him in public. As if they were blaming him for Alicia's disappearance. It didn't matter to him. All that mattered was that Penny was taken care of. Sacrifices were made, but Colin doesn't regret a single one when it comes to his little hummingbird, who was growing into an amazing young lady he was exceptionally proud of. He just wishes he could have done better, given her more.

A flash of lightning erupts overhead and the distant rumble of thunder could be felt. *Looks like the car wash won't be the only place with rain tonight.* Colin laughs a little, thinking about how every customer who came through today is probably cursing the skies right now. He hops into his truck and fires up the ignition. The radio kicks on and fills the cab with the sound of Sinatra. He puts the truck into drive, turns the wheel, and heads down the road toward home.

The drive home is eventless. Same three street lights, same deputy parked at Sam's who pretends to radar the few passing cars; everyone in town knows Deputy Gates is actually sleeping with the radar gun propped up on his dashboard. Colin honks his horn as he drives by the corner store and watches the unsuspecting Deputy Gates startle from his nap, then shoot a quick glare at Colin's truck. *Sometimes you have to take pleasure in the little things, like Sam does with his traffic light*, Colin thinks.

The road is empty tonight. Most of the town turns in pretty early on the weekdays. Even the listless youth of the town tends to call it a night after dark sets in. One joy of small-town life is that there is never very much to do once the stores close, unless you go down to Ellie's for a few drinks, although all the rain lately is probably even keeping the regular barflies at home. Colin turns down the street leading to his house and finds solace in the fact there are only three other houses on his street. The lights are off in all of them as he drives by. Pulling into his driveway, Colin is happy to see the kitchen light and living room lights at his house are on. It means Penny's home, and she is probably making something for dinner. He turns off the ignition, gets out of the truck, and heads inside.

Penny is at the counter in the kitchen, focused on cutting up the tomato she has in front of her without spraying its innards all over the place. Music is playing from the radio on the counter, fighting for dominance with the sounds of the knife on the cutting board. The singer repeats the hook multiple times before the computerized beat takes over again. Colin can't remember the name of the pop singer, but knows he's heard the song before. All the music the kids listen to these days seems to be the same to Colin. The same beat, the same auto-tuned voice singing minimal lyrics with a catchy hook. Penny looks up from the cutting board and grins.

"Hi, Dad!" she yells over the song. She then sets the knife down and dances over to the little portable speaker tube, turning the music down to a more tolerable level. "I hope you like BLTs. I couldn't find much else in the cupboard to make."

Colin nods at her and smiles. "Thank you, hummingbird. You have a good day at school today?" he asks while making a mental note to get up to Bell's to restock the groceries soon.

Her grin expands. Colin's happy that, even at her current age, she doesn't shy away from the nickname he gave her the very first time he saw her after she was born, with her bright eyes darting back and forth between him and Alicia, like a little hummingbird flying from flower to flower. "It was the same. Mrs. Ansly gave us an English paper to write, but it's not due for a few weeks. I spent a couple hours at the clinic helping out after school, but only two people came in. Apparently, Mr. Tams has a cold and he insists his son gave it to him. Only his son isn't sick. And Ms. Page came in blaming the position of the moon for her migraines again." Colin laughs. Ms. Page is the town's very own lunar cycle specialist, or so she calls herself. She's entertaining in small doses, but any conversation with her than lasts over ten minutes makes Colin want to turn and walk away quickly. "As soon as I'm done cutting the tomatoes, dinner will be ready".

Colin gives his daughter two thumbs-up, walks to the fridge, and pulls open the door. He reaches in and grabs a beer. Twisting off the top, he walks into the living room, sits down in his easy chair, and turns on the television. A news reporter appears on the screen, talking about the latest missing body from a cemetery a few towns north. Colin shakes his head. These stories have been all over the news the last few months, and according to this latest report, over fifty bodies have been dug up and stolen since the discovery of the first empty grave site. He frowns. What kind of sick person goes around stealing corpses? *Then again, at least they aren't kidnapping living people*, he thinks, as Penny's voice while she sings along with the song on her radio carries into the living room. He looks at his little girl. He doesn't want to think about what would happen if he ever lost her. Losing Alicia was hard enough, and the lack of any sort of explanation lead to several very rough years, and now Penny is all he has left.

The music in the kitchen abruptly shuts off, and Penny bounds into the living room carrying two plates, each with a carefully made BLT and some potato chips. "Dinner is served, Daddy-o," she quips while handing over a plate. "And I slaved over a hot stove to make this meal so I think you owe me a trip to the mall in Shelton so I can do some shopping this weekend."

"Slaved over a hot stove…or danced in front of a toaster and a microwave for thirty seconds?" he retorts.

She huffs at him, mumbles something about it being more like a few minutes versus thirty seconds, and sits down on the couch, taking a bite out of her sandwich as the reporter launches into the weather report. As the well-dressed man begins to talk about all the rain that would be coming through the area for the next couple days, Colin can only wonder if he is reporting the weather or reporting Colin's life.

With the sound of thunder once again echoing in the distance, Colin finishes his beer and sandwich. He gets up out of the chair, heads into the kitchen, and puts the plate in the sink. He then wishes his little hummingbird a good night and heads into his room to get some sleep.

As he walks into his room, he is again surprised on how bare it looks. Even now, so many years later. After Alicia left, it took Colin almost two years to get rid of everything in the house that belonged to her. Her clothes, her artwork, her myriad of contributions to the décor of the house. He never bothered to replace the empty spots on the wall where photos once hung. The nails were still in the wall, holding nothing at all, a testament to the ever present reality of her absence.

Part of him never wanted to let her go, but another part of him knew holding on would only cause him more pain. He's happy Penny was still too young during those years to see or hear his sobs that would come every night while he came to terms with Alicia's absence. Colin tried everything he could to find her. He reached out to everyone: her best friends, her parents, even her boss, Karen Ellie who ran and owned Ellie's. No one had any idea where Alicia went or even that she was unhappy and wanted to leave. All of them said the same thing: she was happy and always had the same glowing smile when she said her life was exactly what she hoped it would be. It didn't make any sense to Colin. Maybe he missed a sign somewhere that she had been trying to show him. He spent countless nights replaying every little moment they shared in the small chance he could pick up even a glimmer of a hint that would help explain what happened. But that glimmer, that hint, never came. Over time, Colin accepted the fact she was gone forever and began the slow process of trying to move on. Had it not been for Penny and her ever-present smile and laughter, he wouldn't have made it.

Thunder rumbles again in the distance. Colin takes one more look around and walks across the room. He reaches into his dresser and gets a clean pair of boxers, and heads into the bathroom. Even with spending every day in the rain of the car wash, a hot shower in the evening helps him find his center and allows him to relax enough to fall asleep. He strips down out of his clothes, steps into the shower, and lets the water wash away his thoughts and the slightly fruity smell of the chemical soap used at the car wash, which always seems to follow him home.

The thunder rumbles one more time in the distance, as though trying to warn the town of what is about to come.

≈

The alarm goes off as it normally does. Colin groggily reaches over and slaps at the snooze button. The resulting thud and continuous beeping confirms he merely succeeded in knocking the alarm off the nightstand instead of connecting with the small snooze button that was supposed to be conveniently located at the top of the clock. Frustrated, with his face still half buried in his pillow, he wonders if the designer of the clock ever actually tested or used the clock before manufacturing and selling it. The alarm, apparently angry at being abruptly introduced to the floor, continues its furious beeping tone. Colin slides to the edge of the bed, sits up and puts his feet onto the floor. He reaches down and rescues the clock from its new home. He presses the off button. The alarm stops, apparently happy again, and the complete silence of the house takes over. Listening for movement to confirm if Penny is awake, Colin can only hear the patter of raindrops on the roof. He shakes his head. It's going to be a very long, very slow day at work.

After dressing, Colin heads into the kitchen. Penny has already been up and left for school early, it appears. A sandwich in plastic wrap with a small sticky note attached to it labeled "Lunch. Love you, Daddy" in her long cursive scrawl is lying on the counter next to a fresh-brewed pot of coffee. A peanut butter and bacon sandwich he deduces as he picks it up to take a closer look at it. Add some bananas to it and Elvis would be proud. Although Penny harasses him on a regular basis about his obsession with bacon, she always humors him and puts it on just about everything she makes for him. Maybe one day he will put forth some actual effort to give it up, but then he thinks every man has to have at least one vice to balance himself out. He doesn't smoke. He doesn't have more than one or two beers a night. He figures all things considered, a love of bacon isn't the worst vice he could have. Plus, it's delicious. Colin smirks at this thought as he sets the sandwich back down on the counter and gets a coffee cup from the cupboard. A quick cup of strong black coffee does the trick and he is ready to face what today will present.

Colin then grabs his keys from the hook on the wall, the sandwich from the counter, and begins to head out the door.

Before he can open the front door, the phone rings.

The loud ring in the empty house makes him jump a bit, momentarily startled by a sound he didn't expect to hear this early in the morning. His first thought is something has happened to Penny on her way school. He quickly sets down his keys and the sandwich on the table near the front door and hurries over to the phone. "Hello?" he answers, unable to hide the concern in his voice.

"Colin, glad I caught you at home. It's Alan."

Colin audibly sighs in relief. Alan is Colin's boss, working for the car wash's corporate office in Shelton. A nice guy in every way a guy can be nice. He never hesitates to let Colin take a day off when he needs to support Penny with her latest endeavor. "Hey Alan, I thought something had happened to Penny for a moment. What's going on?"

Colin can hear the immediate apology in Alan's voice. "Oh, man, I'm sorry. I didn't mean to scare you. I just wanted to call you and let you know you don't have to go in today. With this rain we have coming through the next few days, the car wash will probably have little to no one using it. I know you haven't had any time off in quite a while, so I wanted to give you the opportunity for a few paid days off work. What d'ya say?" The excitement in Alan's voice when he finishes is obvious. Alan lives for doing what he can to help make someone else's day or life better, no matter how small the gesture was. He's probably the only reason Colin hasn't attempted to find a job at Sam's or at Bell's all these years.

A couple paid days off work sounds great though and a large grin begins to form on Colin's face. "You know what Alan? That sounds exactly like what I need", he responds. "I was hoping to get some time to head up to Shelton and pick up a few things that Penny's been asking for."

He can almost hear Alan grinning on the other end of the line. "The rain should let up in about three or so days, according to the local news. Take the time off and have some fun with Penny, young man. It's a direct order from your boss." Alan then laughs. "I'll give you a ring once the weather starts to break up. You get some rest and tell Penny I said hi." And Alan hangs up before Colin can object.

A day would have been fine. But three days? It's been a long time since Colin has had that much time off work. Colin's grin remains on his face, though. He sets down the phone and looks over at the table near the door. He wonders if it is too early for a peanut butter and bacon sandwich. Deciding it's never too early for anything with bacon, he walks over to the table and grabs the sandwich. Freeing the sandwich from the plastic wrap while he strolls across the living room, he sits down in the easy chair and turns on the television, ready to enjoy some relaxation time.

≈

Penny looks up from her calculus book and to the clock on the wall. Almost three o'clock. School seems to be taking an exceptionally long time today. She blames the overcast, rainy, depressing weather outside. Then again, she didn't get much sleep last night, either. Between trying to maintain her grades and the multiple college applications she submitted to several prominent medical schools out of state, she feels like a nervous mess inside although she is doing her best not to let it show on the outside. Plus, she is worried about what might happen to Dad when and if she leaves. He's been under a lot of stress trying to make ends meet and she is always doing what she can to keep his spirits up, but she knows there is an underlying sadness to him which never seems to go away.

She doesn't remember her mother at all but knows her mom must have meant the world to him. But Penny has a plan. She is going to do what she can to inspire the blossom of a new love between him and Ms. Luna Page before she leaves for college. Ms. Luna is cute and single, and Dad always laughs and shakes his head a little when she mentions Luna to him.

Penny figured that had to mean something, even if Ms. Page is a little off at times when she starts talking about the moon and its latest equinox or solstice. The ring of the final bell interrupts Penny's thoughts before she can develop a plan for her dad's first date with his future girlfriend. She packs up her books and gets ready to head to the clinic for her regular three-hour internship.

The town only has one school bus for the high school, and it runs from the school to the more distant houses to help shuttle the various students who attend Orchard Lake High School. Any student who lives within five miles either has to catch a ride with someone or walk to school. Luckily for Penny, she only lives within a couple miles of the school, so it isn't far of a walk, and she likes the time during her walks in the morning and the evenings to mull over the plethora of thoughts running through her head. And today she was smart enough to bring an umbrella with her. The walk-in clinic is located just a few blocks from the school and was apparently moved there years ago by the city in order to have medical care easily available for the various players on the football and basketball teams. She remembers the stories her dad used to tell her about his high school years. He hasn't talked about those days in years, though, and Penny misses how excited he would get when he would describe successful plays he coordinated during national playoff games. Maybe if he hit it off with Ms. Page, he would start telling the stories again. Penny grins at the possibility. Stepping out the door of the school, she opens her umbrella and heads out into the rain toward the clinic.

"Pen! Wait!"

She stops before she gets ten steps away from the school and turns around. Laura waves at her and comes jogging over to her. Penny smiles. Laura is one of her oldest and one of her best friends at school. They have been in the same grade since kindergarten and both are enrolled in same advanced classes. Laura even applied to the same schools Penny applied to, hoping they would get into the same school and be able to room together on campus.

Laura tries to dodge the rain as she approaches and squeezes under the umbrella with Penny. "So did you talk to your dad yet?" she breathlessly asks.

Penny shakes her head. She had meant to ask her dad about the senior camping trip last night but didn't think it was the right time.

"Pen! Seriously. You need to ask him, like today," Laura insists. "The trip in is two weeks and I do not want to have to put up with Haley by myself. And you know how Haley gets when there are bugs or boys around."

Penny giggles. Haley is the third of their best friend trio, and is the definition of a girly girl, happily proclaiming she is "high maintenance" to anyone who asks.

"Pen! Focus!" Laura continued. "Haley said she is allowed to go, and my mom said I am allowed to go as well, but she said I can only go if you are going because she thinks Haley will corrupt me."

The serious look on Laura's face makes Penny giggle again.

"OK, OK. I will talk to my dad tonight and call you, all right? I gotta get to the clinic, since my shift starts soon and I'm sure Mr. Tams has something new wrong with him that he caught from his son." Both Penny and Laura laugh. Mr. Tams, the local hypochondriac. Besides the occasional cold, there really is never anything wrong with him.

Laura nods, looks Penny in the eye, and adamantly states, "Pen, you better call me later and tell me what your dad says. If you don't call me, I am going to come over to your house, seduce your dad, become your mother-in-law, and then make you go with me."

Penny grimaces. "Laura, that's disgusting."

Laura laughs, reaches into her purse, pulls out a small mirror, and pretends to primp herself, fluffing her long blond hair.

Penny shakes her head, laughing at Laura's mock primping. "I will call you, stop being gross. I gotta go." With that, Penny turns and heads off down the road, taking the umbrella with her and leaving Laura to scramble back into the school and out of the rain.

"Don't forget to call me, Pen," Laura yells after her. "Or you know what will happen!"

Laura's laughter can be heard all the way to the edge of the road, where it then disappears into the sound of the rain. Penny smiles and shakes her head again while she continues to walk down the road toward the clinic. Her thoughts drift off to college next year and she daydreams of what it would be like if she and Laura were in the same room at the same college. The sound of a loud thunderclap overhead pulls Penny back to reality, and soon she reaches the clinic.

She walks up to the entrance, closes her umbrella, walks in, and gets ready for her shift at the receptionist desk. Not exactly the internship she was expecting, but the interaction with patients as they come in reminds her why she wants to go to medical school. The waiting room is completely empty, which does not surprise her. She didn't expect anyone to show up tonight with the weather outside. Not even Mr. Tams, who has made it his job to come to the clinic every other day with a new symptom of some terminal ailment. Penny sits down, sighs, and lets her thoughts drift back to what adventures she might have in college with Laura next year.

As Penny focuses on her usual clinic duties, she doesn't notice someone standing in the rain on the other side of the empty street.

She doesn't see the figure facing the clinic's large front windows without an umbrella, oblivious to the rain.

Someone who is staring directly at her.

CHAPTER 2

THE BUILDUP

Colin wakes up from his nap in the easy chair around noon. He groggily sits up and looks at the television. Some random infomercial is telling him he really needs this new set of knives so he can cut through a steel pipe while he is cooking. The empty plastic wrapper that had once enveloped his sandwich sits lazily on the coffee table, next to his now cold coffee. Shaking the cobwebs away, he stands up, grabs his cup and the plastic wrapper, and heads into the kitchen. Penny should still be in school, he thinks, and she will be working several hours at the clinic tonight. He smiles. If he hurries, he would have time to head up to Shelton and pick up a few things she has been asking for the last few months and get back before she's home. He sets the cup in the sink and throws the wrapper away. The rain makes its presence known by the constant drumming on the window above the kitchen sink. He pauses to look out the window and watches the raindrops fall and build up on the glass, combining until they become fat watery drop and slide down the pane, leaving a wet trail in their wake.

Even at home, the rain continues to follow him. On the other hand, the rain is also the reason for his day off today.

Colin checks the clock once again. Fifteen past noon. He still has time. He grabs his keys and heads out to his truck, avoiding the rain as much as possible, then drives toward the main road out of town.

The roads are empty. Colin pulls away from Orchard Lake, the truck's windshield wipers steadily swishing back and forth with their singular mission, and heads north toward Shelton. Bobby Darin is singing on the radio. Colin smiles a bit, looking past the ever-present rain battering on his windshield. Shelton is a straight shot north from Orchard Lake, about ninety miles or so. On a good day, a trip up to Shelton takes about an hour and a half. On a day like today, it will probably be two hours. He will have to hurry while he is up there so he would have enough time to make it back, especially if the rain decides to come down any harder than it already is. Colin glances at the clock on the truck's dashboard and pushes the accelerator a little farther down. There won't be any cops out in this mess, he thinks, and the ones who might be out in it won't be interested in stepping out of their squad car just to write a small speeding ticket.

He relaxes back into the seat and begins to hum along with the current song on the radio as the miles start to pass.

≈

Penny glances at the clock on the wall of the clinic. She sighs. One more hour until she is able to head home. Tonight's shift was exceptionally slow since no one came into the clinic. As she guessed, not even Mr. Tams braved the weather today.

Dr. Elyse walks into the reception area from the back room. "Anyone come in yet, Penny?" she asks her even though she already knows the answer.

"No one, Dr. Elyse. Everyone is avoiding the weather," Penny replies.

Dr. Elyse has run the clinic for as long as Penny can remember. Medicine is delivered once or twice a month by a courier service out of Shelton. For most, the clinic is the only source of medical care in Orchard Lake. The nearest hospital is located in Rockville, to the east, about twenty miles away. Since the main highway between Rockville and Orchard Lake is seldom used by most of the town's inhabitants, the ambulances are able to make the trip in excellent time without any incidents.

Penny shows Dr. Elyse the calendar sitting in front of her on the desk. No appointments today or tomorrow are written in and only one single appointment is set for the day after. Penny watches as Dr. Elyse looks at the clock, out the front windows at the rain, and turns around to head back into her office. She pauses right before she walks though the doorway. "Penny, you can go ahead and go home. If anyone comes in tonight, I'm pretty sure I can handle checking them in on my own."

Dr. Elyse lives in a single bedroom, single bathroom

apartment attached to the back of the clinic. When the clinic was originally built, the town felt it would be best if the doctor on duty actually lived on the premises and had the contractors build the small apartment into the structure. As such, it's a condition of the doctor on duty's employment agreement that they live on premises in the apartment. Dr. Elyse has never acted like she minds, though, and over the last couple of years Penny came to understand Dr. Elyse is happiest when she is doing her job and treating patients. Living in the back of the clinic keeps her close to that happiness. Plus, from what Penny was able to learn, Dr. Elyse lives there rent free. *Not a bad deal at all*, Penny thinks.

"OK, Dr. Elyse!" Penny quickly says. She relishes the chance to go home early, since this means she will be able to get some more reading in and possibly cook some actual food for dinner tonight. "If anything comes up, just give me a call and I can come back in." she says, but Dr. Elyse had already walked out of sight and into the back of the clinic, toward the sound of two women screaming at each other echoing into the waiting room. There is a small television back in Dr. Elyse's office and she is a self-proclaimed addict to reality TV. Penny is sure Dr. Elyse has already settled down into her large office chair and is once again deep in the world of petty squabbles and drama.

Penny grabs her backpack and her umbrella, once again glancing at the front windows. The rain is coming down harder now than when it was when she first got to the clinic. It didn't matter to her, though, since her umbrella is gigantic and home isn't far away. Penny makes sure the door chime is set on loud so Dr. Elyse would be able to hear if anyone did enter the clinic while she is in the back office. "Bye, Dr. Elyse! See you tomorrow!" Penny yells toward the office door. Her response is only the constant drumming of the rain, outside on the roof. Penny turns toward the front door, steps outside, and heads toward home.

≈

Colin exits the last store on his list just in time to catch the rain transforming from heavy to full deluge. He runs to his truck, opens the door, and leaps into the driver's seat. Shaking off the multitude of droplets that have made their home on his face and hair, he still finds a smile on his face. Penny is going to love what he picked up for her: Several of the latest paperback releases from her favorite author she doesn't have yet. A new designer backpack to replace her old, frayed one she's had for over two years. And the present he knows she will love the most—a gift card that works for any store in the mall, which she can use to buy whatever her heart desires. And not just some any twenty-dollar gift card either, but a gift card to the tune of five hundred dollars, which took him several months to save up for.

She will protest, he knows, but she will ultimately give in. He didn't know what else to get a teenage girl for a graduation present. Alicia would. Alicia was the expert when it came to picking out gifts for people. She would always find that perfect little item to give, no matter who she was buying for. But Alicia was gone, and Colin had to work with what he knew. And he knows Penny loves to shop when she can and when they had the extra money. She already knew she was going to get his truck if she was accepted at a college out of state and needed the transportation. Colin is fine with walking to the car wash every day if it meant his little hummingbird is safe and happy at college. At least this way with the gift card, she could go out and buy some things she wants, and not just things she needs.

A heavy rumble of thunder vibrating through the truck brings Colin back to reality.

The mall parking lot is almost completely empty, as are the roads back to Orchard Lake. The storm has successfully sent most of Shelton, as well as the out of town visitors, back to their respective homes and towns.

Colin glances at the clock on the dashboard. Just after three. He has plenty of time to get back to his little hummingbird before she got home.

The miles pass. The determined swish back and forth from the windshield wipers and the oldies station playing on the radio are Colin's only company. The roads are completely empty and have been since he left Shelton's city limits. His thoughts turn again to Alicia, as they often do when he is alone. Why she left is a mystery he has never been able to solve. No note, no good-bye. No "Fuck you, Colin, I hate you, I found someone else." Nothing.

The local cops were sympathetic but ultimately found nothing to answer Colin's questions.

It just didn't make sense. She took no photos, no clothing, no food. Just her car, which was never located or even re-registered in any Department of Motor Vehicles within a five-state radius. Colin knows because he personally called each and every DMV himself to confirm if she ever renewed the registration. Yet, still nothing.

A grip of sadness momentarily takes hold of him. He wishes Penny could have known her mom. All she has ever known are the stories he would tell when he would pull out the old photo album. *Maybe it's time to dust off that album and look at it once again when I get home*, he thinks. It's been a few years since he'd last opened it. With Penny getting ready to leave him for college, it would be good to reminisce and remind Penny that, although her mom left, Alicia had been an amazingly talented woman who Penny takes after in so many ways.

A bright flash of lightning striking a tree to the right of Colin's vision brings him back to reality. At that same moment, his headlights fall upon a shadowy figure only twenty feet away.

Directly in front of him in the road.

His heart leaps out of his chest.

His hands grip the steering wheel and he turns it hard to the right.

The truck immediately responds, and the force of the sudden turn causes Colin to be thrown to the left, his head hitting the side window with such force that the window cracks.

Then there was only darkness.

≈

The rain is definitely coming down harder than it was before, Penny observes, as she navigates around an ever-growing amount of puddles. She smiles as she walks. *Glad I didn't wear heels and a skirt today*, she thinks, *because that would be an awkward disaster just waiting to happen in this wind.*

The trip home is quick. Penny doesn't run across anyone else out enjoying the weather as she was and she doesn't see any cars pass by. Rounding the final corner on her street, she sees the house through the downpour—a stark white rectangle framed by darkness and blurred by rain. The driveway is empty and the house is dark when she walks up. She is surprised her dad isn't home. She didn't expect the car wash would have been open today due to the rain, and she knows her dad's boss likes to give him time off when he can. Closing her umbrella, she unlocks the door and steps inside. "Dad? Are you here?" she asks into the darkness.

Already knowing the answer, the rain outside is her only response.

She turns on the light switch for the living room and the room bursts into bright clarity. She slips off her wet shoes and rests the umbrella against the table near the door to dry. Walking into the kitchen, she sees the empty coffee cup setting in the sink and an almost full but cold pot of coffee still sitting in its cradle in the coffee machine.

She puts her backpack down on the kitchen table and walks over to the sink to clean the cup and the coffee pot. *Maybe tomorrow I'll only make a half pot since Dad only ever has one or two cups in the morning these days*, she thinks.

She glances around the kitchen. It's quiet, and she's still surprised her dad is not home. She digs into her backpack and grabs her phone, checking to see if there were any missed messages. Five missed text messages from Laura, each one asking her if she talked to her dad yet and if Laura needs to become her new stepmom, and four missed messages from Haley, all asking the same thing. Apparently, Laura has already told Haley of her plan of seduction and convinced Haley to take part in the charade. Penny laughs and sends them both a response, letting them know her dad isn't home yet, but she will be sure to ask tonight when he gets back.

She then walks over to her portable speaker, which is still on the counter from last night, and plugs the cord into her phone. Turning on the latest hit from Taylor Swift, she turns back to her task of cleaning the coffee pot and the coffee mug her dad left in the sink. "Blank Space" fills the kitchen, she soon forgets the worries of a moment ago and begins singing and dancing along to the song while she cleans the dishes.

The rain continues its assault outside and the wind begins to howl. Thunder is once again heard and light flashes across the sky at regular intervals.

≈

Hidden by the dark, the figure standing outside Colin's house doesn't feel the rain. They don't pay attention to the wind, or the thunder, or the lightning. Instead, they are focused on the petite young girl with the doe eyes and the long, straight brunette hair dancing around, framed by the kitchen window and the light behind her.

The figure watches, just as they did while she was working at the clinic. Watches the young girl twirl around. Watches her as she flips her hair and watches her sing along to whatever music may be on in the house.

Thunder rumbles across the sky again. A deep baritone rumble that sends ominous vibrations through the ground and makes ripples spread across the puddles already formed, once again warning of an even bigger storm coming.

Soon, the figure thinks, as another flash of lightning illuminates the house with the pretty girl inside.

Very soon.

≈

Colin opens his eyes. The seatbelt pulls tightly against his chest and his waist, as though gravity was pulling him towards the right instead of down. The dogged swishing of the windshield wipers continues to mix with the sound of the rain. He tries to focus his eyes. One headlight illuminates a tree in front of the truck that appears to be growing the wrong direction.

He reaches down and unbuckles the seatbelt. Falling across the cab of the truck and landing on the passenger side door, he grimaces as his right side explodes in a sharp pain. *That explains the tree growing the wrong way*, he thinks. A cold mix of water, grass, and mud begins to soak into his shirt on the right side. Little by little, lucidity sets in and clears away the fog. He reaches up to turn on the dome light. The light dimly illuminates the cab of the truck.

Colin searches around the parts of the cab he can reach for his cellphone, feeling around gingerly between the overturned bags to make sure he doesn't slice his fingers open on any broken glass from the now shattered passenger side window. Unable to find the phone, and the pain in his right side growing even angrier, he forces himself to get up and try to get out of the truck.

Hunching over, he reaches up and tries to open the driver's side door to climb out. The door doesn't budge. With the limited light reflecting into the cab from the one still-working headlight, the weak dome light, and the occasional flashes of light from the lightning, he can see the muddy ground below his feet, mingled in with occasional sparkles of broken glass from the passenger-side window. He's not going out that door anytime soon, unless he wants to dig himself out. The windshield, although almost fully spider webbed with cracks, is still solid. That left the small rear sliding window, unless he wanted to roll down the driver's side window and try to climb up and out of the truck that way. With the angry fire in his right side, he wasn't feeling up to climbing up and out of anything.

He unlocks the clasp of the rear window and slides the window open. A fleeting memory of a young Penny crawling through the window from the bed to the cab during trips up to Shelton passes him by as he slowly and carefully extracts himself from his overturned truck.

A few steps away from the truck, Colin is forced to sit down. The pain in his side is becoming all-consuming. He lightly touches the source of the pain, feeling a sharp object sticking out of his side that clearly doesn't belong there. Afraid to pull it out, since he isn't sure how deep it is, he sets his mind on finding help. He looks around.

Trying to avoid whatever was in the road caused him to drive off the embankment and overturn sometime during the process. He isn't sure how far off the main road he is, so his first mission is to find the road and pray someone comes by.

The road isn't as hard to find as Colin thought it would be. The swath of destroyed bushes, small saplings, and gouges in the dirt are easy to see and follow with the random flashes of lighting. Finally reaching pavement, Colin estimates his truck slid about fifty feet down the embankment before coming to a stop. He collapses to his knees on the side of the road, sweating profusely from the volume of effort it took to move with the ever-present pain in his right side.

The lightning flashes again. The road is empty as far as he can see. No lights in either direction. Colin wonders what time it is. He doesn't wear a watch and he couldn't find his phone in the truck. With this weather, it could be anytime from seven at night to five in the morning. He wasn't sure how long he was in the truck before he came to. He knew he had left Shelton around three fifteen and had traveled for about sixty or so miles after he left the city limits. Penny would probably be home right now, as it was dark, and is more than likely worried if the time is closer to the morning versus early evening. He didn't leave any notes and has no way of calling the house. He fleetingly thinks about the shadowy shape and wonders what it may have been. Colin attempts to take a deep breath and tries to smile. *It could be worse*, he thinks. *I could be dead right now.*

If he didn't have this souvenir lodged in his side from the most recent event in his life, he could go back and salvage what he could out of the truck and hike the distance back into town. Unfortunately, even the thought of going back to the truck at this point makes him wince. Making it to the road was difficult enough. Even breathing is difficult now. The pain in his right side is white-hot and growing. He starts to find it hard to focus on anything else, and the flashes of lightning above him seem to match its intensity. Colin then begins to feel like he's drifting, probably woozy from the blood loss. He tries to keep the little of the world he can see in focus but it begins to blur.

Another bright flash of lightning, one that feels like it is directly on him. *I'm sorry, Penny*, he thinks. *I guess I won't be making it home after all.*

The latest flash of lightning is still around him and hadn't faded away. His last thought, before he passes out, is about how weird the now permanent lightning seems.

≈

Colin doesn't hear the door slam from behind that permanent flash of lighting, or the outline of a person who comes running out in front of it, yelling, "Hey buddy, buddy, you OK?" The stranger reaches Colin just as his eyes close and he falls over.

Catching him, the stranger says, "Stay with me, buddy. We are going to get you some help."

CHAPTER 3

THE CATALYST

With the dishes done and her music turned off hours ago, Penny looks at the clock again. Two in the morning. *Dad should have been home several hours ago*, she thinks, and she has checked the answering machine and her cell phone at least twenty times in the last two hours just in case a call or message came in that she missed. She has already looked through the house several times to see if a message he had written was misplaced but didn't find anything. It wasn't like her dad to just disappear without letting her know where he was. She had already called Ellie's to see if he was there, and she had also called both Sam's and Bell's as well. No one has seen him today. A panic sets in and a thought she knows would never be true crosses her mind. *What if he's left like Mom did?* Maybe he finally had enough. Maybe he finally gave into the sadness in his eyes and left. No. She shakes her head and clears the thought from her mind. He would never leave like that. Not her dad.

The doorbell rings, breaking through the silence of the house. Penny almost screams. She looks at the door, afraid to move.

The doorbell rings again and the person on the other side of the door begins to knock as well. "Penny! Penny, come to the door. It's Deputy Gates."

Recognizing the deputy's voice, she should be relieved. Instead, her worries intensify. Deputy Gates would only be here if something bad has happened. Worse case scenarios begin to race through her mind. She slowly gets up and walks to the door, opening it just as Deputy Gates is ringing the doorbell a third time. "What happened?" she abruptly asks, trying to hide the panic in her voice and forgoing the normal niceties of "hello, how are you, and good to see you again."

"He's all right, Penny," the deputy states. "He was involved in a car accident and he's at the hospital in Rockville right now. I came by to let you know what happened and to see if you wanted to ride along with me to go pick him up. The hospital called the station because your father is still unconscious from the accident. They said he didn't have any contact info on him beyond his wallet, which only had his address. From what I was told on the phone, he had to have some stitches in his side from a large cut and he had lost a lot of blood. A trucker making a run from Shelton came across him on the side of the road. Apparently, he lost control of his truck and went off the road."

The panic inside her momentarily spikes when she hears the words *accident* and *hospital*, but it begins to subside a little when it sinks in that he is able to come home instead of needing to stay overnight. He's not dead, which was the outcome of every scenario that had just played through her mind. "Yes, sir. Let me get my jacket."

The storm was in full force at this hour, with the wind whipping the rain around in every direction. Lightning and thunder continue their dance of give and take overhead. She huddles under Deputy Gates's umbrella as he walks her to the squad car.

Penny spends the ride to Rockville in silence, watching the rain make intricate patterns on the window only to be swept away by the windshield wipers. Deputy Gates's police radio occasionally sparks up with some random police lingo, and then goes silent again. The deputy doesn't attempt to make any small talk. As they approach Rockville, Penny pulls out her compact and checks to make sure her eyes aren't too red and puffy. Deputy Gates looks over at her holding her compact and nods. The trip doesn't take long, as the roads are empty and Rockville isn't very far from Orchard Lake. The squad car pulls up to the hospital entrance and stops. Penny doesn't wait for the officer to bring the umbrella around to her side of the car. She opens the door and practically sprints into the waiting room, quickly looking around. Her dad is there, sitting in a wheelchair, next to a vending machine. One of the nurses is standing next to him, holding a clipboard and nodding.

"Daddy!" Penny practically yells and sprints over to him, throwing her arms around him and almost falling into the wheelchair with him.

"Hey hummingbird." he said, weakly hugging her back.

The nurse gently pulls on Penny's arm. "Be careful, sweetheart. He has quite a few stitches in his right side."

Penny nods and backs up a bit. She looks at him, glad to see he's alive. He looks tired.

"Sorry I didn't call and tell you I was going to be late." he said, "They let me know you and the deputy were on your way here when I woke up. Luckily, they are clearing me for release. The kind nurse here was just about to do just that, right, Nurse Jacobs?"

The nurse nods again, scribbles something down on her clipboard, and hands Penny the paperwork. "The doctor wrote a few prescriptions you will have to make sure get filled," she tells Penny. "And no playing any sort of contact sports for a bit while the stitches heal. Have your dad follow up with Dr. Elyse in about a week so she can check his stitches. OK?" Penny nods. The nurse smiles, tells Penny her dad will be all right and reminds Colin to take it easy, then turns and walks away.

Deputy Gates walks up and looks at Colin. "Geez, Colin, you look like shit."

"Yeah, I've seen better days." he responds. Colin laughs and then immediately grimaces. "No laughing for a while, it seems."

The deputy smiles. "Ready to head home?" he asks.

Colin nods and slowly begins to get up only to hear Nurse Jacobs yell at him from the nurse's station. "You better stay in that wheelchair until you are outside the door." He then sits back down and Penny steps around him to be able to push the chair.

Deputy Gates steps over to the nurse's station and grabs the two bags of Colin's personal effects sitting there. The tow truck driver who was dispatched to get his truck was nice enough to gather what he could from inside the truck and drop it off by the hospital for Colin. He will have to dig through the bags later to see what was in there. He was hoping the gifts for Penny were still useable, although he had his doubts about the paperbacks with all this rain.

"All right Colin, let's get you and Penny home," the deputy states.

Penny begins to push the wheelchair for the door and Colin waves good-bye to the nurses still standing at their station. The electronic double doors open wide for him as he rolls up to them. The deputy's squad car is parked right out front, under the large awning, but the rain is still trying its best to push rain into the waiting room.

Officially out of the hospital, Penny stops pushing the wheelchair. "OK, old man, no more free ride for you." She giggles, clearly showing her relief.

Deputy Gates opens the passenger door of the squad car and comes back to help Colin into the car. It is a slow, painful process, but with a little help he is able to get seated in the car and the door is closed behind him. An orderly takes the wheelchair from Penny and she hops into the back seat.

"I'm glad you're OK, Dad." she says.

He smiles. "Me too, hummingbird. Me too."

Deputy Gates opens the driver's side rear passenger door and sets down Colin's bags on the seat. He closes the door and opens the door to the driver's seat and settles in for the drive home. "Dispatch, this is car twelve. I will be in route back from Rockville General and will report in to the station upon arrival." he states into his radio.

The radio squawks in return, "Copy that, car twelve."

Deputy Gates puts the car in gear and pulls away from the hospital. Once the car is out from under the awning, the rain resumes its direct assault.

There isn't much conversation on the way home. Colin is grateful for that. He doesn't really feel like talking since the pain in his side continues to remind him about what recently happened.

After a quick, uneventful ride, Colin's house comes into view. The deputy pulls into the driveway, steps out into the rain, and quickly opens the rear door to grab Colin's bags and the umbrella. The door closes and the deputy navigates around the rear of the car, opening Penny's door. Handing Penny the bags, the deputy asks her to go up to the front door and open it. She quickly obliges, disappearing into the dark and rain outside the car. A moment later, the porch light comes on and Penny stands in the doorway, holding the door open. Colin's door opens and deputy Gates leans over to him with the umbrella overhead. "Ready for this?" he asks. Colin nods, and slowly moves his legs out of the car.

Grabbing the door frame, Colin hoists himself up and the

deputy puts a steady arm around his own. Deputy Gates grins. "C'mon, Colin. You'll catch a cold if we keep you out here in this weather any longer."

Smiling, Colin nods and they walk the short distance up to the house and into the living room, away from the increasingly angry storm outside. Sitting down into his easy chair, Colin breathes a sign of relief.

Finally home.

Deputy Gates pulls out a pad from his pocket and scribbles something down on it. Tearing the paper from the pad, the deputy sets it down on the table next to the door. "Here's the number to the tow company that picked up your truck. Give them a call tomorrow and they should be able to give you the verdict. Also, Colin, make sure you call your insurance company tomorrow as well." he says. "Get some rest tonight. You're home and you're safe. Worry about these things tomorrow, all right?"

"Sure thing, boss." Colin acknowledges.

With a tip of his wide-brimmed hat, Deputy Gates turns and heads out the front door, closing it as he walks out.

Penny is still standing next to the couch. "Sit down, hummingbird." Colin tells her, "I'm fine." He could see the worry still on her face, though, even with his reassurances. "The doc said I didn't cut any major organs and I only lost a lot of blood because of how big the cut was. Apparently, I had fallen on a large piece of glass from the passenger side window that got wedged into my side."

Her eyes become even bigger than they already are. Colin

grimaces. *That didn't sound very reassuring*, he thinks. He tries a different tactic to ease her fears.

"Trust me, hummingbird, I'm all stitched up and will be completely fine." He smiles and grabs the remote control from the end table next to him.

At this time of the morning, the only thing on television will be infomercials and B-rated movies, but he's sure he could find something partially entertaining. "So, what does a guy gotta do to get some bacon around this joint?" he asks right before turning the television on.

Penny giggles and shakes her head. "Geez, Daddy!" she exclaims. "Bacon? Now? You are a hot mess."

Colin laughs a little. A quick jolt of pain races up from his side. Penny continues to shake her head, hops up from the couch and heads off into the kitchen.

He hears the fridge open and close, and the rustle of the bread bag from the pantry. On the television, some pretty little blonde actress is screaming and running away from a gigantic fuzzy caterpillar that apparently wants to eat her. Or mate with her. Colin isn't sure which just yet. He sits a little deeper into the chair, looking forward to the BLT he knows Penny is whipping up for him in the kitchen.

Finally home, he thinks again with a smile.

The caterpillar on the television finally catches up with its pretty little blonde prey. And immediately eats her.

≈

Penny opens her eyes to a dark room, barely illuminated by

her clock. Her alarm radio has chirped on, letting her know it's time to get up and get ready for school. She stretches and wipes the sleep from her eyes.

After she and her father ate dinner last night and watched a ridiculous caterpillar horror movie, she helped her dad into bed and went to sleep herself. That was only a couple hours ago. She tosses her legs over edge of her bed and yawns. The thunder rumbles outside and she can hear the wind still howling and whipping the rain against the window. The announcer on the radio starts talking about how power is out in several cities due to downed power lines from the storm, and launches into listing off all the school districts that are closed today. Hers is on the list.

Penny smiles. No school today. That's a small blessing. She leans over to her nightstand and turns off the radio. She rolls back into bed and pulls the covers back up to her chin. Closing her eyes and yawning once more, she quickly falls back to sleep.

The thunder continues to rumble outside. Lightning occasionally lights up Penny's room from her window, casting large shadows all over.

One of those shadows moves, ever so slightly.

The shadow steps from the sheer darkness of the corner and stops at the foot of Penny's bed. Staring at the sleeping girl.

Another flash of light momentarily pulls the room from the darkness, now casting an outline to the figure, and the thunder rumbles. The figure reaches out and lightly touches a bump on the comforter where Penny's foot is. She stirs slightly at the touch. The figure withdraws the hand, steps back into the darkness, and carefully makes their way to the door.

Easing into the hallway, they walk down the hall to the man's room. Light but steady snoring can be heard through the cracked door. The figure slowly pushes the door open and steps into the room. Another flash of light breaks through the darkness of the house, but they do not need any light to know where all the furniture is. This isn't the first time they have been here.

The figure points at the sleeping man and makes a fist. Another flash, and the thunder rumbles again. The figure slowly backs out of the room, pulls the man's door back to its original position, and makes their way to the front door. Timing the front door with the weather, they wait for the flash of lightning. The flash comes, and they open the door at the same time the thunder rumbles, concealing the sound. The figure steps out onto the porch and once again times closing the door with the thunder.

Walking away from the house, they are oblivious to the heavy rain. Keeping their footsteps to the pavement where no imprints will be left behind, they quickly continue down the street. All the houses on the street are still dark and most of the inhabitants will not start stirring for at least another hour. The figure is well-versed on the normal schedules of each inhabitant of the street.

They have been watching a long, long time.

But now, the time for watching is over. Now, it's time to act.

Everything is in place. Everything is ready. A smile crosses the figure's face. A smile even darker than the surroundings which is currently concealing it.

The figure continues to quickly walk away until they have been fully consumed by the darkness of the early morning.

≈

The sound of Penny singing along to some random pop song on the radio rouses Colin awake. He can hear sizzling from the kitchen, which means Penny is going to spoil him with some more bacon. He looks over at the clock on his nightstand. Ten in the morning.

The light pouring in from the window is gray at best and it is pretty evident the storm is still raging outside. School must have been cancelled. Even with yesterday's incident, she wouldn't miss a day of school. He tries to sit up and winces. The pain in his side sharply wishes him good morning.

Wiggling, he works his way to the edge of the bed and slowly works his way onto his feet. He has several calls he needs to make today. The tow company, the insurance company, and, of course, Alan so he knows what happened. Colin hopes it doesn't take long for him to heal up, even though he is pretty sure he would still be able to do his job in his current physical state.

He shuffles out of the bedroom and down the hall into the kitchen. Penny is in her pajamas, standing at the stove while several pieces of bacon sizzle their way to deliciousness.

"Morning, Daddy! It's about time you woke up," she bubbles.

"Mrs. Ellie came by earlier and dropped off a couple large to-go plates with eggs, pancakes, and sausage and just about everything you could think of in them for you. 'Cept bacon. By the way, there isn't any school today. The radio said the storm knocked out power to a lot of places so they canceled schools all over." She points at the two large plastic bags sitting on the kitchen table. "It looks like the word about your accident got around quick, because Mrs. Ellie was all concerned about you not being able to move around very well. She said she is going to come by later tonight with dinner as well for us." Penny smiles and turns her attention back to the bacon.

Colin sits down at the table. Karen Ellie is a godsend. She was Colin's biggest supporter after Alicia left. Mrs. Ellie had always treated Alicia as if she were her own daughter. Most of the artwork hanging up in Ellie's restaurant and bar was done by Alicia. Karen always insisted on buying Alicia's latest work, because she didn't want the "high falootin' galleries" to snatch it all up from her. It didn't surprise Colin she would be the first to come by the house after learning what happened yesterday. She had suffered in the same way Colin had after Alicia left. Colin wonders how she found out about the accident so quickly, but he also knows word travels like wildfire in a small town anytime something happens.

He digs into the plastic bags and removes several plastic containers. Penny wasn't kidding. Scrambled eggs, sausage, pancakes, three types of toast, ham, and hash browns. More food than he and Penny could probably eat in a week. Opening the containers, the kitchen quickly fills with the various smells of the prepared food and Colin's stomach begins to rumble.

Penny grabs two plates from the cabinet and plucks two forks from the drying rack on the counter next to the sink. Handing him a fork and a plate and setting one of each down for herself, she turns back to the bacon and transfers it to its own plate to cool and sets it down next to the rest of the food. She sits down across from him and grins.

Colin looks across the table at Penny. She is waiting for him to lead the way. He looks down at the food, pretends to survey his options, and reaches first for the container with the eggs. He pauses right before he grabs it, then changes direction and instead grabs the dish with the bacon on it.

Penny laughs. "I worked hard on that bacon. You better eat it first," she says firmly.

He winks at her and loads up his plate with the bacon as she grabs the container with the pancakes, and they both dig into the large breakfast spread in front of them.

An hour later and Colin feels as though he is about to explode. Having fully stuffed himself with the delicious eats Mrs. Ellie brought by, it is time to get cleaned up and make a few phone calls. He excuses himself from the table and slowly works his way down the hall to his room. Easing himself down onto the bed, he reaches over and grabs the phone next to the bed. His first call is to Alan.

While Penny is cleaning up the plates and leftovers from their breakfast, Colin finishes up his call with Alan. Colin hears the shower in Penny's room turn on and he makes his next call to the insurance company.

A few moments later, Colin hangs up the phone. The insurance company said they would be sending someone out to look at the truck at the tow yard and they would call him once they had a chance to see it. He hears Penny's shower turn off and mentally agrees a shower is a good idea, even if Penny has already used up all the hot water.

He heads into his bathroom and starts the water for his own shower. Penny is already back in the living room by the time Colin gets out of his shower and dressed. Walking into the living room, he makes his way to his easy chair and sits down.

Penny looks up from the romance novel she is reading and smiles at him. "Feeling any better, old man?"

He nods. He actually is feeling a little better. His side still hurts, but not as much as it did last night. He points over to the bags with his personal belongings in them from the hospital. "Mind bringing those to me, hummingbird?"

She obliges, grabbing both the bags and handing them over. He sets one of them down next to his chair and opens the other one. He pulls out the items one at a time. A jacket. A pair of his work gloves. His cellphone, completely dead and only slightly covered in dried mud. He will have to charge it up and see if it still works a bit later.

He sets it aside with the jacket and his gloves. Reaching back in the bag, he pulls the last item out of the bag. A tightly wrapped plastic bag with the label of the bookstore he had visited in

Shelton. Still dry. Colin smiles. "Hey, hummingbird. Catch."

Penny looks up quickly from her book and gazes at him warily as she takes the plastic bag from his outstretched hand.

"Go ahead, open it." he urges her.

She opens up the bag and sees the three paperback books at the bottom. Her eyes grow big. These are the new releases from her favorite author, Nicholas Sparks, that she hasn't had a chance to get yet. "Daddy!!! Thank you!!!" she squeals. She quickly looks them over and then looks at him, her eyes glowing with excitement. "These are perfect! I am going to start reading them today."

Forgetting about the book she was already reading, she grabs the earliest of the three new books and begins to voraciously devour every written word.

With a large grin, Colin reaches down and grabs the last bag, which is almost full. He fishes around inside it. A few tools and some paperwork from his glove compartment. A well-worn baseball cap from behind his seat. Still hunting around in the bag, his hand makes contact with the last two items he was hoping to find: the bag with Penny's new backpack and the envelope with the gift card. Both dry. He makes a mental note to send the tow truck driver a thank-you card with several free car wash certificates. He closes the bag up and sets it aside. The backpack and gift card will be gifts for Penny at a later date. He looks over at her. She is focused intently on one of her new books, happy as can be.

He smiles and turns on the television and, for the first time in many hours, begins to think it will all work out fine.

≈

The clinic was empty. Dr. Elyse yawns as she stands in the reception area, surveying the weather outside. Not a soul has come through the door today. The storm is still raging outside, though, and Dr. Elyse had expected it was going to be slow. Just not completely empty. Even Mr. Tams is a no show for the second day in a row. Although, she thinks, there is still several more hours remaining today where he may make his appearance with a new malady to address.

She looks around the empty waiting room and sighs, thinking back to the late-night phone call she had received from the shift doctor at Rockville General regarding Penny's dad and his car accident. She reminds herself to make sure she talks to Penny about it when she comes in for her shift.

Dr. Elyse examines the waiting room one last time and turns to head to her office in the back. A new episode of her favorite housewives' show is about to come on. She settles into her large office chair and turns to face the television. Her reality television addiction is what her mom calls her guilty pleasure. Since she doesn't smoke, rarely drinks, and dates even more rarely than she drinks, she allows herself complete indulgence in her shows, mindlessly devouring every new drama-filled episode that is released. And this episode, from the myriad of previews she has been teased with, should be one of the best yet.

The episode begins, and just as she begins to smile in

anticipation, the chime for the front door of the clinic goes off. Dr. Elyse glances at the clock, and her smile fades away. *I can probably catch the rerun later*, she thinks.

Getting up and out of the chair, she heads out of her office and into the reception room. "Hello?" she asks.

The waiting room is empty. *That's odd.* "Hello? Is anyone here?"

The sound of the thunder and the howling wind driving the rain around is her only answer.

She steps around the reception desk and looks again around the waiting room. No one. She walks to the front door and tries the handle. It is securely closed. She opens the door and looks out into the rain. The street is empty. She closes the door, shrugs off a shiver, and walks back toward her office. Must have been a hiccup in the electrical system. With this old building, and the storm outside, she is more surprised the power is still on.

She sits back down and looks at the television. A commercial about how soft the bar of soap on the screen will make her skin if she uses it babbles through its sales pitch. *Good*, she thinks. *I've only missed a couple minutes.* She sinks back down into her chair and relaxes.

The chime for the front door goes off again.

Frowning, Dr. Elyse looks at the door to her office. *Again?* She gets up out of her chair and once more heads to the front of the building. Stepping into the waiting room behind the reception desk, she looks around again.

Still empty.

"If someone is here, and this is your idea of a prank, it's not funny," she announces to the silence.

Once again, the rain and the wind outside is her only response.

A deep furrow creases her brow. More irritated than anything, she turns to head back into the office.

Only this time, there is a person blocking her way.

Her eyes widen in surprise and before she can say anything, the person quickly waves an arm in front of her and a sharp burning sensation immediately explodes from below her chin. Tears form in her eyes, and suddenly she is unable to breathe. A searing pain takes over and within seconds the world begins to turn black.

The last thing to cross Dr. Elyse's mind before she dies is whether the episode she was missing is any good.

≈

The figure watches the light in Dr. Elyse's wide eyes fade away. As the woman's body begins to collapse, the figure quickly reaches out and catches her. They drag the now-lifeless body into the back office and lay her down behind the desk. The first hurdle to obtaining Penny has been dealt with as planned.

Looking down at the body, they watch the blood begin to pool under Dr. Elyse's head on the white tile floor. The pool grows little by little as the blood continues to drain out of the long slash across the doctor's neck, slowly filling the grout lines and outlining the tiles before spilling over and onto the tiles themselves.

The television interrupts the figure's fascination with the pooling blood. Annoyed by the interruption, they reach over and turn the television up louder. Some woman is complaining about how another woman isn't giving her the respect she is due. They frown at the stupidity on the television.

Looking at the desk, the figure grabs Dr. Elyse's car keys and walks out of the office. They close the office door and continue on into the waiting room, pausing only a moment to look at the various bottles in the medicine cabinet along the wall of the examination room to make sure what they need is still here. Locating the bottle labeled Chloroform, they smile and make a note of its location.

The muffled sound of the television though the closed door causes the figure's smile to waver. They look around at the splattered blood on the wall behind the reception desk and on the tile floor, taking note on the most noticeable parts. They glance at the clock. Only a couple hours to go until the doe-eyed young girl arrives for her shift.

Grabbing a roll of paper towels from behind the desk, the figure begins to methodically clean up Dr. Elyse's blood. The girl should be here soon.

Very soon. The figure smiles, steadily cleaning, as paper towel after paper towel turns from a soft white to a dark red.

≈

Penny glances up at the clock, taking a quick break from the latest adventure of her favorite heroine. Almost four o'clock. *Shit*, she thinks. *I need to be at the clinic by four thirty.* She quickly hops up from the couch, taking care to be quiet as her dad is now sound asleep in his easy chair. Walking to her bedroom, she quickly changes into clothing more appropriate for work and puts her long hair up into a ponytail. She frowns. She won't make it to the clinic in time if she tries to do her makeup now. She grabs her large purse and throws a variety of makeup into it. She can always use her compact and do her makeup at work. She smiles. Not like anyone will show up and see how she looks anyway since the storm outside is still going full force. She can hear the wind and the rain and the thunder repeating its mantra over and over. She then grabs the book she is reading that her dad gave her and throws it in her bag with the makeup. At least she will have a great new book to read during her shift.

She walks out of her room, puts on her sneakers, and grabs her umbrella. She scribbles a quick note on the pad of paper on the table next to the door, telling her dad she loves him and she will be home as soon as her shift ends. She adds a PS to the letter: Your turn to make dinner. She softly chuckles a little bit at this. Dad probably won't remember when she told him at breakfast that Mrs. Ellie would be bringing dinner by as well today. So he should be pleasantly surprised again when Mrs. Ellie shows up.

Easing the front door open, Penny steps onto the front porch and opens her umbrella. The wind is strong enough now that the rain is almost being blown sideways. She closes the door and begins to walk briskly toward the clinic. Even in this weather, it shouldn't take her too long to walk there. She hopes Dr. Elyse lets her leave early again today and Mr. Tams decides to take another day off from his various sicknesses. *He's a nice enough guy*, Penny thinks, *but there is rarely anything wrong with him when he comes in.* Maybe he has a crush on Dr. Elyse, which causes a fit of laughter. Her amusement over this thought is lost among the sounds from the wind and the rain.

It doesn't take Penny long to reach the clinic. Walking in the door, she shakes off her umbrella and sets it in the rack next to the first set of waiting room chairs. "Dr. Elyse, I'm here," she announces.

No response. The waiting room is empty. She can hear Dr. Elyse's television on in the back room and the door to her office is closed. *She must not have heard me or the door chime*, Penny thinks.

She begins to walk to the back office to let Dr. Elyse know she is here but changes her mind. Dr. Elyse is pretty serious about her shows. Penny doesn't want to interrupt her and maybe irritate her to the point where she might make Penny stay to the very end of her shift. She smiles. Better to just sit down, open up her book, and wait for Dr. Elyse to make her way out here and notice Penny is busy doing her job at the reception desk.

She sets her purse down on the desk and sits down in the chair. No names were written on the check-in sheet. *No wonder Dr. Elyse is sequestered away in the back*, Penny thinks. No one has come into the clinic today. Penny reaches into her bag and pulls out her compact. *Might as well put a little makeup on anyway*, she thinks.

She pauses a second before she opens the compact. A faint smell of something is lingering in the air. Penny can't place the odor, but it's vaguely familiar. Maybe Dr. Elyse did some cleaning earlier today or yesterday evening. She grabs her eye liner.

Penny concentrates on applying her eye liner evenly and doesn't see someone step from the back room and into the waiting area behind her. She doesn't hear the figure slowly step forward toward her, purposely staying out of view of the compact mirror that holds Penny's attention.

She doesn't see the rag in the figure's left hand or sense them approaching closer and closer.

Happy with her artistry, Penny sets the compact down on the desk and puts the cap on the eye liner. She reaches into her purse for her lipstick, finds it, and begins to pull it out when a rag suddenly appears in front of her face and is tightly clamped down over her nose and mouth.

She screams into the rag. She tries to get up and get away but a forceful arm wraps around her arms at the shoulder, pinning her arms to her side and holding her down into the chair. The lipstick falls to the floor.

Penny struggles against the figure holding her down. She once again screams into the rag and inhales to catch her breath. A pungent, sweet odor invades her nostrils. Recognizing the odor from her biology classes, she tries to hold her breath—but she knows it's already too late. The waiting room begins to spin, slowly at first but soon it spins quicker and quicker. Her arms grow heavy and soon she stops struggling. Her eyes grow heavy and finally close.

≈

Once Penny stops struggling, the figure releases their grip around her, allowing her to slump down in the chair. They put the rag into their pocket and watch the girl a moment. No movement. Slow and steady breathing.

Confident Penny is now completely unconscious, the figure picks her up and lays her down on the tile floor. Binding the girl's arms and legs with large plastic zip ties they pull from one of their pockets, they walk over to the neon open sign for the clinic and turn it off. They also turn the lights of the waiting room off, plunging the interior of the building into dark corners and large shadows. Satisfied the clinic now appears to be closed to anyone passing by, the figure picks up the purse on the counter and then the young girl, carrying both out the front door and into the rain. Glancing around, they make sure no one is out on the street and proceed to carry their captive around the side of the clinic and to the back lot where Dr. Elyse's car is parked. Opening the back door of the car, they lay the girl down on the back seat. They set her purse on the seat, next to the girl's feet, and close the door. The figure walks around to the driver's side, opens the door, gets in, and starts the car.

Time to go.

The figure backs the car out of its parking spot, pulls out onto the street, and soon the car disappears into the rain.

CHAPTER 4

The ringing of the doorbell wakes Colin from his deep slumber on the easy chair. He groggily opens his eyes and looks at the clock on the wall. Six o'clock. The doorbell rings again, almost impatiently, as though he should have already been waiting at the door for the initial ring.

"Yeah, yeah, give me a minute." he yells at the door, hoping the person on the other side can hear him over the storm outside.

He slowly gets up out of the chair, wincing at the sharp hello of the pain in his side. He notices a note from Penny on the table by the door, probably telling him she is at the clinic and will be home later for dinner. Finally reaching the door, he grabs the handle and opens the door just as the doorbell rings again.

"Colin, dear, you look like death," booms a voice from outside in the dusk.

Colin smiles. "Hey there, Karen. Sorry it took me so long to get to the door."

Mrs. Ellie appears in the doorway, her left hand holding two large, plastic carry-out bags. Her normally cheery demeanor is currently replaced by a wide-eye look of concern. "Penny told me this morning you would be OK. You don't look OK. Have you been eating and resting enough?"

Colin chuckles and nods, stepping back so she can come in. "I can't thank you enough for dropping breakfast by this morning," he says as she walks by.

"Honey, we are family. It's the least I could do. Penny told you I was coming by tonight too, right?" she yells over her shoulder as she heads into the kitchen with the plastic bags.

"She did," he answers.

Colin closes the front door and reads Penny's note. His smile widens when he reads her PS. *More like Mrs. Ellie's turn*, he thinks as the smell of meatloaf and mashed potatoes make their way from the kitchen to his nose. "It smells delicious!" he exclaims to her as she diligently unpacks all the plastic containers from the bags and lays them out on the kitchen table. "Penny isn't back yet from the clinic, though, and probably won't be home for another hour or so," he adds.

Mrs. Ellie, happy with the layout from her unpacking, turns and walks back into the living room where Colin is still standing by the door. She sits down on the couch and beckons him over. He slowly walks back over to his easy chair and sits back down. "Seriously, Colin, how do you feel?" she asks.

"Penny really was worried this morning and you know that girl loves you to death."

"I'm fine. I'm just sore and have to take it easy for a couple days." he says.

She scrutinizes him for a moment.

He laughs. "I'm fine, honest. Quit looking at me like that."

The concerned look slowly leaves her face and her normal smile returns. "Fine. Be difficult. I'm not easy to shoo away and you know this, mister," she retorts. "You just relax. The food is fresh from the stove and will stay warm for a while. I will go by the clinic and convince Dr. Elyse to let Penny come home early and I will bring her back here so you two can have a proper dinner."

Colin laughs, then grimaces from the sharp pain from his side, and nods. "Yes, ma'am," he states, giving her a quick salute.

The smell of the food from the kitchen makes his stomach growl. Hearing this from her spot on the couch, her smile graduates into a full grin. "No eating anything until I get back from the clinic with Penny," Mrs. Ellie states as she walks toward the front door. She stops before grabbing the handle and points at Colin. "And no sneaking any bacon," she adds with a smile.

Colin is still smiling as the door closes behind her.

≈

About the same time Mrs. Ellie is unpacking the food at Colin's house, the figure is returning to the clinic. Having left the unconscious girl at a safe location, the figure knows the loose end of the clinic needs to be wrapped up before the game truly begins. A murder investigation would only complicate things, especially after how much time and effort has already been spent.

Pulling back into the same spot in the parking lot, they turn off Dr. Elyse's car. The world plunges into a dusk that, thanks to the dark clouds above, is practically night. The rain quickly obscures and covers the windshield now that the wipers have stopped. It turns the dark outline of the clinic into a distorted rectangle that is constantly changing shape with each new stream of water formed by the ever-steady raindrops. The figure stares out the windshield a moment and then opens the driver's side door and exits the car. They walk to the back of the car, pull out a red canister, and walk back to the front of the clinic, looking around and making sure there are no spectators.

Back inside the clinic, the shadows have now taken over most of the interior. The figure moves around the front reception desk, into the back room, and toward the closed office door. Yet another drama-filled reality show blares from the television on the other side of the door. They open the door and are greeted by the warm, coppery smell of Dr. Elyse's blood which has permeated the room. Her body is in the same position it was left, only now a very large pool of blood is formed around her.

The figure breathes in deeply several times, listening. To the wind howling outside. To the rain on the roof. To the woman on the television complaining about how her best friend had sex with her boyfriend the night prior and how she was going to kick her best friend's ass over it.

The figure sighs.

Opening the cap on the canister of gas, they begin to pour the contents over Dr. Elyse's body, her chair, and her desk. They splash the contents on each of the walls and begin to back out of the office, pouring a small trail from the office, through the exam room, and to the waiting room. The figure continues to splash the contents of the canister over the waiting room chairs. Over the walls. Over the reception desk.

They pause a moment at the desk and set down the canister. They reach down to pick up the girl's lipstick lying on the ground and the compact lying on the desk and put them into their pocket. Picking the canister back up, the figure finishes emptying the remaining fluid throughout the exam room. They walk back to the front of the waiting room and stand next to the front door. Pulling a box of matches from their left pocket, the figure opens the box and pulls out a match. They strike the match on the side of the box and watch the flame burst into life—the flicker of the flame, the light dancing back and forth— as it casts a faint glow and makes shadows dance all over the waiting room. The woman on the television in the back room continues her rant over the events from the prior night.

The figure flips the match toward the reception desk with a simple flick of the wrist.

The match arcs through the air, staying lit as it continues its unique dance. Then it lands on the center of the desk and ignites the gasoline that has been splashed all over. The fire erupts with a vengeance, as though it was waiting for this very moment for far too long.

Following the trail of the gasoline, the fire rapidly spreads from the desk to the floor and to the walls, spreading throughout the waiting room and toward the exam room and the back office, where the idiot on the television is still complaining and Dr. Elyse's slowly cooling body awaits its next fate.

The heat in the waiting room quickly becomes too fierce to bear, and the figure steps through the front door and into the rain. They leave the front of the clinic and heads toward Dr. Elyse's car in the back of the building. Just as they open the driver's side door, the sound of the clinic's front windows exploding could be heard, and the shockwave from whatever exploded in the clinic causes the figure to slip on the wet pavement and fall to the road. They quickly shake off the fall and gets back up. The figure sits down behind the wheel and closes the car door. A smile crosses its face. By the time the fire department arrives at the clinic, any remaining traces of gasoline would be washed away by the storm.

The figure starts the car, backs out of the parking spot, and turns down the street, pulling away from the raging fire at the clinic and heading back toward the young girl. The game is about to begin.

As the light from the fire of the clinic continues to grow, and the taillights from Dr. Elyse's car continue to fade, a small, round, shiny object is left alone on the ground where the car was parked only just moments ago.

≈

Only a few miles away from the clinic that is quickly being engulfed in an inferno, Karen Ellie closes the door behind her to Colin's house. Wrapping her jacket tight around her, she thinks about the events of the past couple days. Her smile slowly disappears and the frown returns.

Poor Colin. He's had a rough time of it since Alicia left, and now this. She can still see his smile about her bacon comment. *He is one tough, stubborn man*, she thinks. Even when Alicia left, he refused to show any grief and always kept a smile on his face for his little girl. But Karen, she knows better. He is hurting inside. Every single day. He might not say it, but it's in his eyes. And she knows Penny can see it as well, particularly now that she is older.

She walks down the porch and into the rain toward her truck. She won't let this family fall apart. She loved Alicia like a daughter and Colin like her son. Starting up the truck, she turns on the headlights and puts it in gear. Pulling out of the driveway and into the deserted street, she turns the windshield wipers on high. The storm is getting worse and the ever-present wind is blowing the rain almost sideways. Although she knows Penny will be fine walking home in this weather, the little girl has been through enough the last twenty-four hours. Karen hopes a large dinner and a ride home in the warm interior of her truck will help ease Penny's worries a bit.

Her frown eases up a little bit and a smile begins to form at the edges of her mouth. Her restaurant has been completely empty anyway the last couple days due to the weather, as the local townsfolk hunker down to weather the passing storm. The weatherman said today and tomorrow would be the worst of it and within another day it should clear up completely.

As she approaches the turn for the street the clinic was on, a car comes toward her going the other direction. She waves at the driver, not sure if they can see her and unable to determine who it is due to the constant stream of water on her windshield. Her poor windshield wipers struggle to keep up with the rain but can only do so much. The car passes and she can see the blurred light of the taillights in her rear view mirror. She slows to make the turn, hoping the other driver gets to their destination without any difficulties.

As she approaches the clinic, the distant light she assumed was a street light quickly begins to get bigger and bigger. A wave of panic races through her body. Something is wrong. As she reaches her destination, she can see where the light is coming from. Flames have engulfed the entire clinic and, even in this rain, repeatedly leap into the air several feet beyond the rooftop. Karen stops her truck in the middle of the street and throws it into park. She leaps from the vehicle and runs toward the building, praying Dr. Elyse and Penny are OK and not trapped inside. As she reaches the front of the clinic, the heat from the flames is too much and it forces her back out into the street. There is glass scattered everywhere on the ground. Karen pulls out her cellphone and quickly dials the number to the fire station. *Please, please pick up*, she silently begs.

"Orchard Lake Fire Department," the familiar voice on the other side of the phone booms.

"Frank! It's Karen Ellie. The clinic is on fire. Please hurry!" she yells, hoping to be heard over the roar of the fire and the sound of the rain.

"Jesus, Karen, seriously? We are on our way. Stay back and don't get yourself hurt."

Karen hangs up the phone and puts it away. Still standing in the street, the rain has thoroughly soaked her through. She looks at the blaze. If Dr. Elyse or Penny were still in there, they would not be coming out alive. Tears begin to form in her eyes. She then shakes her head and strengthens her resolve. They made it out, she knows it. Both women are incredibly smart and would have been able to get out in time.

She looks around to see if there is anyone in the street, but it's still empty. She quickly heads back to her truck and gets behind the wheel. She pulls it over to the curb to allow the fire truck to get through and turns off the engine.

A siren can be heard approaching in the distance, its wail piercing through the storm. Karen reaches down into her pocket and pulls out her cellphone. She pauses a moment and looks at the phone. How is she going to break this news to Colin? He's in no shape to move around and she knows he would sprint here from his house if he thought Penny was in danger, disregarding what injuries he might sustain or aggravate in the process.

She puts the phone back in her pocket. Calling him now would only lead to further stress on his end. She decides to wait.

She needs to know if there are any bodies in the fire ravaged building before she goes back to his house.

The siren grows in crescendo until it passes her truck. The fire truck pulls partially sideways in the street and stops in front of the clinic. The lights from the truck play across the dark storefronts on the other side of the street and seem to get lost when they cross the street and meet the fire from the clinic.

The firemen on board leap into action even before the truck fully stops and begin connecting the hoses to the truck and the fire hydrant across the street. In no time at all, there are two hoses spraying large, steady steams of water full blast at the clinic. Smoke quickly begins to overcome the remaining visibility in the area, rolling in waves from the clinic and, with the help of the rain, covers everything with a gray-tinted smudge.

A figure, blurry through the window by the rain, walks up to her truck and raps on the window, making Karen jump.

"Mrs. Ellie? It's Frank. Are you OK?" the figure asks. The fire chief has to practically yell to be heard over the fire, the storm, and the firefighters valiantly racing to put out the blaze.

She rolls the window down and leans out so she doesn't have to shout. "I'm OK, Frank." she responds.

"What happened here?" he asks.

She shrugs at him. "I don't know. The place was on fire when I got here. Frank, please tell me if you find anyone inside. I didn't see anyone outside when I arrived."

He nods his head and looks back toward the fire. "We won't

really know anything until we get the fire out and have a chance to get inside. I'm sorry, Karen. I'm hoping no one was hurt."

He looks at her and tells her to stay put for the time being. She nods her head and rolls the window back up.

She looks out the window at the fire and watches the smoke rise into the air, fighting the rain for dominance. Watches as water from the hoses cascades over the clinic and in through the windows. Watches the flames get smaller and smaller.

Karen continues to watch, shaking in her seat and fighting back the tears she knows will come in due course once the flames are no more.

≈

After Mrs. Ellie left, Colin doesn't have much interest in what was on the television. With Karen going to pick Penny up, he knows Dr. Elyse wouldn't be able to argue and she would end up letting Penny go early. He forces himself to get out of the easy chair and slowly heads into the kitchen, where the delicious smell of Karen's home-cooked food has taken over.

His stomach rumbles once again. Colin walks over to the cabinet and pulls out two plates, taking care not to drop them since the pain in his side is wide awake and adamant about letting him know it is still present. He slowly sets the table in anticipation of the meal. No need to make Penny do all of this when he is fully capable.

He glances at the clock. He has at least thirty minutes before Karen and Penny get back to the house, which should be just enough time for him to get a shower and clean up. He heads into his bedroom and grabs some clean clothes from his closet, slowly moving from his closet and into his bathroom. He takes off his clothes and carefully removes the bandage on his side. His laceration has stopped bleeding, but it's still red and extremely tender to the touch. The stitches stand out, stark black lines against his skin. He is thankful he doesn't have to go back to Rockville to get the stitches removed. The doc had said something about the stitches dissolving on their own over time and he should be healed up by the time they are all gone.

Colin turns on the faucet and adjusts the water to a comfortable, warm temperature. He steps into the shower and lets the water slowly wash away his worries. An initial, sharp sting erupts from his side when the water hits it, but quickly begins to fade. As he settles into the warm blanket of water that envelops him, he stops thinking about the pain and begins to think about the delicious meal spread out on the kitchen table that awaits him and his little hummingbird.

$$\approx$$

Karen had turned the headlights off on her truck well before the fire was extinguished. Now only the rotating lights from fire truck illuminate the night, throwing shadows here and there as the firemen rush back and forth, trying to eliminate any hot spots while confirming the building structure is sound enough to enter it.

Ten minutes pass. Twenty minutes pass. Karen strains to see what is happening. From what she can see through the blurry windshield, only a few of the firemen are still out at the truck, packing up the hoses and capping off the fire hydrant. She rolls down her driver's side window and looks out to get a clearer view.

She surveys the little bit of the clinic she can see from the lights on the fire truck. It appears now as a hollow, burned-out husk of a building with a blackened facade and small trails of smoke still rising from the remnants of the roof. An occasional flashlight beam is seen shining here and there as the firemen and fire chief inspect the interior. She finds solace in the fact the lights haven't hovered on one location too long in the main room, at least from what she could see. Penny would have been sitting at the reception desk in the front and if she didn't make it out, her body may have still been at that spot.

After waiting what seems to be an eternity, one of the flashlights exits the clinic and walks her direction, cutting a pathway through the rain.

This is it. Karen doesn't notice it, but she begins to shake again. She's afraid of what is about to come. She needs to know if any bodies were found but at the same time, she doesn't want to know, either. Frank reaches her window and looks at her.

"I have some bad news, Karen. We found a body in the back office. From the size of the body, we are pretty sure it's Dr. Elyse. The coroner is on their way from Rockville and will be able to provide a positive identification for us. We didn't find any other bodies, so we are fairly certain no one else was in the clinic at the time of the fire. We don't know for sure what caused the fire, but there was melted television in the back and some melted extension cords next to it. We are pretty sure that may have been the cause but we won't know until we can clean it up a bit. This rain isn't helping at all."

Karen visibly sighs in relief. Although saddened by the news Dr. Elyse appears to have died in the fire, she is relieved Penny's body was not found in the rubble. "Thank you, Frank. I know you didn't have to tell me all of that. I was worried Colin's daughter, Penny, was in there as well. You know Colin, he works down at the car wash. As you have probably heard, he was in a pretty bad automobile accident yesterday, and she was working tonight as the receptionist at the clinic. I was actually on my way here to pick her up and take her home so she wouldn't have to walk in this weather."

Frank looks at her and nods. "Well, she's not in there, if that is any consolation. Maybe she left early and went to a friend's house." he suggests. "Listen, Karen, there is no reason for you to be here anymore. Go on home. We will get everything cleaned up and then in a few days, once the storm passes, we can mourn the loss of whoever is laying in the back room and begin the rebuilding process."

She lowers her head a moment, then looks up at the fire chief and nods her head. She watches as he turns and heads back into the burned-out clinic. She rolls up her window at last, stopping the never-ending stream of water running down the interior portion of her door and soaking the left side of her body. She starts up the truck and takes a deep breath. Dropping the vehicle into drive, she clings to the glimmer of hope Penny is over at one of her friend's houses and nothing else bad will happen tonight. Karen turns the vehicle around and heads back toward Colin's house.

It was time to break the news, and Karen wants to be there in person for it.

≈

Colin steps out of the shower and grabs a towel. He dries off and begins to get dressed. He pauses before putting on his shirt and grabs a new bandage from the bag on the sink. He applies the bandage to his side and wraps the cloth ends around his waist, securing it tightly on the opposite side with the provided clamps. He puts on a loose-fitting shirt and glances at his reflection in the mirror. *Not bad*, he thinks. Besides a few cuts and scrapes, he almost looks like he normally does.

He glances at the clock on the table next to the bed. The shower didn't take him as long as he thought it would have. He quickly combs his short, brown hair and heads back into the kitchen. The tantalizing, aromatic mix of meatloaf, mashed potatoes, sweet corn, and homemade bread all hit his nose at the same time, sending his stomach into a grumbling marathon.

He pauses at the fridge, opens the door, and grabs one of the cold beers on the shelf. He twists the top off and takes a swig. *To hell with not mixing the pain medication with alcohol*, he thinks. Turning toward the living room, he heads back to his easy chair and sits down. The news reporter on the television is talking about massive power outages in Shelton and Rockville. So far the power hasn't gone out here. *Thank goodness for small blessings*, he thinks.

As if he said the blessing in his head too soon, the television goes silent and the house is plunged into darkness.

"Well, that's just peachy," he says to the now quiet house.

Colin listens to the storm outside as it continues its bombardment on the roof and sides of the house. Feeling for the end table, he puts down his beer and stands up from the chair. He slowly makes his way, arms outstretched like a zombie, to the kitchen where the candles are kept. He finds his way to the sink and opens the drawer next to the sink. Reaching in, he grabs several candles and the box of matches. He pulls one candle from the stack and lights it up, instantly bathing the small kitchen in a flickering light. He puts the candle in a holder near the sink and proceeds to light another candle, putting it in a holder on the other side of the kitchen. Six candles later, the living room and kitchen have enough light to actually see where everything is again. Colin walks over to the table by the door and opens the drawer, pulling out both flashlights that are kept there. Turning each one on, he tests the lights to make sure they work. One for him and one for Penny, for when they need to go into the back of the house. Power outages are common in Orchard Lake, so every resident has a good stockpile of candles and batteries for their flashlights.

He sets one of the flashlights down on the table and aims the beam of the other one at the clock. *They should be here by now*, he thinks. He slowly walks around the living room and kitchen, double-checking to make sure all the lit candles don't pose a fire hazard. Happy with his inspection, he walks back into the living room and sits back down in the easy chair. He grabs his beer and takes another swig. After Penny gets home, he can look into getting the coolers from the back room and putting everything in the refrigerator and the freezer into them. The fridge and freezer will keep their cold for several hours as long as they are not opened up a lot. But he can do that after they enjoy dinner.

His stomach rumbles again in agreement.

A set of headlights suddenly shining through the front window interrupts Colin's thoughts. *Good*, he thinks. *Karen and Penny are back.* Colin gets up from the easy chair, and holding both his beer and the flashlight, he walks over to the front door so he can greet them. He hears a car door shut and, shortly after, steps on the wooden porch. He opens the door before the doorbell could ring.

Karen is standing on the front porch. Dripping wet, with black smudges all over her face and clothes, she has a look on her face Colin has only ever seen twice before in his life: first when she lost her son Nick, Colin's best friend in high school, and then when she found out Alicia was gone. "Jesus, Karen, what happened?" he asks, unable to hide the panic in his voice.

She bursts into tears and lunges forward, throwing her arms around him, almost causing him to drop both his beverage and the flashlight. As her words fight for life through her sobs, Colin learns that there was a fire at the clinic and one body was found, but it wasn't Penny.

The initial panic he felt subsides a bit. With the weather as it is, maybe Dr. Elyse let Penny leave early and she stopped by one of her friend's houses before coming home. He forgot to check his cellphone prior to taking a shower, so it's possible she called and left a message. "It's all right, Karen. Relax. Come inside, dry off, and in a bit, you can tell me again what happened."

Pulling away, he sets his beer down on the table and clasps her hand. Leading her into the house and to the couch, she obediently sits down. "Wait here, OK?" he asks and turns toward the door, not waiting for her answer. He walks over and closes the door. He then turns on the flashlight and heads to the hallway closet, intent on grabbing a few towels. He grabs the towels and takes them back into the living room for Karen. He hands the towels to her and then walks back to the table by the door, grabbing his cellphone from the table and opening it up. No messages. Then again, he doesn't have a signal, either. Looks like the power isn't the only thing that isn't working tonight.

Karen's voice breaks the silence. "Did she call?"

"No, no messages," Colin replies. "But then, I don't have any service, either. So tell me again, what happened at the clinic, Karen?"

She lowers her head a second and then slowly begins to explain what she saw and what the fire chief told her. When she is done, Colin hangs his head. Dr. Elyse, presumed dead from a fire at the clinic. She was a nice woman. A little too into her reality television, but a nice woman. Penny, wherever she is, will be devastated when she finds out. She really liked

Dr. Elyse and loved working at the clinic.

"Karen, you are going to stay here tonight, all right?" Colin hands her his flashlight. "My room is the first room to the right down the hall. Go ahead, grab a candle and get a shower. There should be enough hot water in the water heater still. You can sleep in my room and I'll take the couch. Plus, Penny is going to need all the support we can give her when she gets home and she finds out what happened. We will figure this all out in the morning."

She looks at him and nods, gets up off the couch and makes her way to Colin's room.

He then picks up the wet towels from the floor and takes them into the kitchen, laying them over the backs of the kitchen chairs to dry. He refuses to allow any panic set in. Penny wasn't at the clinic, at least that was confirmed. She must be over Laura's house or one of her other friends' houses. He vaguely remembers she had mentioned something earlier in the week about an upcoming trip with Laura anyway. Maybe they were busy planning it and, with the storm knocking out the power as well as the lack of cell service, she decided to stay there. Content with his assumption on her whereabouts, he walks to the table by the door and grabs the other flashlight. As his hand wraps around the flashlight, a heavy knock comes from the front door.

He quickly looks at the door with a puzzled look on his face. He didn't remember seeing any lights shining from outside the house, which would normally indicate someone was driving up. As his thoughts race, his confusion turns to fear. He slowly walks to the door and grabs the door knob. *Please*, he thinks, *please don't let it be Deputy Gates or the fire chief with more bad news.* He pulls the door open.

Only the wind and the rain are there to greet him. He shines the flashlight briefly around the porch and into the rain in front of the house. The beam of light from his flashlight dances over Karen's truck and then back to the porch. No one. Just as he is about to turn back inside and close the door, he sees a rectangular brown package lying on the porch in front of the door. His confusion returns.

He reaches down, picks up the package and once again shines the beam of light from the flashlight around the porch.

Nothing but the rain.

He backs into the house and closes the door, setting the flashlight on the table. Holding the package, he walks into the kitchen and places it on the table. *COLIN* was written across the top with a bold black marker in block lettering.

For some reason, the hair on the back of his neck begins to rise. Something isn't right.

A wave of fear races across his thoughts.

His hands are shaking when he finally reaches out and begins to open the package.

CHAPTER 5

THE GAME

Penny opens her eyes to darkness.

She blinks and her eyes slowly begin to focus. She strains to make out her surroundings. Vague shapes can be seen here and there around her, but without any light, she is unable to determine how large the room is or where she is. Panic begins to set in.

The last thing she can remember is being grabbed from behind at the clinic, and then the world went dark. Questions race through her head. How long has she been unconscious, where is she, and what happened?

"Hello?" she asks into the dark.

No response.

"Is anyone there?" Her panic begins to escalate.

Get a grip, Penny, she tells herself. *You have seen enough movies to know what happens in a kidnapping. But why me?* Her dad isn't rich. She isn't famous. She didn't have any enemies she knew of, and everyone likes her dad.

She takes a deep breath, hoping to clear away the grogginess and stop her head from spinning.

The dark around her is all-consuming. So is the silence. "Hello. If anyone is out there, please, please just let me go" she begs to whoever or whatever might be listening.

She tries to stand up but doesn't make it very far. Her arms and legs are bound to the chair she is sitting in. She struggles to free herself, but her efforts are in vain. Whatever she has been bound by is not willing to allow her to move at all. *Think, Penny*, she commands herself. *The kidnapper always makes a mistake and you have to keep a calm head to get out of this.*

She takes another deep breath. There is a stale but slightly pungent odor in the air she can't place. And the smell of sawdust. She twists her feet left and right on the floor, but nothing moves under her shoes. She taps her foot. The sound and the feel of her taps confirm the floor is solid.

She looks around again, trying once more to identify the dark shapes she can see but is unable to do so. She listens for any noises which might help her figure out where she is, or what time it might be.

Silence.

Just as she wonders if the rain has stopped, she hears and feels the rumble of thunder. The familiar noise of the thunder helps her find just a moment of calm. Steadying herself and resolving to find a way out of her predicament, she rocks back and forth in the chair to see if the chair is secured to the floor or not. The chair moves with her. Hope springs into her chest and she resumes her efforts. Gaining momentum, it only takes a moment of additional effort for the chair to start to overturn, carrying her with it. As the chair begins to fall over, her right foot pushes too hard against the floor and the chair rotates slightly. The side of the chair hits the floor and Penny is unable to stop the right side of her head from hitting the floor.

Sharp, bright light flashes before her eyes and pain erupts from the side of her head, just above her right eyebrow. The world begins to slip away again.

The throbbing from her right temple is the last thing she remembers before she once again fades into unconsciousness.

≈

The figure watches Colin, candlelight flickering in the house behind him, as he shines his flashlight around his porch, looking for who rang the doorbell. The figure smiles. They know Colin won't see as far out at the tree line where the figure is standing. Not in this weather. They watch as Colin notices the package at the base of the doorway and picks it up. They watch as he takes the package inside and closes the door. Soon, he will know. Soon, he will begin the game. And soon, the figure will get the revenge they have been waiting for all these years. The revenge they deserve.

After Colin disappears into the house with the package, their smile fades. The figure turns to leave. They walk slowly through the woods and toward the main highway, where Dr. Elyse's car is parked. It's time to head back to Penny. To make sure she is still where she was left. The last thing the figure needs is for Penny to escape. She is secured extremely well so the figure is fairly confident she hasn't gone anywhere. Still, the thought of her possibly escaping races across the figure's thoughts.

If she did escape, and the figure did not catch her in time, the entire plan would be ruined. After the months, the years, it took to plan.

They shake their head and remove any thoughts of Penny's escape from their mind. She won't escape. There has been too much planning for anything to go wrong. Every step is covered. Every loose end is resolved. The only thing left now is to bring the full plan to completion and enjoy the finale.

The figure smiles again briefly. The revenge they have dreamed about for so long will soon come to blossom.

The breaking of sticks and occasional noise of the underbrush from the figure's footsteps is completely lost in the sound of the thunder and heavy downpour of rain. Soon, even the figure's few lingering footprints won't be seen on the ground at all. And that's exactly what the figure is expecting.

Finally approaching where the car is parked, the figure stops at the tree line. They take a moment to look around, to make sure no other cars have stopped to investigate. Satisfied no one else is nearby, the figure walks to the driver's side door and gets behind the wheel. The car starts, but the figure waits a moment to turn on the lights. They check once again to make sure no other cars are around. The road is completely empty. The figure turns on the lights and puts the car in drive, slowly pulling from the shoulder and back onto the main road. *Soon*, they think. Soon they will be back with Penny, and it will be time to start thinking about the second package and when to deliver it.

The thought of what the second package will contain brings another smile to the figure's face. This time, the smile remains for the duration of the trip. The thought of Colin's upcoming physical and emotional pain is a delicious thought that the figure keeps feasting on over and over in their head.

The smile gets bigger. Both of these types of pain will be very present for as long as the game is being played. *And this game*, the figure thinks, *will be played for quite some time*. They know Colin too well to believe he would give up before the finale. Before the figure finally has the salvation they have dreamed about for years.

The car disappears into the dark and the rain.

The roads, once again, are empty.

≈

Colin takes a deep breath.

Having removed the exterior plastic and the plain, brown wrapper from the package, it now sits forgotten to the side. A simple cardboard box, sealed shut with standard clear tape remains. The fear grows stronger, eating away at what calm sanity he still has. Why would a simple little box cause such a worry, he wonders. Maybe it's merely a care package with some bandages and a book or two from a concerned neighbor. His fear subsides a little at this thought. He has no logical reason to be worried.

He reaches over and pulls a small knife from the knife rack off the counter. Drawing the point of the blade down the tape that still holds the box shut, he breaks the seal on the remaining tape and sets down the knife.

The fear momentarily creeps back into his thoughts.

He forces himself to laugh. *There is nothing bad about this package*, he reassures himself. He reaches forward and opens the package up. Confusion sets in for just a moment. Then Colin recognizes what he is looking at and the lingering fear turns to overwhelming panic.

There is a total of three items in the box. The largest item in the box is the new Nicholas Sparks novel Penny was reading before she left for the clinic. Or, at least, maybe a copy of the same book. Colin is sure it is the same book, though, as he sees the two other items taped to its cover. One of those items is the same kind of lipstick Penny always makes Colin buy when he makes a trip to Sam's store. *That could be a coincidence as well*, he thinks to himself.

The third item, though. That is the item that makes all of Colin's fears come to fruition. The third item is Penny's watch. He knows it is her watch. The watch is taped face down on the book, with the back of it showing. Engraved there are the words: "To my little hummingbird. Love, Dad."

Colin's panic finally takes control.

He stumbles back from the table and backs into the counter, almost knocking over the dishes still in the drying rack. A sharp bolt from his side reminds him his wound is still there.

He tries to reassure himself what he just saw is a hoax. His mind is playing tricks on him. That when he looks back into the box, it will be a different book and something else that resembles the other two items he saw. Plus, he tells himself, the candle light isn't very bright at this spot in the kitchen and he may have imagined everything he just saw.

Colin steps forward from the counter and toward the table. His stomach rumbles. The smell of all the food Mrs. Ellie laid out earlier is still strong. He pauses before looking back into the package. This time, he reaches over and grabs the flashlight he laid down on the table next to the package.

He needs to be sure when he looks again.

He turns on the flashlight. The beam illuminates the far wall with bright white light, overpowering the yellow flicker of the candlelight and erasing any shadows that were being cast there. He slowly moves the beam from the spot on the wall, down to the floor and onto the table, across the table and the food, and into the box.

His fears are confirmed.

Inside the box are the same items he had previously identified. Also inside the box, and what he didn't see due to the dim candlelight, is Penny's name written all over. Writing in big letters. Small letters. In thick strokes and in thin strokes. Like how a teenager would decorate their notebooks with the name of the person they had a crush on.

The steady beam shining into the box waivers a moment, as Colin tries to regain control and slow the panic that is quickly taking over. He forces himself to reach into the box. He grabs the book and pulls it out, setting it down on the table. He stares at it for a moment, and then aims the beam of light back into the box to see if anything else was in there.

A folded, white piece of paper is lying at the bottom of the box.

Colin reaches into the box and picks up the edge of the paper. He can see there is writing on it as he pulls it out of the box. He sets it down next to Penny's book.

"Colin, are you OK?" A voice breaks through the silence.

Colin's heartbeat jumps from panic to complete heart attack in an instant. Karen. He was so focused on the box he forgot she was here. He almost drops the flashlight as he regains control. "Jesus, Karen, you scared the hell out of me," he says.

She looks apologetic in the candlelight. "I'm sorry, just wanted to let you know I feel better now after the shower and as long as you are all right, I think I am going to head home."

He pauses a moment before answering her. Should he tell her about the package, he wonders. He thinks better of it at this time. *Mrs. Ellie has been through enough today and doesn't need to be any more worried than she probably already is*, Colin rationalizes. Plus, he hasn't read the note yet. For all he knows it could be Penny playing some weird prank on him. "I'll be all right, Karen, thank you. I'm just still worried about Penny but I'm sure she's OK." He hopes she doesn't see through his outright lie.

She stares at him a moment longer and sighs. "You are one

stubborn bastard, you know that, Colin? Please make sure you eat some food and put the rest away before it goes bad. You are as white as a sheet."

He nods and forces what he hopes is a convincing smile on his face. "Thank you so much again for everything," he adds.

Karen nods, her smile returning to her round face, and she heads toward the front door. "Please call me if you need anything at all. And you damn sure better call me the second you hear from Penny."

Unable to find the words to respond, he nods at her. He's afraid if he says anything else, she will hear the fear in his voice and demand to know what is going on.

Karen takes one more look over her shoulder at Colin, beams her brightest smile, and opens the door to head out into the storm.

He doesn't move until the lights from her truck illuminate the front window, then fade, and finally completely disappear.

Colin shines the beam of his flashlight back to where the folded paper and Penny's possessions are located. Breaking his attention from where the beam was focused, he looks around. The light from the candles in the kitchen and the living room continues to flicker and cast dancing shadows all over the place. Besides the sound of the rain on the roof and the occasional thunder outside, the house is completely quiet. He refocuses his attention to the folded piece of paper on the table. *Please let this be a joke*, he wishes. He reaches down and grabs the paper and unfolds it. A short paragraph is scribbled on the paper, in the same handwriting that is on the box. He takes a deep breath and begins to read what is written.

Yes, Colin, your "little hummingbird" has been taken from you. She belongs to me now. If you ever want to see her again, and still alive, you must follow three simple rules: First, no one besides you can know she is gone or what is going on. Second, you must follow every instruction you are given from this point forward. Third, you will play the game according to the above rules and not deviate at all. If you break any of these rules, she will die. If you don't play the game I have created for you, she will die. Penny's life is now up to you. Now you know the rules, so the game has begun. I will be in touch.

Colin sets the paper down. His hand is shaking as he does.

His worst fears have come to life. Penny has been kidnapped by some psycho who wants to play some sick game. He feels his knees starting to go weak. He pulls out a chair from the table and sits down. A million thoughts race through his head at the same time. Who would do such a thing? Why her? Why him? Where is she? Is she OK? Is she scared? Is she still alive or already dead? Each and every one of these thoughts start with Colin finding her safe and alive. They end with him forcefully snuffing the life from whoever has taken his daughter, his little hummingbird, away from him.

Among the panicked thoughts of rescue and revenge,

a new thought forms in his head. Call the police. Call every single person in town and let them know what is going on. See if anyone has seen Penny recently at all. Get the entire town looking for her, right now. Colin gets up from the table and walks to the phone setting on the table near the door. He picks up the phone and puts it to his ear. The dial tone is waiting for him to make a choice.

He hits the first couple numbers to the police station and then stops. The note said not to tell anyone she was gone. He looks at the windows and at the darkness beyond.

He could be watched right now.

He sets the phone back in the cradle and walks back into the kitchen. He picks up the letter one more time and rereads what is written on it. *Fine*, he thinks. *We will play this your way for now.*

His stomach rumbles again. He sets the note back down on the table and sits down again. He will need his strength for what is to come. He will be no help to his little girl if he can barely stand or move around. He grabs the nearest container of food and begins to fill the empty plate on the table next to him. He will eat and try to get some sleep, if at all possible, and hopefully tomorrow will bring a little more clarity to what is going on.

His panic begins to subside. He will find his little hummingbird, he knows he will. But right now he needs to build back his strength, and he has no idea where to even start looking to find her.

Colin pauses a moment before grabbing the next plastic container. This person may have control right now, but the moment he has the chance, he will take it from them. Until then, Colin will play along. He opens the next container and scoops out some mashed potatoes.

Penny would love this dinner, he thinks.

He's not able to stop the tears that come next. He sets the container down, holds his head in his hands, and begins to sob.

≈

The figure finally reaches the end of the dirt road they have been driving down and pulls over to the side of the road. They turn off the car and the lights, plunging the surrounding world into complete darkness. They get out of the car and walk to the trunk. Opening the trunk, the figure feels around a moment until they find what they are looking for. They pull out a camouflage car cover they had placed in there previously and patiently cover the car with it, fighting the wind and the rain.

Once the cover is secured, the figure turns from the car, satisfied with the job performed. They head into the woods, following a path that would be barely visible on a clear day let alone at night in a rainstorm. But the figure has walked this path many times. They know every branch and turn, every rock and dip in the ground below their feet. Light was a liability at this point. Should the remote chance exist anyone saw the headlights or taillights from the car, the cover and the complete darkness from this point forward should eliminate any possibility of anyone following.

The figure smiles.

They continue along the pathway for some time until the woods and underbrush break into a large clearing. The figure pauses after stepping from the tree line. Although it is still pitch-black outside, the figure knows in the center of this clearing is the building that currently contains Penny and will ultimately become the location where the final stages of the game will play out.

Lightning races across the sky and illuminates the building. Dark. Stoic. This isn't the first storm this building has seen in all the years it has been around. It won't be the last.

The figure picks up their pace as they cross the clearing. Reaching the entrance, the figure fishes a keyring out of their pocket and unlocks the large metal door. They slide the door open, listening to the screeching of old metal on metal echo through the entrance to the building. They step into the building and pull the door closed. The screeching of the door is lost in the storm outside.

Beyond the rain and thunder from the storm, the figure's only welcome back is the silence after the door is finally closed and secured. They reach over to the nearest wall and flip a switch. The large, open room is slowly bathed in light as the dim overhead lamps hanging from the high ceiling turn on, becoming brighter as they warm up.

Everything is exactly as the figure left it. There is no worry that any of the light would be seen from outside. The figure was very careful to cover any windows or openings to make sure no light from inside the building would ever been seen on the outside.

They walk down the steps and onto the main floor of the building, maneuvering around the various pieces of dust-covered equipment that still remain from the building's former working years when it was an active sawmill, until they reach a door on the back wall of the room. Wet footprints remain behind them on the floor, leaving a dark-colored trail from the main door to the door they are currently standing in front of. Still holding the keyring, the figure unlocks this door and opens it up. The light from the main room illuminates a staircase that goes forward a few feet and then quickly plunges back into darkness as it turns to the right. The figure flips another switch on the wall, and the stairwell is quickly bathed in light. They walk down the stairs and stops at the bottom where yet another door is closed and locked. The figure unlocks that door and opens it, stepping through the doorframe and into the room.

Silence once again greets the figure.

The figure frowns. Penny should be awake by now. They expected yelling. Begging. Pleading. Crying.

They didn't expect silence.

The figure swiftly reaches to the left and a faint click echoes through the room. The overhead fluorescent lights come on, and the figure sees why there was no sound to greet them when they opened the door.

Penny is lying on her right side, still securely strapped to the chair, with a small pool of blood pooled around her head.

That is not how the figure left her at all.

A quick jolt of panic hits the figure. Penny's early death would make the game much more difficult to play.

They rush to where Penny is lying on the ground. They check for her pulse and find one.

A shudder of relief races through the figure's body. They take a slow, deep breath. She's still alive. She needs to stay alive for now. At least until Colin has made it here and the final stage of the game is in play.

The figure grabs the girl and carefully uprights her, setting the chair back in the same location it was previously. The girl doesn't wake.

The figure kneels down in front of the pretty doe-eyed girl. They lean forward and check the side of Penny's head, finding the wound from the impact. After a thorough inspection, they are fairly confident no major damage was caused from the fall. They look around. Nothing else was moved from where the figure had placed it. She must have struggled to free herself, overturned her chair, and hit her head on the ground.

The smile on the figure's face returns. Her attempts to free herself were for nothing. She will not escape. The figure's next thought makes their smile widen even farther.

Unless this doe-eyed young girl considers death an escape.

Still kneeling in front of the girl, the figure reaches forward and brushes the hair hanging in Penny's face to back behind her ears, pausing a little through the parts of the hair that is matted with dried blood from the fall. As the figure brushes the last of Penny's hair away from her face, they pause a moment. Still touching her ear, the figure slowly traces their hand down her ear and carefully traces her jawline. Stopping at her chin, the figure extends an index finger out and slowly traces the outline of Penny's soft lips.

An old, familiar feeling stirs within the figure. A feeling the figure hasn't experienced in years. Their heart starts to beat faster. Their breathing begins to get shallower and quicker. *No,* they silently command.

The figure quickly pulls their hand away from the young girl's face as though they had just felt an electric shock. The figure's hand is shaking.

She is bait, the figure thinks. She is nothing more, never will be, and cannot replace the first. The one. The one the figure spent years with. Through many long nights and many conversations about everything. Until death finally came and took the one from them.

No. She is nothing. She is bait. She is a mere pawn. She is an object. She is the lure that will bring Colin here.

She shouldn't be able to have this effect. The figure frowns. Have they grown so weak they will now give in to every whim or fancy that crosses their mind? No. But the figure has to know. Has to know they will be strong enough for what's to come. Has to know they can make the hard choices when they need to. They must be tested.

Still kneeling in front of the unconscious girl, the figure reaches out both hands for Penny's head. Taking her head in their hands, they lift her face level with their own.

They lean forward toward her, deeply breathing in her scent.

And carefully put their lips to her lips.

CHAPTER 6

THE REALITY

Light pierces into Colin's restless sleep and brings him back to the present world. He opens his eyes and looks up at the ceiling fan above him. He stares at each of the blades and tries to bring his thoughts together. He looks over at the doorway to his room and the brightly lit bulb of the hallway light. This means the power has come back on.

He went to sleep shortly after dinner last night. After putting the remnants of dinner into the fridge, he left the box and the letter sitting in the center of the table as a reminder. As a beacon. As another wound to complement the one already in his side. To complement the one already long existing in his heart.

He stretches his legs and throws off the covers. He swings his legs off the bed and sits up. The pain that greets him this morning is much less intense than yesterday. *That's a step in the right direction*, he thinks. He gets out of bed and heads into the bathroom. He hits the switch and light from the four bulbs above the mirror illuminate the room. He looks at his reflection in the mirror. Haggard. His eyes appear sunken into his face and stubble has taken over his normally clean shaven face. He looks as though he hasn't slept in days and has aged ten years overnight.

He rubs his eyes and grabs his toothbrush. Time to clean up and go visit the box again.

After washing his face and changing clothes, Colin feels more like himself. The reflection in the mirror looks more like himself again. He walks into the kitchen and looks up at the battery-operated clock above the window. It is one of the only clocks in the house still on the correct time. Nine o'clock. He actually, somehow, slept in a couple hours today. He opens the fridge. Normally, he would frown at drinking any alcohol before noon, but something tells him he might need a little liquid courage to face what today might bring.

He grabs a beer from the shelf and pops off the top. Taking a swig, he readies himself and looks over at the table. The box still sits in the center of the table, holding guard over the small piece of folded paper lying next to it. The original wrapper remains discarded next to the box. He closes the fridge door and walks over to the table. He sets down the beer. Picking up the folded paper, he again reads what is written on it. He sets the paper aside and looks through the box. He checks the pages of Penny's book, making sure nothing is buried between the pages. He checks the watch and the lipstick, and puts all the items back into the box.

Nothing.

Colin slams his hand down on the table, causing the objects in the box to jump a bit and almost overturning his beverage. Why would this lunatic send this to him without anything else? Why not give him a timeframe of when he might be able to expect more contact? Was he just supposed to wait indefinitely until this person made contact again, to permanently worry about his little girl's life and whereabouts?

His frustration begins to grow. This inhuman piece of shit takes his daughter and doesn't have the decency to give him any idea on what to expect. His frustration gradually turns into rage. Colin grabs the box in fury and throws it across the room, watching it slam against the far wall. The contents spill out and Colin finds himself staring at Penny's possessions, lying on the floor next to the box.

The back of Penny's watch catches the morning light coming in the window. His attention focuses on this and his rage slowly begins to subside.

He needs to keep a calm head. He's watched enough crime shows to know when you get angry and do something stupid during a kidnapping, the person who is kidnapped usually gets hurt. He forces himself to take a deep breath and relax a little bit. He won't be the reason Penny is hurt any more than she might already be. Colin turns from the table and looks out the window above the sink.

It's the first time he notices it isn't raining anymore. Outside the window, the early morning sun is fighting to break through the clouds. Colin was so accustomed to hearing the rain and the thunder the past couple days that he didn't notice it when it was finally gone. He turns on the faucet, leans forward, and splashes some cold water on his face to help fully quell the now subsiding rage inside him. Grabbing the towel next to the sink, he dries his face off. Just as he turns back toward the table where the note lies, the phone rings.

Colin jerks back a bit when the initial ring echoes through the air. Startled, he looks over at the phone on the table. It rings again. Penny is his first thought.

Colin quickly moves toward the table near the door and grabs the phone. "Hello?" he quickly asks, almost out of breath and afraid of what he might hear on the other end.

"Colin, my friend! How are you this fine, non-rainy day?" the voice on the other end booms.

Colin's hopes crash upon rocky shores. Alan. "Hey. How are you?" Colin replies, attempting to hide the panic and disappointment in his voice.

"I'm good, my friend, I am good. Listen, I heard about what happened. Are you OK?" Alan asks from the other end of the line.

Another new bolt of panic strikes Colin. How did Alan find out about Penny? Colin was sure he didn't tell anyone per the instructions on the note. He waits for Alan to speak again.

"Listen, Colin, I know a car accident is a rough time and the last thing you probably want to see is a bunch of cars, so I am going to keep the car wash closed for a few additional days. That means you need to stay home, get better, and spend some time with Penny."

A wave of relief floods through Colin. The car accident. Beyond the occasional painful reminder from his side, the car accident is the furthest thing from his mind. "Thanks, Alan. That means a lot," he replies. Alan didn't know about Penny.

"You get some rest, all right? I will call you in a couple days to see how you are doing and if you need anything at all, just let me know."

Colin gives him his agreement, thanks his boss for his concern, and says good-bye. He hangs up the line, slowly setting the phone back into the cradle. Colin's attention refocuses back on the folded letter still lying on the kitchen table. Mocking him. Daring him to disobey and play God with his daughter's life.

He walks back into the kitchen and picks up the beer still sitting there, taking another drink. Setting it back down again, he walks over to where the box is lying, with Penny's possessions spilled onto the ground around it. He looks the box over closely once again in case he missed something when he first looked at it. It is a standard cardboard box, about eight inches wide and eight inches long. No distinguishing features, beyond Penny's name written all over the inside of it.

Still holding the box, Colin reaches over and picks up the book, watch, and lipstick. He puts them back inside the box and stands up, returning to the table to set the box back down.

He takes another swig of the beer and sits down at the table. Taking a deep breath, wincing from the pain in his side, he hopes Penny is OK and isn't afraid. He hopes she is still alive. Most of all, he hopes he will have the opportunity to get his hands on whoever is doing this and make them pay.

He takes one last pull from the beer bottle, finishing off what is remaining.

≈

A loud screeching noise pierces through the silence of the building. Penny's eyes slowly begin to open. The right side of her head is throbbing with pain. The lights are on and, as the fogginess around her consciousness lifts, Penny is able to see where she is at for the first time. Trying to move but unable to do so, she affirms she is still securely tied to the chair. She doesn't attempt to rock it this time, though. That was a painful lesson to learn. She takes a moment to survey the room, unaware of what happened when her captor found her on her side. A double fluorescent light is hanging from the ceiling above her, lighting up the room with flickering light, as though one of the bulbs is about to burn out. The room is about fifteen feet by twenty feet, with a solid wood door across from her on the other side of the room and another door made of some sort of metal to her right. A table stands without any chairs on the far left side of the room, with various wood working tools lying around on the top of it. Next to Penny, on her left but thankfully out of the reach of her head should she fall over again, is a large metal chest with a hand sander for wood lying on top of it.

Both the chest and the sander appear to be extremely old and covered in dust. None of the items appear to have been used in years. To her right, in the corner, there is the lonely base of a water cooler, missing the companion jug that would normally be on top. In the other corner between the two doors there are two shovels propped against the wall. Both shovels appear to have been used recently, as there is what looks like dried mud smeared on them both and there is dirt lying on the floor below them. The room smells of wood and dust and the persistent underlying smell she still can't identify.

The metal door on the right side of the room begins to creak and scrape along the ground as it slowly begins to open.

Penny quickly closes her eyes and lowers her head, pretending to still be unconscious.

She can hear the scraping of the door come to a stop, and then start back up again as it is closed. Once the scraping stops, she hears a lock tumble into place and then footsteps. The footsteps get slightly louder with each step, and she can sense the steps are approaching her.

Her heartbeat begins to race. She tries to slow her breathing.

The sounds of the footsteps stop directly in front of her. The smell of dirt mixed with the sharp smell of some sort of cleaning chemical assaults her nose. She concentrates harder on keeping her breathing steady. She hears a rustle of clothing and a metallic click. She feels the heat of another person's skin pass her left cheek and grab some of her hair hanging near her ear.

She can feel her heartbeat raging through her body and its sound is so strong in her ears she is afraid she won't hear anything else. She prays whoever is standing in front of her doesn't hear it as well, as she is sure it is pounding hard enough as though it's about to leap out of her body. She feels a quick tug from her hair and then the hand begins to pull away slowly. As the hand is pulling away, it pauses on her lower cheek and traces a line from her cheek to her left corner of her lips before it finally pulls completely away.

She fights the urge to flinch and scream with every ounce of her being. *Please*, she silently begs, *please just leave*.

A long, heavy sigh comes from in front of her. She hears the rustle of clothing again, and then the footsteps resume. Walking away from her. She hears a door unlock and a door open. The footsteps recede farther away and the door closes. The lock clicks back into place.

The room is silent once again.

Penny hesitates to move her head or open her eyes. She waits. A distant echo of metal on metal breaks the silence.

Opening her eyes, she lifts her head. The room is empty and both doors are closed. She can feel her body shaking from the adrenaline.

Too scared to scream and bring back whoever was just here, she begins to quietly cry. She might almost be an adult, she thinks as the first tear rolls down her right cheek, but right now all she wants is her daddy.

≈

Deputy Steve Gates has seen a lot in his time while he has served as a police officer. He wishes he could say what he is currently looking at is routine, but something doesn't feel right about it. He takes off his hat and runs his hand over his closely cut hair.

Standing in front of the charred husk that remains of the clinic, the deputy knows in his gut this isn't an accident. How does a building catch fire and burn almost to the ground in a heavy rainstorm? It just doesn't make any sense. The fire chief insists it was an electrical fire and told the deputy he was wasting his time doing an investigation.

Gates wasn't always with the Orchard Lake Police Department. He spent five years with the Chicago Police Department before he lost his partner during a routine traffic stop gone bad and decided to relocate to a new city to escape his memories. How he ended up in Orchard Lake was by pure chance. One night at home, after the better part of a fifth of Jack Daniels, Steve decided he would let a dart decide where his new home would be. He grabbed a dart from his dartboard and threw it at the United States map he had hanging up on wall on the other side of the room.

The first dart didn't even make it to the wall. His second dart ended up securely embedded into the wall above the map. His third dart found the middle of Lake Erie.

It was his fourth dart that found Orchard Lake.

And here he stands, six years later. Proud member of the small Orchard Lake sheriff's department and the only black deputy on the force. Staring at the remains of the clinic. The coroner and fire department—which includes the chief—had all left in the early hours of the morning after the fire was fully extinguished. They had ruled it an accident. The fire chief was convinced a faulty television wire had ignited the fire that burned down the clinic.

Still, the deputy was not convinced it was due to a faulty wire. This kind of damage is not caused by an electrical fire alone. This kind of damage is caused by a large volume of accelerant and the deputy has seen this before when he was with the CPD. And when an accelerant is involved, to this extent of damage, it almost always means it was set on purpose. A fire set on purpose and a dead body makes this a homicide investigation, and that is exactly how Deputy Steve Gates is treating it.

Unfortunately, he had already scoured the remains of the clinic's interior and nothing was of use. Everything is charred, melted, and twisted. Any evidence remaining in there would be completely useless or unrecognizable.

The deputy looks around the street and at the few other buildings nearby. The firefighters did a good job of cleaning up all the glass from the windows that had exploded into the street. Almost none of the debris remained on the ground. The few pieces that did remain were only noticeable when they were caught by the sunlight and glinted back at Gates.

He continues his inspection of the outside of the building. Walking around to the back side of the building where there were a few additional parking spots, he notices something on the ground in the spot closest to the building, surrounded by the now drying puddles. The deputy walks over to it and bends down for a closer look.

A makeup compact was lying on the ground.

Steve pulls a plastic bag from his pocket and after turning it inside out, picks up the compact. He seals the bag and inspects the compact. Where did he recently see one of these, he wonders. Then he remembers.

Colin's daughter, Penny.

She had a compact just like this with her when he drove her to pick up Colin from Rockville. *It makes sense, though*, he thinks. Penny works at the clinic.

It wouldn't be unusual for a young girl to drop something.

Except this compact was lying right around where Dr. Elyse parks her car. And Dr. Elyse's car is nowhere to be found, even though her body was found inside the clinic. The fire chief made sure last night to point out his job was to deduce the nature of a fire and not solve the mystery of a missing car. The deputy stands up and completes his search around the clinic. He finds nothing else of use in his investigation. Walking over to his squad car, he opens the door and sits down behind the wheel.

He sets the plastic bag with the compact on the passenger seat. "Dispatch, this is car twelve. Come in, over."

"Car twelve, this is dispatch. Go ahead," the voice chirps on the other end. The hint of sarcasm wasn't unnoticed by the deputy. It took Steve months to get the dispatch operator at the station to stop calling him by his first name over the radio on calls. The dispatch operator has been less than pleasant since.

"Dispatch, just finished inspection of the Walk-In Clinic. Going to go interview the additional employees regarding the whereabouts of Dr. Elyse's car. Requesting BOLO on her vehicle please," Gates asks. He knows the bulletin on the vehicle might be a little premature, but again his gut tells him he is going to want to find that car and quickly.

"Copy that, car twelve. BOLO issued on Dr. Elyse's vehicle," the dispatcher's voice echoes over the line again, issuing a lookout for Dr. Elyse's car, giving the year, make, model, color, and tag number. Steve looks at the laptop in his car to confirm the bulletin was issued and relaxes a little bit.

He pulls his door closed and starts the car. Time to pay a visit to Colin, see if Penny knows anything, and to return her compact. He puts the car in drive and pulls into the street.

≈

Colin doesn't hear the car pull into the driveway. He doesn't hear the car door shut or the footsteps cross his porch to the front door.

He doesn't even hear the doorbell the first time it rings. The second ring of the doorbell snaps Colin back to reality. He has been staring at the folded piece of paper in his hand for the last hour or so. Reading it over and over. Every word. Every line. Memorizing it.

He glances at the clock. Just before noon.

The doorbell rings again, followed this time by a strong rap on the door. Colin gets up from the table and walks to the door, expecting to see Karen standing there with another truckload of food and demanding an update on Penny. Instead, he opens the door to Deputy Gates.

For the second time today, a bolt of panic races through him. "Deputy, how can I help you?" he asks, trying to sound in control.

"Colin, I'm sure you are aware of the fire at the clinic last night. And I'm sure you are aware we sadly have lost a member of our community to it. I was hoping to speak with Penny about it since she was on shift last night," the deputy states.

"She's not here right now, Deputy," Colin responds.

"Do you know when she will be back?" Deputy Gates asks.

"No. You know how teenage girls are. She's probably out with her friends and enjoying the weather."

The deputy looks at him with a sideways glance. Colin knows what he just said sounded forced and very unlike what he would normally say. "Colin, what's going on?" Gates asks with narrowed eyes.

Getting frustrated with the conversation and the deputy's persistent questions, Colin barks a reply a little too harshly. "Nothing, Steve. I'm tired. It's been a long fucking week, my side still hurts, and I keep getting bad news." Colin instantly regrets his tone. The deputy and Colin struck up a good friendship several years back over drinks at Ellie's one night. Steve was also one of Colin's few friends in town who didn't look at him like it was his fault Alicia left.

The deputy's face softens a bit after Colin finishes. "I'm sorry if I upset you. I understand it's been a long week. I'm just trying to do my job, though, and right now my job requires I speak with Penny. May I come in and wait for her with you? It would be better than just me showing up at one of her friends' houses to talk to her. Less for her to worry about."

Colin takes a deep breath. He isn't going to be able to get rid of the deputy now. Not after how he is acting, and he knows Steve can sense something is wrong. "Yeah, come on in."

He steps away from the door and allows the deputy to step inside. As the deputy is walking by him, he remembers the box and the paper still on the kitchen table. "Have a seat in the living room, Steve. I'll grab you something to drink."

Colin closes the door behind the deputy and quickly walks into the kitchen. He grabs the paper and the box, stuffs the paper into the box, and puts them in the cabinet under the sink. "I have water or soda," Colin states. "Pick your poison."

"Water's fine, thank you," the deputy replies.

Colin grabs a clean cup from the cabinet and fills it full of cold tap water. He walks into the living room and hands the glass to the deputy.

"Thanks. So, Colin, what's really going on?" Steve asks. "There's something you're not telling me."

Colin sits down in the easy chair and sighs. Steve is a good friend and an even better cop. Colin can't remember how many times he had wished Steve was on the force when Alicia disappeared. Maybe then the investigation into her disappearance would have been more than two visits and a single "I'm sorry."

"Steve, you have been a good friend," Colin begins. "Yes, there is something going on. I can't tell you everything but here is what I can tell you. Penny isn't here. I don't know where she is, and I plan on finding her. I wish I could tell you more, but I can't."

Colin stares into the deputy's eyes. The deputy slowly nods at him in return and glances around the room.

"Have you told anyone else about this?" the deputy asks. Colin shakes his head. "Good. Don't. In fact, let's assume you never told me, either."

Colin nods.

Steve continues to talk. "Stop me if I am wrong. You have received something physical or a call that indicates Penny is missing. If you tell anyone, she will be hurt. If you don't follow instructions, she will be hurt."

Colin nods again.

"She is going to be all right, Colin," the deputy states. "Dr. Elyse's car is missing, and I think I found some of Penny's makeup near where it would have been parked. I initially thought Penny may have taken the car, but I realize now my initial thoughts were wrong. So now I think it would be safe to assume whoever took Dr. Elyse's car may also be the one who has caused the situation you are now facing."

The deputy could see the obvious relief spread across Colin's face.

Gates stands up. "Colin, how were you notified of Penny's disappearance?"

Colin doesn't say a word. He quietly stands up and walks into the kitchen. He then opens the cabinet under the sink where he had placed the package before going to sleep last night and hesitates before grabbing the cardboard box. Colin shakes his head. Not even a day into what happened and he has already broken one of the kidnapper's rules. *I'm sorry, Penny*, he thinks. *I wish I was strong enough to face this on my own.* He grabs the cardboard box and pulls it out, then stands back up and sets the box down on the kitchen table.

The deputy walks over to the table and stops at the far edge, opposite from Colin.

Colin takes a deep breath and watches the deputy. Steve reaches over and pulls the box across the table to look at it closer. He inspects the box, checking each one of the three items in it, and then finally pulling out the folded piece of paper. He reads the note several times over, and checks the paper thoroughly. Colin observes the deputy intently, searching for anything that might indicate hope.

Seemingly satisfied with his inspection, Steve sets the paper back down and looks at Colin. "She's still alive, Colin. That's the most important thing to remember in all of this. Secondly, you are not alone in this. I know what the note says. Don't let that get to you. She will be all right."

Colin nods at the deputy. He still can't shake the feeling that bringing Steve into this is only going to make things a lot worse than they already are. For all of them.

Steve begins to say something else but is interrupted by the doorbell. Colin jumps at the sound. Steve looks at Colin and then at the door. Neither man moves. The doorbell rings one more time, once again giving off the impression of being impatient.

"Be right there," Colin yells. He steps around the table and heads for the door. The deputy takes a step back from the table and puts his left shoulder to the wall, partially concealing himself with the corner of the wall.

Colin reaches the front door and grabs the knob. He hesitates a moment before opening the door and looks back at Steve. The deputy nods his head at Colin.

Facing the door again, Colin grips the knob tightly, his knuckles turning white from the pressure. Steeling himself for whoever may be on the other side, Colin pulls the door open. "Hello?" he asks.

No one is standing on the other side.

He steps closer to the doorframe and looks around the porch. Empty. Feeling a sense of déjà vu, Colin forces himself to look down at the floor of the porch in front of the door. Nothing. Colin looks back at Steve and shrugs his shoulders.

The deputy comes out from his place around the corner and walks to the front door where Colin is. Colin moves out of the way and Steve steps out on to the porch, looking around.

"Steve, this is the same thing that happened last night, when I found that package on the porch," Colin says. "The doorbell rang, and no one was here." The deputy looks at him and nods.

Colin points at the floor where he is standing. "The box was left right here."

Steve walks over to where Colin is standing and looks around. The rain would have washed anything away from the delivery last night. "Do you remember about what time the box was left here?" Steve asks.

Colin's brow furrows as he tries to remember. "I'm not sure, Steve. The power was out. It could have been any time after nine I suppose. Karen was here and had just told me about the fire. She took a shower and then abruptly left. The box was delivered while she was in the shower."

The deputy nods again. "Does she know about the box or Penny's disappearance?"

Colin shakes his head. *If she did, she made no indication of it when she was here*, Colin thinks.

The deputy finishes the search of the porch and turns his attention to Colin's doorbell. Pausing mid-step to the doorbell, the deputy instead turns toward his squad car. "I have a print dusting kit in the car, Colin. Maybe we will get lucky be able to pull a print from the doorbell."

Colin nods, his hopes returning for the first time since he opened the cardboard box. "Do you think you can get anything from it?"

Steve throws up his hands, as if to say who knows but we have to try.

Colin turns to face the doorbell, looking at it like it may

offer the only salvation available.

The deputy begins to walk to toward the squad car in the driveway and stops in his tracks at the foot of the stairs. "Colin," Steve practically whispers.

Colin looks back at the deputy, who is staring at the car. Colin follows the direction of Steve's stare.

A plain brown box is sitting on the hood of the squad car, directly in the center. Wrapped with black ribbon pulled together at the top in a large bow.

CHAPTER 7

THE RULES

Around the same time Deputy Gates is inspecting the burned-out clinic, the figure is closing the door to the building where Penny is being kept. Locking the door, they walk down the steps and head across the clearing toward the path in the tree line, carrying a small cardboard box. The box is wrapped with plain brown paper and tied with a flat black ribbon. The rain has finally let up and various sorts of wildlife are enjoying the few rays of sun poking their way through the clouds and creating bright spots on the ground around the building. The figure pays no attention. They are focused on the next step in the game.

Reaching the edge of the clearing where the tree line begins, they plunge into the brush without hesitation and skillfully follow the small trail they have followed many times previously. Penny is still unconscious. That's good, although the figure knows she would need to be awake for the next part.

She isn't going to like the next part. At all. But the next part is a necessary evil in the game. The figure feels a smile forming at the corner of their mouth at what is to come but hesitates before the smile fully forms. They stop walking a moment. Why are they hesitating? This is the part that they had been relishing for days.

For months. For years.

They shake off the momentary hesitation and start down the path again, stepping from shade to small patches of sunlight as the light breaches through the leafy canopy above and shines down on the forest floor in little spots here and there. Their thoughts drift back to the first. The one. They wish the one could see how everything is smoothly playing out so far. The one might be proud, over time. Impressed. In awe, even. Of course, there would be the begging. The pleading for the figure to stop and think about what they are doing. But the one and the figure both knew stopping is not a possibility. Even when the one finally died. The figure could not, and would not, stop.

The cracking of a piece of wood underneath one of the figure's footsteps brings them out of their reminiscing. Dr. Elyse's car is up ahead and parked at the end of the unmarked road, tucked away between two trees and next to the figure's own vehicle. Both vehicles are covered with camouflage covers and are almost unnoticeable unless someone is practically on top of them. The figure exits from the forest and steps onto the road. Although calling the two barely noticeable ruts on the ground a road—overgrown with hanging branches and crushed bushes—is a very loose interpretation of the term.

The figure approaches Dr. Elyse's car and checks to make sure it is still fully covered now that the storm has passed. Content her car is still well camouflaged, they set the wrapped box down on the back of the car and walk over to the other vehicle parked among the trees. Bending down next to the side of that car, they unhook the securing straps to the cover and pull it off the car. The figure takes the cover, folds it up, and puts it securely into the trunk of the car. They walk back to Dr. Elyse's car, pick up the box from the back of her car, and return to the other car. Opening the driver's side door, the figure gets in and sets the box carefully down on the passenger side seat. They close the door and take a deep breath.

Even now, after all these years, the scent of the one lingers in the air inside the car. The scent is faint as so much time has passed, but the figure would recognize it anywhere. Even in the building where Penny is being kept, the figure can still catch the occasional whiff on the air of the light flowery scent that marked the one. That scent is probably the only reason the figure has kept the car for so long. The smile finally returns to their face.

They start the car, back it out onto the road, and begin to head to the next destination. The ruts are bumpy and the figure is constantly jostled around in the seat as they progress down the road. Overgrown bushes rub against the sides of the car and low-hanging branches scrape across the top. The noises are familiar and welcoming to the figure. As familiar as each and every one of the bumps in the road. Only a few more miles and they will reach the highway. The figure is careful to check the box each time the car jostles over a bump or dips through a rut in the road. Although the box and its contents will be perfectly fine should it overturn onto the floor, the figure wants to make sure it arrives in the same condition as it was when they prepared the box. Placement is everything, the figure thinks. Perfect placement will ensure the game and the finale goes according to plan.

The highway comes into view through the trees and brush only a few yards in front of the car. The thick foliage makes the road difficult to see for any passing motorist. Unless someone is intentionally looking for the road, they would not see it as they drive past. The figure is not worried about being seen though. The highway in front of them is rarely used this far out of town, with the exception of the occasional lost tourist or someone taking a scenic drive. They pull from the obscured road onto the highway and head toward town.

They pass the road that leads to Ellie's and a mile later passes the post office on the left. The figure reaches one of the stoplights the town is so proud to have. The road is still empty, even in what could be considered the center of town. Sam's could be seen a little bit down the road to the figure's left. The parking lot is devoid of any other cars with the exception of Sam's beat-up Ford pickup truck. It is still early. Most of the residents are still in their homes, probably still sleeping or cleaning up from the storm.

The figure waits at the light, the click of the blinker the only sound inside the car. The light finally changes and the figure pulls onto the main road though town. A couple miles farther and the figure is already out of the city limits and headed toward the junction that splits the main road between Shelton and Rockville. The road is still empty when the figure reaches the next turn.

Making a right, they pull down a road they have been on hundreds of times. They pass the street to Colin's house and continue a little farther down before pulling off the road and onto the shoulder. They are taking a risk by leaving the car here during the day, but this next part of the game is imperative and the figure could not leave Colin waiting too long for the next piece of the puzzle. The figure knows Colin is weak. So weak he might not be able to follow the rules the way the figure has designed them if he is left to wonder for too long. The figure could not risk another player in the game although should that happen, the figure is already prepared.

They turn off the car and pick up the wrapped box. They exit the car, closing and locking the door behind it. Walking around the car, the figure plunges into the woods. They follow the same path they have followed many times before when they visited Colin's home. Watching him. Watching Penny. It is a short walk until Colin's house is visible through the trees.

The figure approaches from the back side of the house. Unless Colin is standing at the sink in the kitchen and looking out the window, he will not see the figure approach. It's a risk the figure is willing to take. Reaching the edge of the woods, they survey the house and the window. No lights are on inside the house and no one is seen moving near the window. The figure must be sure not to be seen.

They carefully move along the edge of the trees until they are angled toward a corner of the house. This will limit the figure's visibility from anyone who is inside the house. They look out at the street and the few other houses that are visible from their location. No one appears to be outside or along the road. The figure gets ready to step from their cover and into Colin's yard when the sound of a vehicle coming down the street reaches their ears. They quickly duck back into cover. An irritated frown forms across their face. A police car comes into view on the street and pulls into Colin's driveway.

The figure watches. They don't move a muscle. *Why are the police here?* the figure wonders. They narrow their eyes. Is Colin really so weak that the first thing he does is call the police? Has he already broken the rules? A wave of heat flushes across the figure's body as their rage begins to form.

A deputy gets out of the police car and walks up the steps to Colin's porch and disappears out of the figure's view. Deputy Gates. The figure recognizes him even from this distance. They are familiar with Gates and his friendship with Colin. Former city cop who had enough and came to a small town for escape.

The figure can hear voices from the direction of the porch but cannot hear what is being said. Moving quickly and as quietly as possible, the figure moves from cover and clears the distance between the woods and Colin's house. They hug close to the siding and edge toward the front of the house and the side of the porch, concealed by a large trash can. Colin's voice can be heard clearly now, as well as the deputy's. The figure stops and listens. After a minute or two of listening to the exchange, the figure's rage fades and a rush of relief crosses their body. *Good boy, Colin*, the figure thinks. *Keep up the ploy Penny is merely over a friend's house and not home.* The figure listens as the deputy presses the issue and almost insists on going inside to wait. *Pushy bastard*, the figure thinks. Maybe when the game with Colin is over, they will play a game with the deputy. The thought of this brings a smile back to the figure's face. The sound of Colin's door closing as both he and the deputy go inside brings the figure back to the present and away from the daydream of what the figure could do with Gates.

They listen carefully. They can hear the two men inside talking. They can hear the weakness in Colin's voice. Weakness that does not deserve Penny. Weakness that will allow the figure to control every part of the game and get the much-anticipated finale they want. The men stop talking a moment and the outside sounds of birds chirping fill in the void. Then the deputy begins to talk. The figure strains to hear him clearly.

What the figure hears erases any traces of the smile from their face. Colin's confirmation after the deputy is done makes the figure shake with rage. *Colin, you weak piece of shit*, the figure thinks. You will pay for breaking the rules. The figure stops mid-thought. *No, Colin, you won't pay.*

Penny will pay. And you will learn.

The figure, done with listening to the men's conversation inside, steps from their hiding spot on the side of the house and walks to the police car. They set the wrapped box down on the center of the car's hood. Content with the box's location, the figure turns to the porch, quickly but quietly climbing the steps and crossing the porch, stopping at the side of the door, next to the doorbell. The two men are still talking inside, discussing the contents of the first delivery.

The figure rings the doorbell. Their rage at Colin for already breaking the rules holds the figure in place. Daring Colin or the deputy to open the door and see the figure there. To maybe even recognize a face that has been long forgotten. The men are now silent inside the house and the figure hears no footsteps coming toward the door.

They ring the doorbell again. This time, Colin's voice answers the ring. The figure, breaking their defiance and realizing the game can't be played if they are caught, turns and exits the porch on the far side, leaping over the railing and quietly landing on the other side, back near the trash can.

Their rage subsides. They quickly cross the remainder of the yard and secure a new hiding spot in the trees where they can watch the next step in the game. The deputy's involvement is troublesome, the figure thinks, but will not affect the final outcome. The figure will merely have to get rid of the deputy before getting Colin out to the building for the finale.

The figure's smile returns. It looks like they get to play a game with the deputy after all. They wait in the cover. Both men are on the porch now, and the figure can occasionally see the deputy coming into view as he walks around the porch. Too far away now to hear what the men are saying, the figure sees the deputy walk down the porch steps and abruptly stop at the bottom, staring in the direction of his squad car. He must see the box, the figure thinks. Good.

The figure waits for what feels like an eternity until Colin comes into view, racing down the steps and toward the box. The deputy grabs him and pulls him back. The men exchange words, but the figure is still unable to make out what they are saying. The figure watches as both men walk up to the box together and look at it. After several minutes, the deputy reaches out, picks up the box and looks around. The figure freezes as the deputy's eyes scan the spot where they are crouching. The deputy's eyes continue past them and after he is done surveying the area, both men turn and walk back into the house. The figure waits until they hear the door close before slowly backing away from Colin's house, deeper into the woods. Once the figure is confident they have reached a safe distance, they turn from the house and head back to where the car is parked.

The figure is still smiling by the time they reach the car. Unlocking the door, they get in and start the engine. It's time to prepare the next package, and to prepare the deputy's part in the game. They pull from the car's spot on the shoulder and back onto the road, heading back to the building. The figure needs to make a quick stop first, though, before going back to the building where Penny is still waiting.

≈

Karen Ellie opens the blinds to her restaurant and pulls the switch to turn on the green neon open sign. She looks around her little business. A medium-size bar lines the far back wall with six bar stools in front of it. The dining room is adorned with five wooden tables with four chairs each. The kitchen is off the back of the bar, and above it all is where Karen lives. Upstairs is a nice little two-bedroom, two-bath home where she has lived for decades. The furnishings in the restaurant are simple enough with modest artwork of mountains and lake scenes, most of them painted by Colin's wife, Alicia, decorating the wood walls. Karen prefers a simple, uncomplicated way of life, and her restaurant and bar reflect her style perfectly.

She turns back to the front of the building and looks out the window at the empty parking lot. Besides her, the restaurant and bar are completely empty. With Orchard Lake being such a small town, she didn't have the need to employ a regular employee anymore during the weekdays. Not since Alicia left, anyway. Nor did Karen need to keep any kind of regular hours. Only on the weekends would she have a couple of the high school kids here to help clean dishes and wait on the tables when necessary. Most of the time, however, there are only a few regular diners and they would sit at the bar when they are here. On days like today, Ellie's will be just about empty all day long with the exception of the occasional tourist stopping in or a regular who is looking for a cold drink or two.

She smiles. She likes her little oasis on the outskirts of town. A beautiful view of the actual lake the town is named after greets her patrons from the back patio of the restaurant and her faithful regulars normally spend just enough money here to keep her in business. She is happy with her life. Unfortunately, she thinks, she appears to be the only one in Orchard Lake who is happy with their life.

She takes one more long look out the front windows at the empty parking lot and turns to head back behind the bar. Once there, she grabs the bottle of tequila behind the counter and pours herself a shot. She slowly shakes her head. *What a horrible week*, she thinks to herself. Colin's accident, then the fire at the clinic and the apparent demise of poor Dr. Elyse, and little miss Penny's whereabouts are unknown. Hasn't this poor town had enough already?

Karen slams the shot back and pours herself one more. "This round's on the house," she announces to the empty room. She finishes off the shot and walks over to the bar sink to clean the shot glass. She makes a mental note to call Colin sometime this morning to see how he's doing and if he has heard from Penny. And to apologize for abruptly leaving last night. She should have stayed after the shower to make sure Colin was OK, but the moment she stepped out of the room and into the kitchen and saw the look on his face, she knew she needed to leave.

She also didn't need Colin to know she recognized the box sitting on the table.

He needed to be alone with what was going on and her

presence would only complicate things. She makes another mental note to make sure she clears up that no deliveries should ever be made when she is present. She glances at the clock on the wall in the dining room. She should have some company any moment now.

She walks from the bar and back into the kitchen. She opens the fridge and grabs some of the lunchmeat off the bottom shelf, as well as some cheese. Closing the fridge, she sets the items down on the counter and grabs some bread from the breadbox. She begins to make some sandwiches for her upcoming visitor. After she finishes making the third sandwich and is wrapping it in cellophane, she hears a car pull past the restaurant and to the back where her truck is parked. A door opens then closes shut, and after that, the back door to the restaurant opens. A silhouette frames the doorway and looks into the kitchen where Karen is standing, now holding three wrapped sandwiches.

A stern look spreads across her face. "About time you got here. What took you so long?"

She gets no response in return. She doesn't expect one, though. She knows her point is being made.

She grabs a large paper bag from the stack on the counter and stuffs the three sandwiches into it. She walks over to the silhouette still standing in the doorway and hands over the bag. It is taken from her without hesitation.

"You need to get your head out of your ass." she admonishes the silhouette. "Don't you ever make a delivery when I am present. Ever again."

The silhouette's head hangs down and a meek voice responds, "I'm sorry."

"You are damn right you are sorry." she harshly states. She pauses before saying more. "Here, let me grab you a few drinks to go with the sandwiches, and then you can get back to what you have going on."

The silhouette nods, head still hanging down.

Karen walks back into the kitchen and opens the cooler to pull out two cans of cola and two bottled waters. Pausing at the counter, she also grabs two straws. Walking back to the silhouette, she places all four drinks and the straws in the open bag, taking care not to crush the three sandwiches already inside.

"Now go, get out of here," she states. "And don't make another stupid mistake like you did last night."

Her only response is another nod.

The silhouette turns from the doorway and heads back to the car. Karen watches until the car drives away, and turns to go back into the restaurant. She walks to the front windows and looks out, making sure the car is gone and no other cars have shown up. *That fool is going to be the death of me*, she thinks. She shakes her head, turns, and walks back behind the bar. Picking up the phone, she dials Colin's number.

≈

The phone on the table rings loudly through the silence in the house. Colin once again practically jumps out of his skin at the sound. Deputy Gates and Colin have been standing at the kitchen table studying the bow-wrapped box for the last half hour without attempting to open it when the phone interrupts them.

The deputy looks at Colin and over at the phone. Nodding, Colin walks over to the phone and plucks it from its cradle just as the second ring comes through. "Hello?" he asks.

A familiar voice booms at him from the other end of the line. "Colin, dear, it's Karen. How are you doing?"

Colin relaxes a bit. Another familiar voice is just what he needs right now. "I'm fine, Karen," he lies.

"Good, good, I'm glad to hear that. Have you heard from little miss Penny yet?"

Colin hesitates a moment, holding back the initial intake of air that accompanies tears. "No, not yet, Karen. I'm sure she should be home any time soon. With the power out last night, and the way she uses her phone, it's probably dead. And she's a typical teenager, so she wouldn't remember the number to the house without her phone."

"I'm sure that's it," she states. "Listen, Colin, I'm sorry about last night. I wasn't feeling well and with all the stress of the day I just wanted to be in my own home. I hope you understand."

He nods while holding the phone, although the action is more for him than for Karen on the other end of the line. "It's all right, I understand. It's been a rough week for us all."

She gives her agreement and asks him to make sure he calls her the moment he hears from Penny. He promises he will and hangs up the phone. Steve is still standing in the kitchen, looking back at Colin, the latest delivered box still laying on the table in front of him.

"You did good, Colin." the deputy states.

Colin nods, quietly confident his voice didn't sound too shaky when he was talking to Karen.

"You ready to finally open this and see what's inside?" Steve asks.

Colin walks back to the kitchen table and stops next to the deputy. He takes a deep breath and looks at the box on the kitchen table. He reaches out and grabs the two loose ends of the large black bow, slowly pulling them apart, almost if the package might explode if he moves too fast.

The bow finally unravels and falls to the sides of the box as Colin lets the ends go. He grabs the box and slowly breaks the strip of tape on the top, folding up the two portions of cardboard that keep the box shut. The two men are breathlessly and hesitantly waiting to see what is inside the box.

Colin pauses a second after the box is open. The only thing visible after the lid is open is a bunch of crumpled pink tissue paper. The tissue paper has black lettering all over it, but due to how crumpled the paper is, what is written on it is illegible. Colin lets go of the cardboard piece on the right side and reaches forward to remove the pink tissue paper and see what, if anything, is underneath it.

Just before his hand reaches the tissue paper, the deputy starts forward with his own hand and then hesitates, as if to stop him. Colin turns his head to his right and looks at the deputy. Steve shakes his head as if clearing a thought and then nods once at the box, indicating for Colin to go ahead and delve further into what the box may hold.

Colin looks back at the box and finishes reaching for the tissue paper. He lightly grabs part of the paper in the middle of the box and pulls it away, revealing a small, black velvet–covered case lying in the center of the box with more pink tissue paper underneath it. The paper underneath the case also has thick black lettering written all over it. Still unable to actually read what it says, Colin can make out the letters N and E at various unrumpled spots on the tissue paper. The hair on the back of Colin's neck rises up. His pulse quickens. The black velvet case is identical to the type of case you would put an engagement ring in.

Colin's hands begin to shake. *Please don't let me find part of a finger with a ring in that box*, he begs to himself. He sets the tissue paper he's holding down on the table, to the right of the box. He reaches into the box once again and gingerly grabs the ring box by the sides and pulls it out. As he is removing the ring box, he feels a hand set down and rest on his right shoulder. Steve must have seen how bad he was beginning to shake.

Colin looks once again at the deputy, who nods. "Open it, Colin," he states.

Colin reaches forward with his other hand, clasping the ring box at the top and holding it at the bottom with his other hand. Trying to steady his shaking hands, he opens the box, revealing what is inside. Lying in the center of the box, secured by a small black band, is a thick lock of brunette hair. Colin audibly exhales in relief. He sets the ring box down on the table and tries to calm the shaking of his hands.

Steve breaks the silence. "I know what you were thinking. I thought it was going to be the worst possible scenario, too. But it's not, it's only hair. And if it really is Penny's hair then there is a good chance she hasn't been hurt, right?"

Colin looks at the deputy and nods, relief written all over his face.

The deputy motions his head toward the ring box and the package. "May I check it out?" he asks.

Colin nods, unable to find any words at this time. His eyes focus again on the ring box and the lock of hair lying innocently inside it. There is no doubt in Colin's mind that the hair inside the small box is Penny's. His mind wanders through a wide variety of scenarios as to how that lock of hair might have been taken from his little hummingbird and if she was hurt at all when this monster sending the packages took it from her. A small, burning, hot coal forms in Colin's stomach and slowly begins to grow. *Once I get my hands on you, whoever you are*, Colin vows to himself, *I will wring every ounce of life from your body.*

As the burning coal inside him begins to turn into a raging fire, Colin's hands slowly begin to steady and finally stop shaking completely. He watches the deputy inspect the latest package.

Steve begins his inspection by opening up the top, crumpled

piece of tissue paper lying to the right of the box. Spreading it out flat, the block lettering is finally legible. *Penny is MINE* is written over and over on the tissue paper. Large letters. Small letters. Filling almost every available space but not touching another repetition of the phrase. Flipping the tissue paper over, the lettering is the same. Covering almost the entire paper.

Penny is MINE.

The deputy leaves the paper where it is and moves his inspection to the ring box. It is a standard ring box, soft velvet on the outside and black in color, with no distinguishing marks or branding. The lock of hair is secured by a black band to the inner partition, which the deputy is able to pull out with ease. Nothing is underneath the partition when Steve lifts it up. He sets the partition back into the ring box and checks the lock of hair in the box. Satisfied there is no dried blood or any other substance on any of the hair in the small ring box, he turns his attention to the remaining tissue paper still in the package. The deputy reaches in and pulls out the tissue paper. Underneath the remaining tissue paper and lying on the bottom of the package, is a neatly folded piece of paper.

The deputy looks at Colin, who in turn is now raptly staring at the folded piece of paper. "Colin?" he inquires.

A few moments pass before Colin seems to acknowledge what the deputy said.

Colin reaches forward for the paper lying in the bottom of the package. His hand is still completely steady thanks to the burning fire inside him. He grasps the piece of folded paper and pulls it from the box. He sets it down on the table and unfolds it. Both men lean forward and read what is written on the paper.

The rules have been set. The game is now being played. Penny's hair is my gift to you, so you know she is still alive and has not been hurt. Get some rest tonight, Colin, for tomorrow will be a busy day for you. I will be in touch soon. And Colin, should you break any of the rules, I will find out. And when I find out, Penny's hair will not be the only piece of her you will start to receive.

Colin's burning meteor of rage in his stomach is quickly extinguished. Although the letter doesn't indicate it, the deliverer has to know Colin has already broken a rule.

Because the package was left on the hood of the deputy's car.

Colin's hands begin to shake once again.

CHAPTER 8

THE PUNISHMENT

The figure quickly walks the pathway toward the building where Penny is. Even carrying a large bag in their right arm, they are able to deftly navigate the overgrown path. Rogue branches claw and scratch at the bag, occasionally catching it and leaving little tears. The figure pays no attention to these distractions. They are focused on the new addition of the overzealous deputy to their little game.

Colin has broken the rules. He must now be shown the consequences of doing that. Stepping from the trees and into the clearing, the figure pauses and gazes upon the building in front of it. Their smile is once again gone, and they are allowing their anger to continue to grow at the events which have transpired over the last few hours.

Taking a slow, deep breath, the figure tries to ease the rage once again building inside and concentrate on what will happen next. They will not let the deputy's involvement interfere. The figure takes a moment to think, frowning. Standing still, looking at the clearing and building in front of them. Listening to the birds chirping and the various noises of the woods. Surveying the surroundings. Formulating a fitting end for the deputy.

The frown quickly disappears. They have figured out how to best deal with the deputy. A large smile begins to form, showing discolored and ragged teeth. The figure resumes walking and continues on to the building. Reaching the door, they try the handle, making sure the door is still locked before reaching into their pocket with a free left hand and fishing out the ring of keys that allows access to the various parts of the building.

Unlocking the door, the figure puts the keys back into the pocket they came from and slides the large metal door open. The familiar screeching echoes throughout the big main room of the building once again. The figure steps through the doorway and slides the door shut, securely fastening it once it reaches the end of its short journey.

The small, dirty windows near the top of the walls are completely covered, barring any light from entering the building at all. Except today. One window is allowing a thin beam of light to arc across the room and rest on the far wall. Dust dances within the beam of light, amplifying its unwanted presence. The figure's grin fades a little. They will need to fix that before dark falls upon the building tonight.

Shaking their head, the figure walks across the room and around the equipment, finally reaching the locked door on the other side of the room. They again fish the keys from their pocket and unlock the door, opening it up and stepping through the door into the darkness beyond. Closing and locking the door behind them, the figure turns on the light revealing a small hallway and a stairwell. They walk down the stairs and stop at the door that leads to the room where the pretty little brunette girl is waiting. Still holding the keys in their left hand and cradling the large bag in their right, they hesitate before inserting the key into the lock.

They listen. Listens for any noise on the other side of the door. Silence greets the figure. A frown replaces the partial grin on the figure's face. Where is the screaming? The yelling? The begging and pleading? The crying? The frown returns to the figure's face.

The one begged and pleaded. The one screamed and yelled. The one cried. For years. The frown on the figure's face hardens. If the pretty brunette does not want to play along, they will make sure she has a reason to. Especially now, since the figure needs to teach Colin a lesson on how to follow rules.

They insert the key into the keyhole and unlock it. Grasping the door knob, they swing the door open wide and step into the room. The fluorescent lights above are still ablaze. Penny is still in her chair, head down. The figure turns, closes the door, and re-locks it. The figure puts the set of keys back into the depths of their pocket.

As they turn back around, they are greeted by a now alert Penny. Her head is up and she is staring right at them. She finally speaks for the first time since she has been here. "Let me go, you piece of shit."

The hard look on the figure's face softens up a bit. As if she was sensing this momentary weakness, she continues to speak. "What do you want with me? Why am I here? Who are you?" The questions from the pretty young woman begin to come as a flurry once the initial silence is broken.

The figure stands motionless until she stops talking. Once she is silent again, the figure moves toward the table to their right. The figure sets the large bag down on the table. They reach into the bag and pulls out the three wrapped sandwiches, setting them in a stack to the left side of the bag. The shiny cellophane wrap on the sandwiches looks out of place next to the various antique, dust-covered tools on the table. Pulling two bottled waters followed by two cans of cola from the bag, the figure places them next to the sandwiches. They reach one final time into the bag and pulls out two straws, setting them next to the colas. The figure crumples the bag into a small ball and tosses it onto the large chest just a short distance from Penny. The bag comes to a rest against the old sander sitting there.

The figure finally speaks to the pretty young girl with a slow, deep voice. "Eat. You are going to need your strength."

The expression on Penny's face when she finally hears his voice pleases the figure.

He grabs one of the sandwiches and removes the cellophane wrap from it. Setting the sandwich down on the stack of the other sandwiches, he grabs a can of cola and opens the top, plunging one of the straws into the cola and bending the top part at a ninety degree angle so it would be easier to drink. The wrapper of the straw is now forgotten on the floor.

The figure grabs the cola with the straw in it and the sandwich. He turns toward Penny and walks over until he is standing directly in front of her. Holding both items in front of her, he waits.

Penny finally nods her head toward the cola and the figure holds the cola with the straw sticking out of it close enough for the young girl to reach. She drinks greedily from the straw, almost emptying half of the can. The figure pulls the can away and offers the sandwich, close enough for Penny to lean forward and take a bite. Looking at the figure, Penny hesitates but finally leans forward and takes a large bite of the sandwich. The process is repeated until the cola is empty and the sandwich is gone.

The figure points at the stack of two sandwiches still remaining and looks at Penny. She shakes her head. Nodding, the figure then points at the remaining cola and water bottles. Again, the pretty brunette shakes her head. Satisfied, the figure takes the empty soda can and tosses it onto the chest with the crumpled-up paper bag. The sound of the aluminum can as it strikes the metal chest echoes throughout the room.

He turns from the girl and walks to the metal door on the other side of the room. Pulling the keys from his pocket, he unlocks the door and pulls it open. The door slowly opens, scraping along the floor the entire way. He can feel the heat of the young girl's eyes burning into his back the entire time.

Right before he steps through the doorway, the figure turns

and looks directly at the pretty brunette. She quickly averts her eyes and stares at the floor in front of her. The figure smiles quickly, allowing the fancy to play across his thoughts that Penny is merely looking away in flirtatious embarrassment instead of fear. He stares a moment longer, waiting for the hesitant raise of the head and the soft doe-eyed look that normally follows flirtation, but Penny's head does not raise and her eyes continue to remain affixed on the floor. The figure's smile remains regardless.

The momentary daydream gone, the figure turns and steps through the doorway. He pulls the metal door closed behind him and the sound of the latch finding home echoes through the silence. In the darkness of the room on the other side of Penny, the figure easily finds the keyhole and inserts the key. The metal door locks with a loud click and the figure continues on in the darkness to get the next items he will need.

≈

Penny stares intently at the floor. After seeing how those hollow eyes looked at her earlier while she was being fed, she wants nothing to do with them ever again. She continues to stare at the floor while the sound of the metal door scraping across the floor greets her ears. The scraping sound finally stops and a loud click is heard.

She forces herself not to look up and instead to continue to stare at the floor in front her. At the bits of sawdust and dust scattered all over. At the myriad of faded footprints all over the floor. Her eyes drift to the right and she can see a dark red stain on the right side of the floor, just at the edge of her peripheral vision. She wonders what could have caused a stain like that, although she is more afraid of learning why the stain is there.

Penny is alone with her thoughts, unaware of how much time is passing, until she again hears a click and the metal door finally begins to scrape again along its set path and stop. Refusing to look up, a slight clang is heard and then the scraping of the resumes. Penny focuses on the footprints and sawdust until she hears the solid thud of it shutting once again. The loud click of the lock engaging follows shortly after.

She allows herself to finally look up and look around the room. The wooden and metal doors are both closed. On the table to the left of her, the two bottles of water, an unopened can of cola, and two sandwiches wrapped in their shiny cellophane from earlier still sit by one another. On the chest a little closer to her left, the ball of the paper bag and the empty can of cola lie next to the dust-covered sander. A straw lays next to the can with a few spilled droplets of cola soaking up the dust that has made a home on the chest.

She looks at the stain on the floor to her right. The large, dark red shape discolors the floor where she had previously fallen, only now there is a slightly smaller shape overlapping the older one, adding what seems to be an updated coating of the red color. Only this smaller shape is from her, when she hit her head on the ground.

Penny sighs. Still tightly bound, she is unable to move and is unwilling to rock the chair after the last experience. There was still a dull throb from the right side of her head. She tries to wiggle right and wiggle left. The wrappings around her arms securing her to the chair don't give at all. Her legs are also secured in the same way. Unless she wants to overturn the chair again, she isn't going anywhere.

Hours seem to pass. Penny's sense of time melts away. Her eyelids grow heavy multiple times and she occasionally catches herself dozing off.

The metallic click of a key being inserted into a lock brings her back to reality.

The bolt on the metal door clicks loudly as it is slid free from its housing. Penny quickly lowers her head and focuses her attention on the dirty floor in front of her feet as before. The loud scraping sound of the door moving begins and after a few moments stops. Silence retakes the room. Then, like an uninvited guest to the party of silence, the scraping of the metal door's hinges begins again until it finally ends with a thud and the solid click of the bolt finding its home one more time. Penny continues to focus on the ground at her feet, refusing to look up or acknowledge what is going on.

The hollow, dead eyes of her captor are too horrific to look into again.

Footsteps echo on the floor until Penny can see dirt-crusted boots walking in front of her from the right side, step by step, until they walk out of view on her left side. She fights the urge to follow the footsteps as they exit her field of view.

The steps finally stop, and she hears a rustling noise from

the direction of the table. The noise in the room suddenly stops for a moment. A metallic clink from something being set down on the table lets her know her captor is still there. A hissing starts, almost like air escaping, and is quickly followed by a loud scraping noise. The hissing noise gets deeper in tone and stays that way. A wave of heat can be felt on the left side of her face from the direction of the hissing noise. The sound abruptly stops, and a metallic clink is heard again.

The footsteps begin again until they finally stop directly in front of her. The dirt-encrusted boots now face her, only inches from her own sneakers. A pair of dirty blue jeans cover the top of the boots, but Penny doesn't dare look any farther up in the event she will see those horrible hollow eyes again. She feels the warmth of her captor's hand pass her cheek on the right side of her head and then something wraps around her hair. A sharp pain accompanies her head jerking back as her hair is pulled harshly away from her head. She closes her eyes, avoiding contact with those dead eyes that will forever haunt her dreams.

With her head forcefully pulled back by her hair, Penny fights the urge to struggle. The strong grip in her hair pulls farther back and then sharply pulls her hair to the right, forcing her to tilt her head to her right and exposing the left side of her neck and her left ear. She fights to keep her eyes closed tightly, even with pain screaming from every hair follicle on her head. The grip and force is so strong she couldn't move her head even if she wanted to.

Minutes tick by. They feel like hours. She finally feels heat on the left side of her face. The heat is followed by the sensation of lips that gently caress her cheek. Lips that slowly move from her left cheek to her left ear. She fights the urge to gag and scream. She squeezes her eyes even more tightly shut.

The caresses cause an unwanted biological response, a warmth that begins to form between her legs she refuses to acknowledge. The heat from her skin feels like a furnace, and the heat between her legs is growing in intensity. She begins to breathe faster, loathing her body's natural reaction and the reason for the arousal. The lips finally leave her ear, allowing the cool air of the room to quickly replace the heat that was building there. The pain from how hard her hair is being pulled slowly returns to her, after momentarily becoming a morbid addition to her want of ecstasy. An ecstasy unwillingly caused from the slow kisses across her cheek to the warm, wet pulling of her ear lobe by unfamiliar teeth.

Penny fights to slow her breathing as well as tries to keep her eyes closed. Her body screams for more and that simple want makes her feel even more disgusted than she has ever felt before. The heat and wetness between her legs makes her sick to her stomach.

The hand entangled in her hair refuses to budge at all and continues to hold her head tightly back and to the right. Moments pass, and she finally hears a voice whisper a single statement: "I'm sorry."

Fear races through her body. She finally opens her eyes and

finds herself staring directly into the hollow, dead eyes she dreaded seeing again, within mere inches of hers. Unblinking. Unfeeling. Staring.

Penny screams. The figure's eyes don't even blink.

Penny's eyes flicker around in panic. The figure's deadpan face is horrifying and she is unable to look into it anymore. Unable to move her head, she looks right at the closed metal door, and then looks left toward the table. Before her eyes could alight upon the table, she sees the figure's right hand dangerously close to her face, holding a large knife. The shiny silver blade glints from the fluorescent light up above. She screams again.

A smile appears to form on the man's face in front of her. The hand with the knife moves closer to her face until she can feel the cold blade on the side of her left cheek. She closes her eyes and begins to beg the man in front of her to just let her go. To not hurt her. Tears begin to force their way free from her closed eyes and run down her cheek. She squeezes her eyes shut tighter, trying to stop the flow of her tears and feeling the cold blade sliding across her cheek to her left ear. The knife blade stops at the front of her ear and then is lifted away.

Moments pass. Penny's sobs and pleadings are now the only noises in the room. She fights to gain composure. The sharp pain of her hair being pulled to the back and right reminds her that her captor is still there.

Suddenly, the cold sharpness of the knife is momentarily felt on the backside of her head and behind her ear.

A sharp, exploding pain erupts on the left side of her head. Penny screams and her eyes force their way open. The pain causes fireworks in her vision and she is unable to focus on anything in front of her. Except those eyes. The hollow, dead eyes staring into hers. The pain becomes all-consuming. It feels as though the entire left side of her head is on fire.

Her head is jerked forward with a sharp pull and the fire turns into lava. The pain quickly takes over and Penny soon stops thinking about her captor's eyes. The pain is all Penny can focus on. She feels herself getting dizzy and the edges of her vision begin to turn black. The blackness soon takes over.

≈

The man watches the young girl's reaction after he finishes the cut of the blade and pulls the knife away from the side of her face. He watches her tears, her eyes, her screams, how she finally goes limp. He watches the red streams of blood running down her cheek and neck, soaking her shirt in an ever-growing pattern.

Breaking from his trance at the multiple tracks of red racing down the pretty doe-eyed girl's neck, he grabs the flat metal bar lying on the chest. With one end still slightly glowing red from the torch earlier, he presses the flat metal bar to the left side of the girl's head. The hiss, following by the familiar smell of burning skin and hair greets him. He breathes in deeply, taking in a scent he has missed for so long. This act of pain was a necessary evil which needed to happen. To teach Colin his lesson.

He watches as Penny's fair-colored skin on the left side of her head turns to a dark brown and the bleeding from where her ear quickly stops. He pulls the flat metal bar away and sets it back down on the chest. He inspects the wound. Convinced it is fully cauterized, he releases Penny's hair. Her head falls forward on to her chest with her now free hair falling forward to cover the angry, red damage to the left side of her head.

A tinge of remorse overtakes him. *This is your fault, Colin*, he thinks. He looks down at the floor and where the remnants of Penny's left ear now lies. Splatters of blood dot the floor all around where her ear sits.

He reaches down and picks up the ear. He momentarily marvels at his handiwork. The warmth of the ear in his hand makes him smile. It almost looks like it was surgically removed, he thinks. He takes another look at the unconscious girl and turns back to the table where the portable butane torch is setting. Next to the torch is another cardboard box. The lid is open and pink tissue paper peeks out from the top of the box on either side. Sitting behind the torch and the box on the table are the two remaining sandwiches and the drinks from the paper bag.

The figure grabs the cardboard box and carefully places the bloody ear in the center of the tissue paper, taking care not to get any excess blood on the paper or the outside of the box.

Time to teach Colin a lesson about rules, he thinks. He sets the box back down and picks up a rag from the table. He slowly cleans away the blood from his hands and sets the rag to the side. He then reaches into his right pocket and pulls out a small notepad and a black pen. He turns and sits down on the metal chest with the sander and sets the pad on his right leg. He begins to write, slowly at first but soon finds a steady rhythm and quickly finishes the message he means to convey.

The figure clicks the pen closed and looks at what is written. A smile forms on his face. *Perfect*, he thinks. Just enough to teach Colin the lesson he needs to learn and just enough to get the deputy to where he will need to be to end his part in the game.

The figure folds up the paper neatly in half, then folds it once again in half. He turns to the box, lifts up the tissue paper and the prize lying on top of it, then places the folded note on the bottom of the box and replaces the tissue paper and its gruesome present back to their original location. He closes the lid of the box and, holding the box closed with his left hand, picks up a small roll of tape from the table. He tapes the lid shut and puts the roll back where it came from. He takes a moment and looks at the plain brown box now sealed shut. No ribbon this time. He writes *TO COLIN AND STEVE* on the top of the package.

Pleased, the figure picks up the package and stands up. He looks over at Penny. Her head is still hanging on her chest. Lines of bright red blood now streak the left side of her visible neck where her hair is not hanging down and covering it. He takes a few steps in the direction of the young girl and again stops in front of her. The figure hesitates a moment before he turns to leave, reaching forward with his right hand to brush the girl's hair back behind her ear. Only now, the ear isn't there. The figure stops his hand halfway there, then pulls it back. *Soon*, he thinks.

The figure finally turns and walks to the wooden door. He transfers the box to his right hand and pulls the set of keys from his left pocket. Unlocking the door, he pulls the door open and steps into the hallway, closing the door tight behind him. The loud click of the lock sliding back into place is the last noise before silence once again fills the room.

The figure follows the familiar route out of the building, opening and closing each of the doors he comes across, making sure each door is completely locked before moving on to the next. Finally outside in the morning air, the figure quickly walks across the clearing and onto the pathway in the tree line. An evening and a night has passed while the figure was inside the building, and now with the coming day, it is time to deliver a new package.

He walks the pathway with ease, dodging hanging branches still laden with the morning dew. Finally reaching the two covered vehicles hidden among the trees at the end of the road, the figure contemplates which vehicle would be the best to use for this latest delivery. He smiles and chooses the vehicle that still occasionally smells like the one, his first prize, that he lost. The vehicle that will have the most impact on Colin. He sets the package down on the back of Dr. Elyse's car. He removes the camouflage cover from the one's car and opens the unlocked trunk, placing the cover and the securing cords in it. With the trunk still open, the figure grabs an old license plate with an expiration sticker well over fifteen years old and a screwdriver from the right side of the trunk. He quickly exchanges the plates and closes the trunk. Happy with the outcome, he grabs the package and gets into the one's car, setting the package on the passenger seat. Closing the driver's side door, he smiles. It is finally time to show Colin something he has spent over a decade of his life searching for.

The smile on the figure's face grows larger and larger until his crooked, yellowing teeth are once again showing. He puts the car in reverse, carefully backs out from the spot in the trees, and proceeds down the partially hidden road to the highway.

The figure's smile continues. It's going to be a good morning.

The drive to Colin's house is quiet. No other cars on the road, even in the center of town at the traffic lights. Just as the figure expects. Only this time instead of parking along the tree line on the main road away from Colin's home as he normally does, he pulls down Colin's street and drives past his house to the last house on the street. The Aryns, who live there, are away on vacation this month and no one would be home to notice the car pulling into their driveway, stopping momentarily while someone gets out and sets something on their neighbor's porch slightly down the street. The Aryns, probably in Aruba right now, would also not be near any windows at their home to notice the same car back out of their driveway and stop just slightly in front of Colin's driveway, just far enough away to make it difficult to see who is driving but close enough to clearly show the car and license plate off to whomever was inside the house.

The figure, having dropped the latest package on the porch, waits a moment in the running car. He takes a deep breath and for a moment, he can smell the one once again. The light flowery scent the figure can only rarely smell anymore seems to, for a second, flow from one of the air conditioning vents and allows the figure a moment of reminiscing. The scent quickly fades and he is brought back to reality. The reality where it is six in the morning and he is parked in the one's car in front of Colin's house. The reality where there is still a police car parked there as well. The reality where Colin will soon never break the figure's rules again, and the one in which the deputy's involvement will soon come to an end.

A large smile crosses the figure's face. Time to wake up Colin and his deputy friend.

The figure reaches forward and presses down on the horn of the car. The obnoxious sound permeates the morning, echoing off the nearby houses. He continues to hold down the horn and doesn't let up until he sees Colin's front door open in the side mirror.

Not until a bewildered Colin, with a sleepy deputy standing next to him, spill onto the front porch. With both men staring at the car.

He finally lets off the horn, steps on the gas, and quickly drives away.

CHAPTER 9

THE RECOGNITION

After the inspection of the bow-wrapped package, Steve insists on staying with Colin through the evening and into tomorrow until the next package arrives. Colin doesn't fight the deputy's request, since whoever had Penny obviously already knows the deputy is now involved. The two men eat leftovers from what Mrs. Ellie had brought over from the night before, and while the deputy is speaking with dispatch, Colin brings out some spare pillows and a couple blankets so the deputy can sleep on the couch. Both men end up going to sleep without saying much else at all.

Colin doesn't sleep much, as each time he closes his eyes, he sees horrible things happening to Penny. After what feels like a never-ending mix of tossing and turning, Colin finally gives up on trying to sleep and gets out of bed, heading into his bathroom. He glances at the clock on the nightstand on his way there. A few minutes after six in the morning. Reaching the bathroom, he turns on the light and is greeted by the reflection of a tired, haggard man in the mirror. *That can't be me in that reflection*, he thinks.

He walks over to the sink and turns on the faucet. Leaning forward, he splashes some of the cold water onto his face and runs his fingers through his hair. A familiar throb from his side reminds him his wound is still present. He stands up straight again and takes a deep breath, ignoring the sharp hello from his side. He stares into the unfamiliar eyes looking back at him in the mirror for a while. He searches those eyes for an answer, for strength.

Get ahold of yourself, he commands the reflection. The eyes staring back at him appear to disregard his order and offer nothing of what he is hoping to find in them. He closes his eyes and shakes his head.

Reaching down, he turns off the faucet. He reaches over and grabs a hand towel from the rack, drying his face and his hair. He returns the towel and takes off his shirt. He inspects the bandage over his wound. A little blood has seeped through the dressing and has left a small portion of it stained maroon. He removes the bandage from around his side and lays it down on the bathroom sink. He carefully removes the cloth dressing from the wound and inspects it to make sure the stitches are still holding in place. Satisfied with what he sees, he cleans the jagged cut with some hydrogen peroxide from the medical kit on the counter and applies a new cloth dressing over the stitches. He picks up the bandage and rewraps it around his midsection. Once he is done and the bandage is again secure, he turns and heads back into his bedroom, walking over to the dresser. He removes some clean clothes from the various drawers and quickly changes, taking care not to aggravate the wound on his side.

Opening his bedroom door, he steps into the hallway and walks toward the kitchen, intent on getting a pot of coffee started. As he reaches the counter, he looks over into the living room and sees the deputy still asleep on the couch. He turns back toward the counter and reaches for the coffee pot. Before he has a chance grab it, a loud horn begins to blare outside.

The abruptness of the horn's intrusion into the quiet of the morning startles Colin. He turns and starts to walk toward the door to see who is outside. The deputy is already sitting up on the edge of the couch, clearing the sleep from his eyes. "What the fuck is that?" he asks.

The horn's obnoxious sound continues its steady song without reprieve.

"No idea, Steve," Colin replies. "But we are about to find out." Colin opens the front door and steps out onto the porch, the deputy only a step or two behind him.

Two steps out the door is only as far as Colin is able to get before he sees the car, the sight of which stops him in his tracks.

Before either of the men can speak, the horn's steady drone stops and the car takes off down the road and out of sight. "Who the hell was that?" the deputy asks. "Is that one of your neighbors?"

Colin is unable to answer him. His heart is in his throat and he can't stop staring down the road in the direction the car just disappeared.

"What an asshole," Steve remarks. The deputy walks over to Colin and puts a hand on his shoulder. "Colin, you all right? You are as white as a sheet."

Colin shakes his head. It couldn't be. It can't be. He turns and quickly heads back inside the house, brushing off the deputy's hand without acknowledgement. He rounds the corner to his bedroom and drops to his knees in front of his dresser. He opens the bottom drawer and digs under the folded jeans, pulling out a large photo album.

The deputy appears in the bedroom doorway. "Colin, what the hell is going on?"

Colin doesn't pay any attention to the deputy's question and quickly opens the photo album. He frantically flips to the back of the album and stops on the last page of photos before the news articles begin. He quickly peels the cellophane cover back and removes one of the photos. A photo of a young woman standing at the trunk of a car, smiling and holding a large paper bag with both arms.

He holds the photo out to the deputy. Steve walks over and takes the photo from him. Colin watches as the deputy looks at the photo and then takes the photo back when the deputy holds it back out.

"It's the same kind of car as the one that was just outside. Same color and everything. Who is that, Colin? An ex-girlfriend you pissed off recently?" the deputy joked.

Colin shakes his head. "That's Alicia. And that's her car in the photo."

The deputy looks at Colin and looks down at the photo again. "Now I know why you looked like you saw a ghost outside," Steve states.

Colin frowns, as if the deputy is trying to merely humor him. "You don't understand, Steve. That color on that car. It's a special order. When I was trying to find her after she left, I checked with the DMV in five states in either direction and there were only two other cars of this year, make, and model registered with this exact paint color. Neither of them were within five hundred miles of this town and neither were registered to anyone with family in this state. I know because I spoke with both of the owners."

The deputy looks into Colin's eyes and slowly nods. "Colin, listen carefully to what I am about to say and ask yourself how this sounds. You are saying that the car that was just outside is the same car of your ex-wife who left you well over a decade ago. Who just happens to be in the neighborhood this morning and wanted to wake you up with a car horn and then decides to speed off when you come outside."

Colin looks at the deputy. "I know it sounds crazy, Steve, but what are the odds?"

The deputy looks once again at the picture still in Colin's right hand. "Colin, I just—" The deputy's words are cut off by the ringing of the telephone.

Colin watches the deputy as he closes his mouth and nods, apparently deciding not to say anything more on the subject. "OK, then," Steve concedes.

Colin puts the photo of Alicia and the car in his back pocket, returns the album to the dresser drawer, and closes it. The phone keeps ringing. He gets up from his kneeling position on the floor, wincing from the quick stitch of pain in his side and heads into the living room to grab the phone.

The phone rings once more. Colin finally reaches the phone and picks it up. The voice on the other end of the line introduces themselves as an adjuster from the insurance company, explaining that they would be inspecting his vehicle today at the tow yard.

Steve walks into the living room and begins to put on his uniform top and holster. Holding the phone and only partially listening, Colin walks into the living room and looks out the front windows onto the porch and into the street. The voice on the other end of the line advises they will call again after the inspection and wishes Colin a good day. He disconnects the line and lowers the phone to his side. The accident is the furthest thing from his mind right now.

Still looking out the window, he looks down the road until it disappears into the tree line. Wishing he had the chance to get a better look at the car that was just here. It was Alicia's car, or at least the identical match to her car. But why? His eyes follow the road back to his driveway and skip across the deputy's car in the driveway. Looking over the porch, his eyes pass over a brown box sitting on the railing near one of the corner banisters as he begins to turn back in the direction of the kitchen. He stops mid-turn. His eyes quickly dart back to the brown box.

A plain, wrapped brown box. Another delivery.

Afraid to lose sight of the box balanced on the railing, he sets down the phone on the television near the window. "Steve, get over here."

The deputy finishes latching his belt and walks over to the window. Colin points. Steve follows the direction of Colin's finger and his eyes alight upon the box on the railing. "Shit," the deputy exclaims. "Now we know what the car was doing here."

Colin takes a few steps forward, finally removing his stare from the package and quickly opens the door. He steps outside and looks around to see if anyone is watching him. Looks around to see if he can feel any eyes on him. Nothing beyond the morning birds chirping in the trees.

He steps forward onto the porch and up to the box resting on the railing. *TO COLIN AND STEVE* is written in block lettering on the top of the box. Colin's heart sinks. They knew. Whoever is doing this is aware the deputy knows what is going on. Maybe seeing the car that looks just like Alicia's car is the punishment for telling another person, Colin hopes. Maybe whatever is in this box is the punishment.

Colin turns toward the front door, holding the box in both hands as if it might explode. The deputy is standing at the doorway, looking out into the tree line, as well as up and down the street. Looking for someone who might be watching, as Colin initially did before he stepped onto the porch to get the package.

Colin walks across the porch and the deputy steps aside to allow him to enter, then continues to look around outside as Colin goes on to the kitchen table.

He sets the new box down on the table. He pushes yesterday's box farther back on the table and closer to the first one he received, clearing room for whatever may be inside this latest delivery. He hears the front door close behind him and the deputy walks over and stops next to him.

Steve leans forward and reads the top of the box. "Colin, do you want me to open this one?"

Colin shakes his head. "I'll open it, Steve. I made the decision to share what is happening with you. If there is something horrible in this box, I will need your help to deal with it." Colin hopes he sounds as though there is strength in his voice, because there was none in his body at the moment. He is terrified to open this package. Terrified to find out what the kidnapper would do, or already has done, knowing the rules they laid out were broken.

He looks at the box. This one is square, with no wrapping and just a wide strip of masking tape holding it shut. With the block lettering written in pen this time, instead of marker like before. Forcing his fear away the best he can, Colin reaches out and begins to break the tape seal that is holding the box shut. After breaking the seal, Colin takes a deep breath and opens the box. Pink rumpled tissue paper once again lines the box. Only this time, there isn't a velvet ring box hidden in the center. No, this time it isn't a ring box at all.

It's an ear.

Blood has soaked a large portion of the paper underneath the ear, where it would normally be connected to a head. Small splatters of blood dot the rest of the ear and a few spots inside the box. The ear is pierced, and the earring is still in the lobe: a pink heart with a small diamond in the center. The same kind of earrings Colin bought Penny for Christmas last year. The ones she loved. The same ones she wore all the time.

Colin stumbles back from the box, refusing to believe what he's just seen. It can't be his little girl's ear lying in the box in front of him. Still backing away, his movement is stopped when he bumps into the back of his easy chair. With his movement now stalled, he falls to his knees on the floor. Any strength he has remaining left when he saw what is in that box. He begins to cry, holding his head in his hands.

The deputy continues to stare at the box and the bloody gift inside. He doesn't say a word.

The only sounds inside the house now are Colin's sobs and the tick of the clock in the kitchen. The tick of the clock seems to slow and soon, for Colin, time feels like it comes to a complete stop.

≈

The intense throbbing coming from the left side of her head finally brings Penny back to reality. She opens her eyes and tries to find focus. The fuzziness of the world around her begins to fade and objects sharpen as she regains perception. The pain from the left side of her head is unlike anything she ever experienced before. A heavy, throbbing pain occasionally accented with sharp lightning bolts racing across her skin.

She struggles to move her arms and legs to see if the latest events have given her any opportunity to get away. Still securely tied to the chair, she stops struggling. She looks around the room. The table now has a red-stained rag and a butane torch sitting on it. The dusty tools that were previously scattered across the surface have been moved to the right side of the table. The chest near her now has a long, flat metal bar lying on it next to the sander. On the floor, around her feet, is a large splattering of dried blood spots. The left side of her shirt is stained maroon. The flickering of the fluorescent light overhead seems to be in tune with the throbbing inside her head. She stares at her shirt, trying to surmise how much blood she must have lost to stain her shirt to this extent.

Her bravado from earlier completely disappears and she begins to cry. The sound of her sobs seems off to her, as she can only hear the sound from the right side of her head. The realization she may never hear again from her left side sets in and she begins to cry harder. *What did I ever do to deserve this*, she begs to the silence through her tears. The silence doesn't respond.

Between the throbbing pain from the left side of her head and the oppressive silence in the room, Penny's hopelessness begins to turn into anger. The tears and sobs begin to slow. Her anger grows, blooming into a scorching bonfire of rage in the pit of her stomach. Her tears stop completely. She opens her eyes and focuses them on the door in front of her, vowing to find a way to get free and get away from this hell.

She renews her struggle against the bonds that hold her to the chair. Wrestling her arms and legs to the left and right. Up and down. The bindings that keep her restrained soon begin to cut into her clothes and then into her skin as she continues to struggle. The pinpoints of pain from her bonds only add fuel to the fiery rage now inside her and she struggles harder.

A loud crack permeates through the room. Empowered by the sound, Penny struggles harder, concentrating her efforts on the right side where the noise came from. Another crack. And another. And then the right arm of the chair breaks free from where it connects to the seat.

With the arm of the chair still connected to the back rest of the chair, Penny begins to move her right arm in a circular pattern, trying to completely break the right arm of the chair. A few more cracks echo throughout the room and her right arm is suddenly free from the chair, although still bound to the broken arm of the chair. She quickly reaches over and fights to remove the bindings of her left arm. Once they are removed, she removes the bindings on her right arm, freeing it from the broken chair arm.

The chair arm clatters loudly as it hits the floor.

Penny freezes. The sound created by arm of the chair is

exceptionally loud in the room. She wonders how loud the other noises from the chair were during her struggle to get free. She stares at the door in front of her, praying she doesn't hear the click of the lock being slid back from its position. Praying the door doesn't open and the hollow, dead eyes of her captor appear from the darkness beyond.

Minutes pass. The silence is almost thick enough to cut. Forcing herself into action, Penny leans forward and removes the bindings from her legs. She leans back after freeing her legs and attempts to stand up. Dizziness overtakes her and she sits back down before she can fully make it on her feet. She must have lost more blood than she expected. She has also been sitting in this chair for countless hours. She tells herself she has to take it slow so she doesn't make herself black out before she can get away.

Catching her breath while still sitting in the chair, she hesitantly reaches her left hand up to the throbbing spot on the left side of her head. As her fingers gingerly touch hardened, disfigured flesh, her fears are confirmed. That inhuman piece of shit cut off her ear. Penny fights back the tears that instantly begin to form. She needs to remain strong. She needs to get out of here.

Penny forces herself to stand up, steadying herself by holding onto the remaining arm of the chair. After finding her balance, she stumbles forward and to the door. Trying the knob, she confirms what she expected. The door is locked.

She walks over to the table and looks around to see if there is anything she can use to get the door open. On the table are the drinks and remaining sandwiches from earlier. A variety of dusty tools are spread out on the back end of the table, their intended use mostly unknown to Penny. Closer to the front of the table, a small butane torch sets among a few pieces of pink tissue paper and the blood-smeared rag.

Glancing around the remainder of the room, her eyes fall upon the flat metal bar lying on the chest. She quickly moves to the chest and grabs the bar, testing its weight. She walks back to the door and pushes one end of the bar in between the door and the jamb. Pulling with all her strength, she tries to separate the deadbolt lock from its home in the door frame. The wood frame cracks and splinters a bit where it meets the bar, but the bolt remains securely where it is. Penny eases her pull on the bar and relocates it to a new position between the door and the frame. She pulls once again with all her might and once again is met only with some cracking from the frame.

The deadbolt remains in its position, unmoved by her efforts.

Dizziness sets in due to the exertion from her efforts. Penny drops to her knees in front of the door, trying to stop the world from spinning and making sure she doesn't fall over. She fights to breathe slow and steady. Passing out is the last thing she can afford to do, especially after getting this far. She closes her eyes. While the outside world continues to spin, Penny focuses her thoughts on how she can get out of this room.

She can try the metal door on the other side of the room

and see where it leads if it is unlocked. If the door is locked, there's no way she is going to be able to force it open. Her only real option is to find a way through the door in front of her. *Think, Penny, think*, she tells herself. Maybe she can use the torch on the table to cut through the deadbolt, providing she can clear enough of the frame away to reach it with the flame of the torch. Maybe she can use one of the larger tools in the room to break the doorknob away or even break through the door to get out. She takes a deep breath and opens her eyes. The world has stopped spinning. The intense throbbing from the side of her head, however, still remains.

The sound of a key sliding into the keyhole on the other side of the door greets her, and the click of the deadbolt sliding back into its home in the door echoes loudly in the silent room.

≈

After driving away from Colin's house, the figure heads through town to Ellie's. There are no other cars on the road this early in the morning as usual, and he is confident Colin and the deputy are both busy looking at the latest package. A light fog has settled in from the lake and gives the town an eerie feel as the figure drives through it.

Stopping at the red light in front of Sam's, he marvels at the hazy red circle reflecting on the fog from the red light. The light's slow dissipation from the epicenter of the signal reminds the figure of what fresh blood seeping into the surrounding snow looks like. His reminiscing is broken up by a new green hazy circle abruptly replacing the red one, and the figure proceeds to make the turn toward Ellie's.

One more turn and a couple minutes later, the bar comes into view. The fog is much heavier this close to the lake and the figure carefully pulls the car around the front of the bar and into the back, parking next to Ellie's truck. He turns off the ignition and takes a deep breath. The scent of the one eludes him this time. Frowning, he opens the door and steps out of the car.

A light illuminates from inside the building and shines through the haze from the small window in the back door. The figure walks to the door and before he can turn the handle, the door swings open and Karen steps from the threshold. "Why are you here this early? And why would you even think about driving her car in this town?" Karen demands.

The figure hangs his head. Driving the one's car is a very large risk here, he is well aware. But he needed to. He needed to make sure the game goes accordingly to plan. "The car was necessary," he softly responds. "I was careful."

Karen shakes her head in disagreement. "And why are you here and not with your latest toy?"

The figure hesitates a moment before answering. He knows Karen will be upset when she finds out the deputy is now involved and will have to be dealt with. "There was a hiccup. Deputy Gates is involved now and is going to be playing the game, too." He waits for the yelling. The hitting. The punishment he knows he deserves for not fully controlling the events like planned.

Patiently waiting, nothing happens. The figure stops cringing, slowly opens his eyes, and looks at Karen. She hasn't moved from where she is standing. A half smile is on her face. A look of confusion crosses the figure's face.

"You need my help, don't you?" she asks.

He nods. Although he can control the game easily with one person, an armed police officer showing up with Colin presents an additional variable that only complicates things. He needs someone or something to distract Colin while he deals with the deputy alone.

"So what do you need me to do? I'm not luring another young woman into one of your games like last time," Karen states.

The figure shakes his head, then whispers, barely audible, "I need you to go to Colin's house, tell him and the deputy that you saw the car. Saw the car going down the old lumber mill road. Make sure only the deputy leaves to check it out and keep Colin at home. I will then remove the deputy from the game." The smile returns to the figure's face.

He watches Karen's face. Looking for agreement. Acceptance. Understanding. A wave of relief washes over him when Karen's smile gets bigger.

"Of course I can do that, honey. I was planning on going to see Colin today anyway," she says. "I will just have to go a bit earlier than I planned. Go. Get ready. I am going to clean up here and then head to Colin's." Her right hand reaches out and softly touches the left side of the figure's face. "Don't fuck this up. You have done so well for so long."

He nods. He turns from her touch, gets back into the car, and pulls away from the restaurant.

The drive from Ellie's to the end of the logging camp's road is brief, only a few miles. The figure pulls the one's car in between the trees beside Dr. Elyse's car and turns off the ignition. The world becomes silent, with only the occasional sound of a loon echoing through the woods. The figure exits the car and pauses before walking to the trunk. He doesn't need to cover the car now. He needs the deputy to recognize the car and know he's in the right place when he gets here. The figure turns from the car and heads down the pathway toward the building he has called home for many, many years.

Finally reaching the clearing, the figure checks to make sure no one is around and steps from the tree line, heading directly to the front door of the building in front of him. Unlocking the metal door, he slides the door open, the familiar screeching of metal on metal welcoming him home like a faithful pet patiently waiting by the door. Stepping inside, he slides the door closed, taking care to lock it once again, then turning and proceeding down the steps and to the far door that leads to the stairs.

A sliver of light still shines from the one solitaire window the old newspaper has peeled away from. The figure again reminds himself that it needs to fix the window.

He reaches the far door and unlocks it, carefully pulling it open and stepping into the hallway before the staircase. He closes the door behind him and once again locks it. He needs to remain vigilant and careful even at this part of playing the game. The figure then proceeds down the hall and begins down the steps when something out of the expected happens.

A muffled cracking noise from the bottom of the steps breaks the silence.

He stops in his tracks. Another muffled cracking noise comes from below. And one more.

Cautiously and slowly taking step after step, making sure each step is silent, he arrives at the door leading into the room where Penny is being kept. He stops before the door and listens.

A clattering of something wooden echoes from the other side of the door. The figure listens curiously. What is she doing in there? He wonders. He leans closer to the door and waits.

After a few moments, the sound of something being pushed into the space between the door and the door frame can be heard, followed by a soft grunting noise and the noise of wood creaking. The noise stops. The figure smiles. She's gotten free and is trying to pry the door open.

He wonders what she is using, what was still in the room with her when he left earlier? He wonders if she realizes no matter what she might be holding in her hands, it will not help her get away. A smile forms at the corners of the figure's mouth.

The creaking noise stops, and then a moment later the soft grunt and creaking noise starts back up again. *Good for her*, he thinks. She still has some false hope. For now.

The noise stops again and the figure hears a muffled thump. She must have worn herself out. Leaning back from the heavy, aged wood of the door, the figure quietly fishes the keys out of his pocket and gets ready to unlock the door. The deputy should be here soon, and the game cannot be played if beautiful Miss Penny is running around free of her bonds.

He slides the key in the lock and turns it, sliding the deadbolt back into the door. The figure's smile widens in anticipation of what is about to happen in the next room. A little extra play in the game never hurt anyone. Much.

CHAPTER 10

THE SIDE GAME

Steve stands at the table, looking at the latest box and its contents. The clock on the wall ticks along as the minutes pass. He can't imagine what Colin is feeling right now, but he also can't just stand here staring at the ear lying in front of him forever. "Colin, I need to see what else is in the box." he states, moving his gaze from the table to where Colin is sitting on the floor.

Colin looks up from his hands, tear stains down each side of his face, and nods.

"Thank you. I'll be careful," Steve assures him. Turning back to the table, Steve steps up to the edge and gently removes the tissue paper with the ear on it from the box. He sets this to the side, taking extra care to make sure the ear is not disturbed from its resting place among the paper.

As he reaches into the box to remove the rest of the tissue paper, Colin's voice breaks past the ticking of the clock. "Steve, wait."

He pauses and turns back to Colin again, who is now standing up. He waits as Colin walks over next to him and stops. "I need to see this as well," Colin says.

Steve nods and waits until Colin nods in return before he returns his focus to the box. In any other situation, Steve would secure the scene, call it in, and make sure none of the evidence was disturbed until forensics had a chance to dust everything for prints and confirm the DNA of the ear. Which would take hours. Maybe even days. Steve knows Colin will not wait for the standard red tape and bureaucratic fanfare that comes with a kidnapping. And he is worried the involvement of additional law enforcement would only result in Penny's death. With the contents of the latest package, it is clear whoever has Penny would not hesitate to cause her pain.

Reaching back into the box, Steve removes the remaining tissue paper and sets it to the side, revealing a folded piece of paper nestled at the bottom of the box. Like the last one. He reaches in and grabs the paper, pulling it out of the box and opening it up. He lays the unfolded paper on the table so both he and Colin can read it.

I am disappointed in you, Colin. So quick to crack. So quick to disregard what I have instructed and dismiss my rules as trivial. Well, I hope the contents of this box will show you I am not trivial. Maybe an extra ear for you, provided by your daughter, will help you hear better and pay attention. You break the rules again and I might have to provide one of her eyes to help you see better as well. There are many more body parts I can send you that she can live without. It was nice seeing you today. Seeing the look on your face when you saw the car. You're not seeing things. It's her car. Take some time to let that sink in. More instructions will be sent soon. As for your deputy friend, his involvement in our game will be ending soon. See you soon, Deputy Gates.

Both men stand in silence while they read the note. Steve's eyes harden a bit at the last line. If this lunatic thinks he is just going to sit back and watch what happens, they are severely mistaken.

Colin's voice penetrates his thoughts. "It was her car. They have my daughter and my ex-wife's car. Why…" Colin's voice trails off and Steve is unable to make out what he says after that.

He looks at Colin. Staring at the paper, his face is a mix of anger, fear, and confusion. He knows there is nothing he can say that will help ease Colin's fears. Rationally, he knows the use of the car and the reference in the letter may just be a scare tactic. It's easy to use the Internet these days to learn a lot of information about a person. Colin's search for his missing wife and what she was driving when she disappeared would be easy to find. The ear, on the other hand, is more concerning. If it really is Penny's ear, then there is a terrified young lady in severe pain somewhere out there who may or may not still be alive at this time.

The deputy continues to look at Colin, who is still staring at the paper, immobile and silent. "Colin, I—"

The ringing of the doorbell cuts the deputy short. He turns to the door and stares at it. It rings again.

A voice calls from the other side of the door. "Colin? It's Karen Ellie. Are you awake? It's really important I speak with you. And why is there a squad car in front of your house?"

Steve looks back at Colin, who is still standing statue-like at the table. Steve quickly gathers up the contents of the latest box, and carefully places them back to where they were previously. He puts the lid on the box and picks it up from the table.

"One minute, Mrs. Ellie," Colin yells toward the door.

Steve skirts the edge of the table and picks up the other two boxes, being careful not to drop any of them, and carries them into Colin's room. Kneeling down in front of the dresser, he places all three boxes in the same drawer he saw Colin pull the photo album from and closes it after covering them with a folded shirt. *Karen does not need to know about any of this*, the deputy thinks. He stands up and goes back into the kitchen.

"Everything OK? What's going on?" impatiently asks the voice on the other side of the front door. The doorbell rings again.

Steve pauses next to Colin as he passes him. "Colin, listen, I need you to not say anything to Mrs. Ellie about the packages, Penny's disappearance, or the car. Do you understand?"

Colin nods, now staring blankly at the empty table in front

of him. The deputy isn't exactly sure at this point if Colin is even still with him in the room.

Steve crosses the few remaining steps to the front door and opens it up. Mrs. Ellie, in all her glory, is standing at the door. A look of concern is drawn upon her face instead of her normal cheery disposition.

"Deputy Gates! I was not expecting to see you here. Is everything OK?" she asks. The look on Mrs. Ellie's face goes from concern to surprise and right back to concern.

"Everything is fine, Mrs. Ellie. I was here speaking with Colin about the fire the other night," Gates replies.

She nods and cranes her head to see past the deputy to where Colin is still standing. Steve hasn't moved from the door's entrance and wasn't planning on letting Mrs. Ellie in unless Colin allows it.

She looks back at the deputy and frowns. "Deputy, do you mind if I have a few words with Colin. In private?"

Steve opens his mouth to tell her that now is not a good time and ask if she can come back later when suddenly Colin's voice chimes in next to his right shoulder. "What's going on, Karen?"

Slightly startled, Steve was not expecting Colin to be standing next to him. Not after the seemingly comatose condition he was in just a short time ago. He moves to the left to allow Colin to step up closer to the door.

Mrs. Ellie's frown disappears when Colin steps into view. She hesitantly glances over at the deputy and looks back at Colin. "Colin, what I have to tell you is just for you, but I guess you should probably hear this too, Deputy Gates, because it is a police matter. Although I'm not sure how much you know about Colin's past and the disappearance of his wife, Alicia. She was like a daughter to me and worked in my bar up to the day she disappeared. And Colin, I don't want to tell you this because the very last thing I want to do is dig up painful old memories, but I saw Alicia's car pulling down the old logging camp road earlier when I was out taking my morning walk. I know in my heart of hearts it was her car, because I would recognize it anywhere."

The gears in Steve's head began to spin into overdrive the moment he hears the car was spotted driving down the old logging camp road.

He must have been wearing the same bewildered look on his face as Colin, because Mrs. Ellie pauses a moment and then asks, "Deputy, are you alright?"

"Yes, Mrs. Ellie. I'm fine," Gates replies. He turns to Colin and looks directly into his eyes. "Colin, I think it's best a uniformed police officer checks this out to verify the car and who may be driving it. And if something that has been missing is found, that officer can bring it back to you. Don't you agree?"

The deputy tries to will Colin's agreement with every ounce of his being. Colin nods, and Steve hopes he is catching the hint the deputy is giving him.

He turns to Mrs. Ellie. "Would you mind staying here with Colin until I come back?"

Now it's her turn to nod. "Of course I will, Deputy."

Satisfied, Gates turns and walks past Colin to the couch, where his hat and gun belt are still lying. While he is putting on the belt, Colin lets Mrs. Ellie in, closes the door behind her, and walks with her to the kitchen table, where they both sit down. Steve's attention is focused on getting out to where Karen saw the car as fast as he can. Putting on his hat, he hears her asking Colin if he's hungry and if he's heard from Penny yet.

"Please stay here until I return," he states over his shoulder to the two in the kitchen as he walks to the door, opening it, and stepping outside. He doesn't wait for a response from either of them.

Closing the door behind him, the deputy quickly bridges the distance between the door and his patrol car, which is now flanked by Karen's truck. He tries to make sure he doesn't squeal the tires as he's backing up and pulling away from Colin's house, but his adrenaline is racing and he can't be sure he didn't end up leaving a trail of rubber behind as he left. He will apologize later for it if so.

≈

Penny stares wide-eyed at the door in front of her. The click of the deadbolt is still echoing through the room. Frozen in place, she waits to see the door knob turn.

Move, Penny, she screams in her head. *Move your ass NOW!* She wills herself into action, standing up and stepping back from the door. She stands in the middle of the room and holds the metal bar in her hand. She grips the bar with both hands and tries to steel her nerves, preparing to swing the bar at the head of whomever or whatever comes through the door. The dizziness begins to set back in due to her standing up so quickly. *Not now*, she begs. *Please not now.*

The door knob turns and the door slowly swings open about six or seven inches. Nothing emerges from the dark beyond the door. No horrid, dead eyes anchored in a sallow face appear in front of her. Her hands begin to shake from her grip on the metal bar. The world begins to spin. *Please no, please no*, she prays.

Feeling her strength begin to fade again, her panic sets in. "Open the damn door and face me!" she screams at the slice of darkness between the partially open door and the door frame.

Silence is only one of the responses she receives. The second response is a hand that quickly reaches into the room from that same slice of darkness and hits the light switch, plunging the room into complete black before Penny has a chance to react and swing the metal bar. She freezes.

She strains to hear any sound that would give her a direction to swing the bar, but the black is all consuming. Not a single bit of light is visible. The pounding of her heart is reverberating in her one remaining ear, only adding to her growing panic.

The creaking of the wooden door swinging the rest of the way open in front of her focuses her attention. She swings the metal bar wildly from the right to the left, and then from the left to the right. She connects with nothing but air on both swings. She sets up again for another swing.

Her heart is now racing, and the strain of listening coupled with her adrenaline is causing her palms to sweat. She focuses, listening for any sound, trying to hear past her pounding heart. She can feel the world spinning, but thankfully the darkness removes the visual effect that accompanies the feeling.

The door in front of her creaks again and she hears the door slam shut. Another swing to the left and back to the right. Only the air and the darkness meet her efforts. Afraid to move, to give away her position, she waits. Agonizing minutes pass, made of nothing but complete silence and darkness.

A loud clatter of something hitting the wall to her right pierces through the silence and she turns in that direction, again swinging wildly back and forth. Only this time, her sweaty grip on the bar gives way as she swings it back to the right and it slips out of her hand, sailing away from her and into the perfect black of the room. A loud boom echoes through the room as the bar connects with the far wall. Penny's heart sinks. Now weaponless, she digs inside for the courage to fight with every ounce of strength remaining in her body.

Disoriented as to what direction she is facing now, she spins left and right trying to hear anything that would allow her to get her bearings.

The room suddenly fills with blinding white as the lights turn back on. Penny instinctively closes her eyes from the light and two strong arms quickly wrap around her body from behind. A hand with a rag clamps over her face and she screams into it. A strange feeling of déjà vu settles over Penny as the dizziness returns full force and the world once again begins to fade away. As her legs begin to get weak one more time, she wonders where she will wake up this time.

Then it all goes black.

≈

The figure feels the girl go limp in his arms, the chloroform once again doing the job it was meant to do. He lays the unconscious girl down on the floor and looks around the room. The chair that Penny was secured to is now missing an arm. Her bindings lie in small piles around the chair with the splintered piece of the chair's broken arm nearby. The metal bar is on the floor, against the wall, lying near the spot where Dr. Elyse's car keys also lie. The keys the figure threw to distract Penny.

He walks over to the keys and the bar, picks them both up, and puts the keys back into his pocket. He walks back to the table and puts the bar down near the bottles of water. Turning, he walks across the room to the metal door and fishes out another set of keys. Unlocking the door, he pulls it open. The familiar sound of metal on metal echoes throughout the room. The figure disappears into the dark beyond the door and comes back a few moments later with a metal chair. He swaps out the broken wooden chair and sets it in the corner of the room. Turning to Penny's limp figure lying on the ground, he walks over and picks her up and maneuvers her into the new chair. After replacing her bindings and confirming they are once again secure, the figure turns back to the current task at hand.

The deputy should be arriving soon.

He closes the metal door, ensuring it is locked once again.

Before exiting the room, the figure pauses in front of Penny. He reaches down, putting a hand under her chin, and raises her face up. Tear stains and blood splatter dance an interwoven dance upon her pretty face. Tracing her lips with his thumb, he leans forward and softly kisses the unconscious girl. A single word escapes his lips after the kiss ends.

"Mine."

He pulls away from Penny, and heads to the main floor of the building upstairs. He plunges the room back into darkness and locks the door behind him. He heads up the staircase, repeating the unlocking and locking process with the door that separates the stairwell and the main floor.

He crosses the main floor and, after unlocking the large sliding door, slides the door open. The fog is still present, lying low to the ground. The overcast sky blots out the sun's rays and doesn't allow them to burn away what fog remains. The figure smiles. He turns back into the building and walks to a nearby wall where several large steel traps are hanging. Old bear traps with massive jaws and ragged, rusty teeth, used by the loggers who once worked here to keep the wildlife at bay.

He takes two of the traps down off of their hooks and grabs the clamp tool he will need to set the traps. Stuffing the tool in his back pocket, the figure walks outside, closing the large metal door behind him, and heads across the clearing to the pathway. Reaching the tree line, he sets one of the traps on the ground and then continues on his way. The figure quickly navigates the pathway until he reaches the end, where the cars are parked. He waits a moment, listening and watching, still hidden by the brush of the pathway.

Although the deputy shouldn't be here yet, the figure needs to be sure. The sounds of the forest in the morning sing their usual symphony. Still smiling, the figure bends over and sets the second trap on the ground. He walks over to the one's car and opens the trunk, pulling out the camouflage cover. After closing the trunk, he heads back to the trap lying on the ground. He sets the cover down and turns to Dr. Elyse's vehicle. The figure walks over to the second car and also removes the cover, placing it in the back seat. No reason to hide the cars anymore.

He then turns and walks back to the trap, picking it up from the ground. Spying a suitable spot on the pathway, the figure sets the trap down and pries the jaws open, arming the spring of the trap with the tool. He partially covers the trap with leaves and underbrush and steps back to survey his work. The trap is still visible yet gives off the impression it is meant to be hidden. His work with the second trap done, the figure picks up the camouflage cover and then turns, heading back down the pathway to the clearing.

He reaches the end of the pathway and picks up the first trap. A large tree borders the end of the pathway, right where the pathway meets the clearing. The figure slowly climbs the tree, with the cover tucked into his jacket, carefully hauling the trap up the tree by its chain. Reaching the necessary height and stretching out onto a branch that hangs over the pathway, the figure hauls up the trap and takes a couple of practice swings.

Judging the distance of the swing. Judging the height of the swing. Judging the length of chain the figure will need to use for the intended result.

Once he's satisfied with the results, the figure prepares for the deputy's arrival. He wraps himself in the camouflage cover, being careful not to allow any edges to hang down or look unnatural. Resting the trap on the branch, the figure carefully sets the trap and secures the chain to the branch leaving just the right amount of chain.

The figure picks up the trap by the edges and holds it out until the chain is taut, turning it and facing the spring portion of the trap downward.

The waiting begins.

Waiting for the deputy to make his way down the path. The path which leads directly under the spot where the figure is now perched, concealed.

The sounds of the morning forest take over. Snapping twigs and footsteps can be heard in the distance. He doesn't have to wait long.

≈

Disregarding the traffic lights, Deputy Gates races through town at speeds the roads probably have never seen before. He is careful not to use his lights or his sirens, as he does not want to cause any alarm to anyone who may see him. Nor does he want to give away the element of surprise and announce he is on his way after this kidnapping lunatic.

Finally reaching the old logging camp road, Steve slows

down, almost missing it, and makes the turn. The road is overgrown and looks as if it has had little to no use in years. Grass and shrubs grow wild through the large chunks of split concrete where the road used to be. The concrete is completely missing in several large stretches.

Steve carefully maneuvers the car down the road, driving slowly, keeping a sharp lookout for any movement or indications of something or someone other than the nature around him. After driving several miles, he finally sees two cars parked among the brush and the trees to the side where the road ends and the forest takes over completely.

He stops the car about thirty feet from the end of the road. He surveys the area. Due to the density of the underbrush and trees, he isn't able to see far into the woods on either side of the road. The two cars in front of him were parked far enough into the brush that the front end of each car is almost fully concealed. A pathway, located to the left of the cars, disappears into the forest. Looking at the cars, he is surprised he is able to recognize both of them. The first one is the car from this morning. The car that allegedly belongs to Colin's ex-wife, who disappeared. The second car looks like Dr. Elyse's.

The hairs on Steve's arms and neck stand up.

Dr. Elyse's car. He remembers picking up Penny's compact off the ground in the back parking lot of the clinic. In the same spot Dr. Elyse normally parks her car.

The clinic that was burned to the ground. The clinic where Dr. Elyse's dead body was discovered.

He doesn't want to think this psycho murdered Dr. Elyse and then set the clinic on fire to cover their tracks, but at this point he is almost one hundred percent positive that is exactly what happened. And it's also more than likely the clinic is where this monster got their hands on Penny.

Steve is sure of it. Just as he is sure this murderer's little adventure is about to come to an end.

Turning off the car, Steve opens the driver's side door and gets out, quietly closing the door behind him. The call of a loon carries through the forest. Its lone, eerie sound drives a shiver through him. *Fitting*, he thinks. He pulls his service weapon, making sure the safety is disengaged, and cautiously walks over to the two parked cars.

The car presumed to be Colin's ex-wife's car is at the end of the road. Steve approaches it. Heat from the engine can still be felt as he gets closer, although he would have to fight back some brush to actually get to the front of the car due how it is parked. He turns his attention to the second car, Dr. Elyse's car. A purse is overturned on the back seat with the contents spilled onto the floor. Penny's purse. Steve recognizes it, as she fidgeted with it the entire trip to Rockville when they went to pick up Colin from the hospital. Among the contents, he sees her cellphone. A little white light near the top of the screen flashes furiously every few moments. In addition to the purse and its contents, a bundled-up camouflage cover rests on the passenger side rear set. The rest of the car is empty.

Steve turns his attention from the cars and to the pathway

which leads away from the road and into the underbrush. He thinks back to the rumors at the station about an abandoned logging camp out this way in the woods that is considered haunted by the local population. Even the more mischievous teenagers in town avoid the spot, which is why he has never had to come out this way before.

He walks up to the entrance of the pathway and stops, looking down it as far as he can see. Over time, the underbrush and low hanging tree branches have framed the path with makeshift walls and a ceiling of green, black, and brown. The path has clearly been used on a regular basis, as the ground is well-compressed with broken twigs, trampled grass, and ferns snapped back at the base. His eyes follow the path up to where he is currently standing, stopping at one spot in particular about two feet away from him where it appears some underbrush has been spread out recently. In an attempt to cover something on the pathway.

Something made from curved, rusty metal with large, jagged teeth.

Steve pauses a moment when he realizes what he is looking at. He looks around where he is standing to see if any other traps have been laid. The area around him is clear.

"Nice try, asshole," he whispers.

He scolds himself for not being more careful when he checked out the cars. He could have easily stepped on a trap lying next to one of the cars and, based on the size of those teeth, he would have probably bled out before he could get help out to his location.

The disturbed underbrush scattered over the trap looks recent, so it would be safe to assume Penny's captor is expecting company. Steve steps forward onto the path, carefully sidestepping the trap and leaving it undisturbed for now. He moves cautiously, quietly down the path. Paying very close attention to the ground in front of him, looking for any more traps or wires stretched across the pathway.

The path seems to go on forever, or at least that's what it feels like to Steve. The fear of stepping on a trap keeps his attention focused downward, and several times his hat is knocked off by a low-hanging branch. Finally, a break in the thick underbrush tunnel appears about sixty feet in front of him, opening up to what appears to be a large clearing. The corner of a building is visible in the distance.

He stops. The abandoned logging camp. With its stigma among everyone in town, it would make the ideal spot for a murdering psycho to hide and torture a poor innocent girl.

The rage begins to race through his system again. Holding his gun with both hands, aimed at the ground about five feet in front of him and at the ready, he proceeds toward the end of the path at the tree line and where the clearing begins. Slowly, one step at a time, eyeing every inch of the ground along the way to make sure he doesn't step on a trap or set an alarm off to give away his position or proximity to the camp.

Ten feet away.

Five feet away.

One foot away.

Steve pauses at the edge of the pathway where it meets the clearing. Hesitant to step from the cover of the tree line, he surveys the area. The clearing is a lot larger than he expected it to be, with large, decaying tree stumps dotting the landscape. In the center is a large warehouse-style building with a loading dock at one end. A run-down antique truck, windowless and overgrown with small shrubs and moss, is parked next to the dock. A large sliding door with a small concrete platform and steps in front of it breaks up the monotony of the building's weathered siding. The low-lying fog, although quickly lifting as the day wears on, still gives the scene in front of him the feeling of a bad horror flick. *No wonder everyone thinks this place is haunted*, he thinks.

Steve's rage subsides a bit as he contemplates what kind of horrors might be waiting for him beyond that door on the side of the building. Mutilation? Multiple bodies? Unspeakable atrocities you only read about in books or see in movies?

He forces the thought that Penny may already be dead from his mind and makes one more thorough search of the ground in front of him. It's time to stop this fucker's little game and get a young woman back home to her father.

Steve steps forward into the clearing.

≈

The figure lies in wait for the deputy, perched on the branch and still holding the trap. Seconds turn to minutes. He doesn't have to wait long, though. Out of place among the familiar sounds of the forest, the occasional twig snapping and crunch of underbrush is easily heard from his position. Slowly, steadily, these noises come closer, until the figure can clearly identify each footstep. Hesitant footsteps, clearly being set down with care. Someone has seen the trap at the beginning of the path. The smile returns to the figure's face, the chapped lips parting and again revealing his yellow stained teeth. His anticipation for what is about to happen overpowers the burning sensation forming in his shoulders from holding the trap out in front of him for so long.

The steps continue to get closer until finally the brim of a hat comes into view below the figure. A hat clearly belonging to a deputy of the Orchard Lake sheriff's department.

The top of the hat stops almost directly below the figure. Two arms are partially outstretched, holding a handgun. *Your gun won't help you here, Mr. Deputy*, the figure thinks. He makes sure he outstretches his arms to full length, careful to avoid any noise from the trap's chain secured to the branch and takes one final look at the hat below it. *Good-bye, Deputy Gates*, he voices in his head.

Opening his hands, the figure lets the trap go.

As if in slow motion, the trap slowly drops down and begins its inward swing toward the deputy, the trap's chain fully extended and guiding the arc. At the same time, Steve starts to take a step forward into the clearing.

His foot never completes the step.

The armed spring of the trap connects solidly with the

deputy's face. In the split second following the initial impact, the trap and the deputy separate slightly, with the weight and momentum of the trap causing the deputy's head to begin to move backward.

Then the split second is over and the trap's jaws slam shut. The jagged teeth on each side of the trap disappear into the sides of the deputy's head, slightly in front of his ears on either side. The force from the closing jaws causes the left side of the man's face to collapse inward, ejecting his left eye from the now-shattered socket.

Several gunshots rip through the forest, scattering the birds from the nearby trees as the deputy's body convulses and his finger, still on the trigger of his service pistol, jerks during his final moments of life.

The figure watches from above in fascination. Watches as Deputy Gates's body twitches as the life within is extinguished. Watches as blood furiously pours from the man's mangled head and down his body, staining his uniform in an ever-growing design of tan being overtaken by a dark red.

He continues to watch until the deputy's now-lifeless body stops twitching, still suspended by the trap and the chain secured to the tree branch. The figure chuckles slightly. It looks like Deputy Gates is still standing, with a bloody trap for a mask.

"Stand up straight, sir," the figure admonishes the deputy, chuckling a little harder.

Content with the outcome of the deputy's part in the game,

he can get back to Penny and Colin and continue with his original plan. He gathers up the camouflage cover and climbs down out of the tree. Leaving the deputy as is, the figure turns toward the building and heads to the door of the logging camp.

He opens the door and steps inside, closing the door and locking it. He returns the trap's clamp tool back to the hanger on the wall and sets the camouflage cover on the floor, turning and heading across the room to where Penny is still being kept. *Time to see if the gunshots woke her up*, he thinks. He wasn't worried about anyone else hearing the shots. The forest around here is always full of hunters, regardless of whether or not it was hunting season. Gunshots are not an uncommon thing to hear in the morning hours around Orchard Lake.

≈

Back at the tree line and the start of the path, Steve's body is still slightly swaying, his limp eet dragging back and forth on the ground, ever so slightly. His hands finally loosen their grip a bit, and his service pistol falls to the blood-stained dirt of the pathway.

His hat, once again lying on the ground, is not picked back up this time.

CHAPTER 11

THE SETUP

Colin sits down at the kitchen table, trying to avoid Karen's stare as she sits across from him. A muted squealing of tires is heard outside as the deputy heads off to the old logging camp road. He hopes Steve finds this monster and kills him, and brings his little hummingbird back home to him. Alive.

He stares at the wood grain patterns in the table in front of him. The swirls of light and dark lines dancing an elaborate dance with one another. The various dents and scratches in the surface from years of use. Karen's voice breaks through his thoughts.

"It was her car, Colin. I know it was," she says softly. "I would recognize it anywhere."

He remains silent. He knows she's telling the truth. He knew it was her car the second he saw it. He doesn't need to look inside that car to know there is a permanent red smudge on the passenger side sun visor from Alicia's lipstick due to a large bump in the road and him driving a little too fast one day when she was putting on her makeup. He doesn't need to lift the trunk lid to know it has *C & A* scratched into the metal underneath, with a large misshaped heart around the letters. That was Alicia's handiwork with a screwdriver on the day he proposed to her.

What he doesn't understand is why this monster, who has his little girl, also has Alicia's car. A shudder races through his body as the thought that this monster may have something to do with the disappearance of his wife crosses his mind.

"Colin, talk to me. What are you thinking? Is there anything I can do to?" Karen's voice cuts through his thoughts again, an unwelcome intrusion.

Colin almost wants to tell her to just shut the fuck up for a bit and let him be with his thoughts, but his manners get the better of him. "I'm trying to process this," he practically barks at her.

Karen quickly looks away from him. And shuts up. Maybe his tone was a little too harsh. He will apologize some other time.

It isn't completely untrue, what he said. He really is trying to process what he saw and what is going on. Trying to find any connections between the two. Any similarities which might help explain it all. And the biggest question of all: why his family?

Colin slams his hand down on the table, the loud noise tearing through the silence of the house and making Karen jump. "I'm sorry, Karen," he says. "I didn't mean to frighten you. I'm sorry if I sounded harsh earlier. It's been a very long couple days."

Karen avoids eye contact and nods. It's a few moments before she speaks. "I am going to go now. You clearly need some time alone, and I think I do as well. I miss Alicia too. And seeing her car being driven by the same person who was delivering those horrible packages scares me to my core."

She gets up from her chair and heads for the front door. He doesn't get up to stop her. Nor does he say anything as she opens it and leaves. His silence continues until he hears her truck door slam shut, the truck start up, and then pull away.

"I never told you about the packages."

His words fall upon an empty room, with only his ears hearing them. His eyes narrow. How did she know? He replays the last time Karen was over. He had just received the first package and she was in the shower. The package was on the table when she came out of his room, but nothing would have seemed out of the ordinary. Karen is a very upfront woman. She would have asked outright about what he was looking at. Instead, she had excused herself and left almost immediately afterward.

She never even inquired where Penny was the last time or two she was here, did she? Colin couldn't recall exactly, but he's pretty sure she didn't. He knows she didn't this morning.

A grim thought crosses Colin's mind. Did she recognize the package on the table the last night? Even worse, did she have a part in it?

His mind is going a million miles a minute. One scenario after another plays out in his head. Could Karen actually have played a part in Penny's kidnapping? Or is she covering up for the monster who did it? Did she know anything at all about Alicia's disappearance?

His brow furrows. He needs answers. He takes a deep breath. A quick, sharp pain in his side lets him know he hasn't healed yet. The accident. Colin hasn't really thought about it since Penny was taken from him. *How many days has it been?* he wonders. Two, three days since it happened? He can't remember. It feels as though it has been ages. He can't even remember what day the insurance company called him.

Another familiar feeling comes over him as his stomach rumbles. Colin tries to remember the last time he ate. Standing up, he walks over to the fridge and opens the door. He pauses while looking at all the containers of food Karen had brought over for Penny and him. She couldn't have had a part in his little girl's disappearance. She couldn't have known anything about his wife's disappearance. She wouldn't have brought the food. She wouldn't have done a million other things she's done over the last decade if she was involved.

Then a new thought creeps into Colin's mind: unless she was sent a package, too, with the same rules Colin was given to follow.

His eyes widen a bit. That has to be it. She knows about Penny missing but not because she's a part of it. Because she's a pawn in this thing's little game, just like he is.

The rumble in his stomach visits again, sounding angrier than last time. Colin makes a mental note to call Karen as soon as he's done eating and after he's heard from Steve. He reaches into the fridge, grabs a couple of the containers from the top shelf and sets them on the table. Turning back to the fridge, he digs through the remaining containers, checking to see if there is any bacon left.

≈

A loud hammering noise pierces the dark silence Penny is floating in, bringing her back to reality. Once again securely fastened to something, she is unable to move her arms or legs. She slowly opens her eyes and lifts her head to look around.

The room hasn't changed much since she last saw it. The lights are back on, and the large metal door to her right is open. Her sight beyond the door is limited due to where she is positioned, but she can see there is a hallway beyond the door with lights hanging from the ceiling every few feet. She is unable to see anything else beyond that. She looks around again. The metal bar that escaped her hands earlier is laying on the table now. The chair that finally offered her the freedom she desperately wants is sitting in the far corner on the other side of the room from the table, near two shovels. The chair's broken arm is resting on the seat.

The hammering noise echoes from down the hallway. She wonders how long she was out and what has happened since then. She tries to move her arms or her legs. There is no slack this time and the new chair seems to be made from metal. She looks down at her blood-and-dirt-crusted clothes. The crotch of her jeans is now a darker color than the legs. That's a new development.

She shakes her head and tries to fight back the tears which begin to well up in her eyes. Here she is being held captive by some monster who will probably chop her up into little pieces over time, and she's probably permanently disfigured on the left side of her head. But to top it all off, she's pissed herself. She wonders what Laura and Haley would say if they saw her like this. What her dad would say.

Unable to hold back the tears anymore, she begins to softly cry. The hammering noise echoes again from down the hallway, like a distant bass drum to accompany the tune of her sobs.

She cries until she is unable to cry anymore. Sniffling, she blinks her eyes a few times to clear the remaining tears away. How long has it been, she wonders. Ten minutes? Twenty? An hour? The hammering noise permeates the room once again, only this time there is another sound to accompany it. The sound of something metal clattering to the ground. She strains to listen for any other noises and watches the hallway for any movement. Silence greets her. She sniffles once more to clear her runny nose, her head still throbbing in pain. She waits and watches the door.

It isn't long until she can hear footsteps coming toward her from the hallway. Footsteps that keep approaching until finally her captor comes into her view. Smiling as he walks into the room where she is being held a prisoner.

"You are awake," He says as he stops directly in front of her. "Good."

Penny says the first thing that comes to her mind. "Fuck you."

The man's smile gets bigger. Showing the stained yellow teeth. She shivers. Although there is a smile on his face, the eyes remain dead and hollow. It's like watching a corpse smile at her. Penny finally looks away and down at the floor.

He speaks again. "It's time to prepare you for the next part," He says.

Her captor gets down on a knee and puts a hand under her chin. She pulls her head away from the touch. Undeterred, the hand reaches out again and grabs her chin. His fingers dig into her jaw on either side of her mouth. Forcefully. He pulls her face forward and levels her face with his own.

The unblinking, dead eyes inch closer to hers until she can feel the heat from his face. The steady warmth from his breath. Breath that has the smell of death upon it. He speaks again, his lips almost touching hers. "I am going to untie you. Then we are going to take a little walk and get you cleaned up. If you try to run or try to fight, it will result in a great deal of pain for you."

She nods, or the best she can with her chin in the figure's iron grip, more surprised at how many words she just heard him say than she is about what he said.

"Good girl," he says, leaning forward the rest of the way and putting his lips to hers. She struggles to pull away but is unable to. Luckily, the kiss is brief. The man pulls away, letting her chin go, and then focuses on untying her legs.

Penny fights the urge to vomit. She can still smell his breath. Feel his lips.

She watches as he finishes untying her right leg and then moves to her left leg. She flexes the toes on her right foot, getting the blood flow back and fighting off the little tingles that are beginning to form on the bottom of her foot. The man pauses after untying her left leg. He looks at her and stands up. She flexes the toes on her left foot, the familiar tingle replacing the dull numbness that was there a moment ago. She continues to look down, refusing to look up and into those eyes once again.

He stands in front of her for a minute or two. Unmoving. Silent. She stares at his boots. Dirty and aged. The silence is finally broken.

"I am going to untie your hands. If you try anything…" He takes a long pause. "If you try anything at all, I will cut off every finger of the first hand I untie and feed all but one of them to you. I will mail the last finger you do not eat to your father. Do you understand?"

Penny continues to stare at the floor. She nods, thinking it's best to just play along for now and wait for her opportunity to really try and escape.

The monster in front of her bends over and begins to untie her right hand. He pauses once again before fully removing the restraint. Words echo from the figure. "Remember. Anything at all."

A moment later, her right hand is free. Unwilling to move it unless directed, she closes her eyes and pretends she is still bound. Hands deftly remove the bindings holding her left arm and suddenly she is free.

The urge to instantly jump up and fight races across her mind, sending adrenaline throughout her body. She feels the hair slightly rise on the back of her neck in anticipation. Her body tenses, ready to leap into action. She fights to keep her eyes closed.

Her adrenaline continues to surge while her body prepares for the fight or flight. Then softly whispered words from her captor reach her ear.

"Do it. I know you want to. Give me another opportunity to take a part of you away and give it to your father."

The words pierce her bravado, causing her to lose all confidence in herself. The man's last five words bring the tears right back to her eyes. *Give it to your father.* She takes a deep breath and tries to relax, allowing a sniffle to be her only answer to his cutting words. This means he sent her ear to Daddy. Her poor father, who has given everything he could for her for as long as she can remember. Who, even in her later teenage years, still calls her by her nickname she had when she was very young.

His hummingbird.

She musters what strength she has left to stop the tears that have already started following the existing tracks down her face. Her eyes are still tightly closed. She forces herself to speak.

"I won't try anything".

Two hands roughly grab her by her arms near her shoulders. "Stand up, then, and let's go. It's time for you to get ready. We will have company soon."

She opens her eyes, still staring down, and stands up with the help of the hands digging into her upper arms. The tingling in her feet has finally subsided. The man's breath falls upon her face, as she is only a few inches away from him once again now that she is on her feet. He lets go of her arms and takes her right hand, hanging by her side. She cringes at the touch of his skin on her own. "It's almost over, Penny."

The words offer her no comfort. She fights to keep her eyes averted. The man begins to walk toward the long hallway, pulling her along. Penny doesn't fight the pull and follows him meekly, refusing to grip his hand at all with her right hand. He doesn't seem to care. They walk past the large metal door and she takes her first step into the hallway. Then her second step. Her third step.

The first hanging light passes by overhead and she continues down the hall, approaching the next hanging light. She will soon be beyond the point she could see while sitting down in the room she was held captive in for so long. Another light passes overhead. And another. And another. A seemingly never-ending stream of lights pass by overhead as she is led along by the man. She refuses to look up, staring intently at the floor and counting the reflection of lights above as she passes them to get an idea of how far she has traveled. Ten. Eleven. Twelve.

Then the smell hits her.

A smell so pungent it makes her forget the smells she was already becoming used to. The smells of wood, of dust, of dried blood, of burned hair and skin, and of her own urine.

This smell is acrid. Of earth and decay. Overpowering. Like someone decided to mix together a bunch of fresh dirt with week-old, super-heated roadkill, made a paste of the combination, and painted the walls with it.

Thirteen. Fourteen. Fifteen. Her captor, leading the way, must have stopped as she fails to notice and walks into him due to the fact she is focusing hard on the lights and trying not to gag from the smell. She glances up and sees they are standing in front of another door. This one, unlike the one they passed through to reach the hallway, is covered with a festive poster adorned with colorful brush strokes and musical notes. And balloons. Inflated, colorful balloons, taped at random intervals to the door poster.

Penny can't stop staring at the door. Confusion races across her mind. The lighthearted, jovial decoration of the door is extremely out of place. The pink and red and blue balloons haphazardly taped at different spots on the door are a stark contrast to the muted gray walls, harsh unfiltered yellow light from the fixtures above, and dark dirt-colored floor. The man reaches out and turns the knob on the festive door and swings it open.

The strength of the smell is the first thing that hits Penny.

Pungent. Overwhelming. As though the dirt and overkill paste was locked in a small, airless room for the entire summer. Cooking and building in strength. Penny blinks to clear the tears from her eyes. Her captor seems unaffected by the smell, as though he doesn't even notice it's there.

The room beyond is dark, and the light from the hallway only penetrates a short distance beyond the now open door. The floor beyond the door shines, a highly polished light colored wood. Clean, minus a bit of dirt here and there. A clean floor is also completely out of place given what Penny has seen so far. The right end of a large dust broom can be seen to the left of the doorway, catching a bit of the light from the hallway.

The man steps forward into the room, pulling Penny in tow and into the darkness beyond. Once she is through the door, he turns back to the doorway and closes the door behind them.

Complete black takes over. A total and utter void of light that rivals any darkness Penny has experienced before. Her eyes fight to adjust to the lack of any light. Fight to see anything. To focus on anything at all beyond the black.

The man's hand is still locked on hers. She hears him take a few steps away from her. She doesn't follow and her arm is pulled a bit away from her. Not far enough to make her have to follow. Penny is thankful for that. She's terrified to move from where she is standing. Unsure what else is in the room. Unsure what the smell is that constantly assaults her nose and clogs her throat. Unsure what is in store for her. She couldn't try to escape now even if she wanted to. She doesn't even know what direction the door is anymore. A weird, although unwelcome, comfort comes from the man's hand grasping hers.

The click of a switch echoes through the room. Large lights quickly illuminate from above and Penny is suddenly blinded by the flood of light. By the shine of the polished wood and light colored walls. She squints her eyes shut and waits for them to adjust to the now overabundance of light. Her arm is still extended away from her. Her hand still in the man's grip. She cautiously opens her eyes.

The man is standing in front of her, facing her and looking directly into her eyes. She quickly averts her gaze and looks around where she is standing. The floors. The walls. The décor.

The confusion sets in once again. It's a gymnasium. It looks just like her high school gymnasium. Even the school flag is draped on the wall above the door, next to a banner proudly proclaiming the school football team was this year's state champions. Streamers are hanging from the ceiling in organized patterns. Three large disco balls are hanging, unlit, in the center of the room.

More balloons dot the walls, tables, bleachers, and floor. Decorated like one of the dances she's been to.

She turns to look at the rest of the room.

The sights that greet her are more than she is ready for. An eerily quiet, large group of people sit at each of the tables and in the bleachers. Her eyes begin to dart around the room, from face to face, attempting to make sense of everything, but her mind refuses to acknowledge what she is seeing and the room begins to darken at the edges of her vision before she can put any of the pieces together. She can hear her heartbeat racing in her ears, overpowering any other sound. She doesn't hear herself screaming. She stops feeling the throbbing from her left side. The dizziness has returned in full force. Soon, the room goes all black again.

Penny wasn't conscious to know if she hit the floor when her legs gave out or when her screams stopped.

≈

After turning the main lights on, the man watches as his young captive finally opens her eyes and looks around her surroundings. He observes as she turns to see the rest of the room and glances around. Listens as she begins to scream. Screaming for help. Screaming at the myriad of faces around her. Exhausted, screaming, the girl begins to slightly sway. He also watches as her screams slowly stop and her knees begin to buckle. Letting her hand go as she falls, the man watches as the girl crumples to the floor.

He smiles. The screams were expected. Running and fighting were expected. The fainting was not expected and it was a pleasant surprise to him. It will make the next steps a bit easier if she isn't fighting back. The man steps forward, bends down, and gathers the now unconscious girl in his arms. Carrying her limp body, he walks toward the stage in the back of the room. The smile, still hinting at the corners of his mouth, gets larger as he reaches the far left of the stage where the stairs are located.

Taking care with the pretty cargo in his arms, he slowly

climbs the steps to the top and reaches the center piece on the stage. He slowly lays Penny down on the stage and stands back up. The man steps forward, stopping at the front of his masterpiece. He reaches forward and opens the door, the metal hinges creaking as it swings open. The man turns and walks back to Penny, bending down and picking her up once again.

He carries her into the enclosure and places her on a small bed on the left side. He lays her down on her back, brushing her hair away from her face. Several strands, matted to her face, refuse to move without extra coaxing. He looks down on the unconscious girl. Even now, she is still beautiful. Maybe more so, smelling of sweat and piss, covered here and there in blood and dirt. His eyes trace a path from her forehead to her nose, her nose to her chin, her chin to the hollow of her neck. He pauses at the hollow of her neck, hesitating to look farther, as though he is breaking a visual taboo.

He takes a deep breath and continues the path with his eyes, slowing moving down away from her neck to the soft swell of her small breasts, and down farther past her stomach to the dark blue stain at the crotch of her jeans.

The man's heart rate quickens as his eyes move down her body and a familiar stirring begins to form in his groin. A reaction he hasn't experienced since the one.

He reaches out a hand and touches the top button of Penny's jeans. A shiver runs up and down his spine. *Not yet*, it says to itself. *Soon, but not yet.* He pulls his hand back and takes one last lingering look at the young girl lying in front of him.

Yearning for more but knowing there are still things he needs to do before Colin gets here, he takes a final look around the enclosure.

A large metal cage with thick reinforced bars that has been placed directly at center stage. A bed, which Penny now occupies, is against the left side of the enclosure. A bucket is sitting in the back right corner, designed to be a rudimentary bathroom. A small roll of toilet paper is placed on the floor next to the bucket. The smile returns. The cage will make the perfect display location of Penny for Colin when the final roll of the dice in the game is made.

He turns and walks out of the cage, closing the door behind him. The metal squeals a bit as it closes, echoing throughout the large room. He pulls the ring of keys from his pocket and locks the door to the cage. He tests the door, making sure it is secure.

Satisfied, the man turns from the cage and walks to the steps on the far side of the stage. He heads down the steps and quickly crosses the room to the hallway. A noise behind him causes him to pause before he reaches the door to the hallway.

"Please." A single word reaches the man's ears. He turns around and sees Penny standing at the door of the cage, holding onto the bars. "Please don't leave me here."

He watches as she waves at the other people sitting at tables scattered throughout the room. People who were watching. Staring. Unmoving.

"Please, someone, anyone, will one of you please help me?

Why are you just sitting there?"

The pitch and desperation of her voice continues to increase as she keeps asking for help. Asking why no one will answer her. The man knows why none of the audience will respond. Penny's pleas escalate into yelling and sobbing. The sounds reverberate throughout the room. She's soon screaming. Screaming at the figure. Screaming at the audience. Screaming for her daddy.

Soon, my Penny, he thinks. *Very soon.*

He turns back to the next task at hand and opens the door to the hallway. He pauses as he walks through the doorway and reaches over, turning off the lights. The room plunges into complete blackness once again and the man pulls the door closed behind him, cutting off the last bit of light and leaving Penny alone in the pitch-black, screaming, with her silent, staring audience the only witnesses to her show.

CHAPTER 12

THE PREPARATION

Leaving Colin's porch, Karen quickly walks across the driveway to her truck. The gravel crunches underneath each of her footsteps and seems to grow in volume until she reaches the driver's side door. She opens the door and hops into the seat, turning the key. The engine roars to life.

She shakes her head. Colin knows something is up, she can feel it. The look on his face the last few minutes she was there said it all. She puts the truck in reverse and backs out the driveway. She makes sure to lightly hit the horn a couple times as she pulls away from his house, in one additional effort to make everything seem as though it is normal.

She drives back to her restaurant on auto pilot, lost deep in thought.

What if he was able to figure it out? Colin is a smart man. Too trusting, clearly, but smart. It was stupid to be so adamant about seeing Alicia's vehicle. A slight wave of panic races through her body and causes the hair on her arms to stand up. What if Colin figures out she had a part in Alicia's disappearance? What if he finds out she had a part in Penny's, too? She has worked so hard over the years to stay close to Colin and his family without being discovered. It's too close to the end for her to be found out now. She has to keep up her image. Remain outside and innocent from what has happened. From what is going to happen.

The facade of Ellie's comes into her view. Warm. Welcoming. Like the arms of a loved one after you haven't seen them in weeks. Much like the facade she puts on every day for everyone she meets. She pulls the truck around the building to the back side and brings it to a stop.

The morning sun reflects off the lake, painting a serene scene of water and trees. She turns the truck off, leaving the keys in the ignition. Her thoughts drift across the all the events that have happened. She tried to intervene, tried to save Colin from what was going to happen. Even risked her own life by stepping in front of Colin's truck the other night, intentionally causing his accident and preferably his death, or her own if he hadn't swerved as he had.

He wasn't supposed to survive that crash.

She stares at the lake, watching the occasional fish break the surface of the water, causing ripples to fan out across the surface of the entire lake and finally reaching the opposite shores. She marvels at how one little fish can affect the whole surface of the large lake with one single action.

A short, nervous laugh escapes her lips. Just like life now. One little fish, her little fish, affecting the whole lake. The only difference is that these ripples will last forever.

Karen breaks away from her thoughts and opens the door to her truck, still staring at the lake. Taking a deep breath, she hops out of the driver's seat and plants her feet on the ground. Familiar ground. Ground she has crossed over thousands of times. Closing the truck door behind her, she starts walking to the back door of the restaurant. The sound of an approaching car interrupts the morning symphony of birds, wind, and buzzing insects that filled the void left by the truck engine shutting off.

She pauses in her tracks. What if it's Colin and he's come for her? Come to demand answers. Maybe even force the truth out of her. What if it's Deputy Gates? What if he found out everything? Her panic sets in again and she quickly traverses the remaining distance to the rear door, whipping it open and stepping inside just as the approaching car reaches the side of the restaurant.

Closing the door behind her, she slowly steps back away from the door one step at a time, staring at it, refusing to look away, blindly feeling around the nearest shelf for anything she can use to defend herself. The car outside has stopped and the engine turns off. A car door opens and closes.

Footsteps slowly make their way toward the back door of the restaurant.

Karen's blind searching of the nearest shelf hits a frantic

pace. She knocks a large pan off the shelf and onto the floor. An explosive, hollow boom rips through the restaurant, echoing on the walls. She practically jumps out of her skin at the sound.

The footsteps outside, only feet away from the door, abruptly stop. Karen freezes, afraid to make any more noise. She is still staring at the door, hesitant to avert her eyes and miss valuable seconds to react if whoever is outside chooses to charge in. Her right hand, still blindly searching the shelf, comes to rest upon a large metal stirring spoon. She hastily grabs it and pulls it close to her, hoping it has enough weight to actually protect her if she needs to swing it. She strains to listen for any sound, any sound at all, to identify if the person outside is still there.

The steps' methodical song on the gravel once again resume until they reach the back door. A shadow, an outline of a person, appears in the small window of the door and the knob begins to turn.

Karen tries to ready herself, tries to focus herself, tries to calm the thunderous pounding in her ears from her heartbeat. *Lord Jesus, Karen, you are going to give yourself a heart attack before you even know who this is*, she thinks.

The doorknob stops its designated turning path and the door is pulled open. The shadowy silhouette steps from the morning light outside and into the restaurant. Into her view.

The sigh of relief she lets out is more than just slightly audible. "Are you trying to give me a heart attack?" she scolds. Taking a few deep breaths, Karen begins to try to calm her nerves. "Why are you back here already?"

The figure, still in the doorway, lowers his head and shrugs his shoulders.

Frowning, she sets the spoon back on the shelf and bends down to pick up the soup pot lying on the floor. "Is the officer going to be any more of a concern?" she asks as she places the pot back on the shelf.

The figure looks at her and shakes his head.

"Good. At least that's one less thing to worry about." She pauses to look at the figure. The resemblance is still there, even after all these years. He always did look more like her than his father, she thinks. She turns and walks into the bar area of the restaurant, stopping next to the lowball glasses lined neatly up on the shelf, her son following in tow.

His father never really amounted to much. Dead-end job, dead-end ambitions. Dead-end life once Karen finally had enough of his shit. "You need to deal with Colin soon," she states as she picks up one of the glasses, flips it over, and sets it down on the counter. "I have a feeling he suspects my involvement. And if that is the case, you need to shut him up before he can talk to anyone else."

She reaches to her left and wraps her fingers around a bottle of Jack Daniels. She pauses a moment before picking it up. "Are you paying attention to me? You already fucked things up when you allowed him to talk to the deputy. We can't have anyone else becoming a part of this or it will get too much attention." She picks up the bottle and begins to pour herself a drink.

"You would have never gotten this far if it wasn't for me," she continues, talking to the display in front of her while her son stands silently back behind her. It's probably good she isn't able to see him right now. It is his fault Gates got involved and it is his fault Colin may think she might be a part of the game. The fear inside her from earlier begins to bubble into a fiery rage.

She sets the bottle of Jack back down in its spot on the shelf. "It was stupid. I should have never agreed to tell the story to Colin about how and where I saw Alicia's car. You should have thought of some other way to separate the two men since you were the moron who let the officer to get involved in the first place. I really have no idea how you will, or have ever, survived without me." Karen reaches forward and picks up the glass, raising it to her lips. She doesn't get the chance to taste it.

≈

As Karen is leaving Colin's house, the man is making his way down the corridor. He reaches the room where Penny has been kept in while he orchestrated the parts of the game leading up to the finale. The familiar metallic screech permeates the silence as he closes the corridor door, making sure to lock it. Taking care to lock each door as he goes through them. Room door. Stairway door. He finally reaches the large sliding door that serves as the entrance and pauses a moment, looking back behind him.

The next time these doors are unlocked, they will be left that way for Colin as he heads to where he will finally make amends for what he has done. The man's smile returns, excited to finally have so many years of planning come to life. Excited to finally exact the payback he has desperately dreamed of for so long. The man slides open the large metal door to the building, steps outside, and slides it shut. The noise echoes throughout the small clearing. He watches a few birds fly across the sky. Oblivious to what recently happened here. Oblivious to what happened here years before. Oblivious to what is to come.

He walks down the steps and crosses the clearing. He pauses at the deputy's lifeless body, still suspended from the tree by the chain of the trap. The body begins to slightly sway again as a breeze blows through the entrance to the pathway. The man admires the dark beauty of his work and then proceeds down the rest of the pathway, winding around the twists and turns, dodging branches until he finally reaches the end of the path and where the road begins.

He deftly avoids the trap still armed and lying on the ground near the entrance and steps to the edge of the road. The deputy's cruiser is stopped in the middle of the road, almost blocking both Dr. Elyse's car and Alicia's car. The man wonders if he will have to move the cruiser out of the way. And if the keys are still in the car. A smile creeps across his face. At least he won't have to look hard to find the deputy should the keys not be in the car.

He crosses in front of the cruiser and walks around to the driver's side door. The key is still in the ignition. He smiles and gets in. He doesn't need to travel very far for the next step in his plan. He backs up a bit down the road, slowly, until there is a spot between the trees it can pull the cruiser into.

He backs into the spot between the trees, crumpling the underbrush underneath, turning the vehicle around, and heads down the road toward Ellie's. He has one more loose end to tie up before the final part of the game with Colin is played.

The drive to Ellie's is quick and uneventful. The man doesn't pass any other cars on the road during the short trip to the restaurant. Soon, he's pulling into the parking lot and proceeding to drive to the back. Karen's truck is parked in the normal spot. The man pulls the squad car up next to her truck and turns off the vehicle.

He takes a deep breath.

The man steps out of the cruiser. He feels the gravel grinding together underneath his shoes. He begins to walk toward the back door of the restaurant. Halfway to the door, a loud noise erupts from inside the restaurant, followed by silence. The man halts in his path and listens. Listens for yelling. For any other sounds. Could Colin have figured it out and come after Karen?

The man, hearing nothing else, cautiously proceeds onward to the door. He grabs the door handle and slowly turns the knob, freeing the latch and pulling the door open. Stepping into the back of the restaurant, he sees Karen standing with a bewildered look on her face and holding a large spoon in her hands. No Colin. Just Karen, who appears to be terrified. He almost smiles at the sight, but he knows if a smile is to grace his face at this moment, she would probably use that spoon on him.

She questions why he has returned. Instead of an answer,

he merely shrugs his shoulders. She sets the spoon down and picks up a pot lying on the floor. He watches her move, as if in slow motion. He vaguely hears her ask if the deputy will be an issue anymore. The man absentmindedly shakes his head, trying to think of how the next ten minutes will play out. Of what needs to happen. Of what will happen.

Karen turns to walk into the bar and the man follows obediently. She stops in front of the glasses and begins to pour herself a drink. Chastising him. Correcting him. The man positions himself just outside of her view, slightly behind her. He looks around the bar while she talks and sees a small paring knife lying next to the fruit garnish tray for drinks. Slowly, carefully, he reaches over with his right hand and picks up the knife.

Karen's voice changes from worried to angry the more she talks. *Don't worry, Mother*, he thinks. *Soon you won't have to be worried or angry ever again.*

As Karen lifts her drink to take a sip, he quickly swings and plunges the paring knife deep into the right side of her neck. Before she has a chance to react, he quickly jerks the knife backward, ripping the knife through the side of her neck and out the back, leaving a large gushing laceration that is now spraying blood all over the display, the floor, and the bar.

The drink she is holding falls to the floor, the glass shattering into hundreds of pieces and spilling brown liquor all over. Karen stumbles forward against the display, knocking over several glasses as well as a couple bottles, adding to the symphony of glass shards already on the floor.

She half turns to the left, facing her son, one hand gripping the edge of the bar display and her other hand now holding the right side of her neck in an effort to try to stop the constant spurts of blood. He doesn't hesitate, moves the knife to his left hand and steps forward, swinging the knife once again and stabbing it deep into Karen's throat. Again, he jerks the knife backward and this time the blade rips out the left side of her neck.

A new gushing spray of blood erupts from the left side of her neck. Her left hand leaves the display ledge and reaches for him. He steps back, out of her reach, watching. The look of surprise on Karen's face brings him immense pleasure. The wide, fear-filled eyes. The mouth, simulating a fish with no sound coming out beyond a gurgling noise. She stumbles forward a step and drops to her knees, then finally crumples to the ground at his feet, lying on her right side and looking up at him.

He looks down on her. Looks into her eyes. She weakly raises her left hand toward him one last time and then it drops to the ground, unmoving. The light in her eyes fades and then finally disappears completely. He watches her for a while longer. Waiting to see if any life returns to her. Waiting to make sure she is truly dead.

Satisfied his mother will no longer have any power over him, he marvels at all the blood on the floor and sprayed all over the bar counter and display. The wet glass shards scattered across the floor sparkle like diamonds, many with a red hue from Karen's blood.

He cleans the paring knife with the bottom of his shirt, wiping away all the blood. Setting the knife back down in its spot on the bar, the man squats down, resting on his heels. Reaching forward, he slowly caresses the dead woman's face. He looks into the now lifeless eyes of his mother. Eyes that have seen him through his entire life until this point. Never actually seeing him. Never actually knowing him. Or those eyes would have known what was going to happen.

He reaches out and pushes her body onto her back, her eyes now staring, blank and lifeless, at the ceiling. Taking one last look at Karen's lifeless body lying in a pool of liquor and blood, he stands and steps over her body, carefully walking to the stairs that lead up to where he once lived, a long time ago. He leaves a trail of partially wet, bloody footsteps across the hardwood floor and halfway up the carpeted stairs before they begin to fade away. It doesn't matter to him. The final game is almost here.

There is no reason to hide anymore.

He reaches the top of the stairs and walks to his old room. Opening the door, he sees the bed is still made. Clean clothes are laid out on the foot of the bed. Not that anything in here has been touched in most of the years that Karen has played the part of the caring mother. Always cleaning, making, folding. Over the last several years, he only changes when necessary and sleeps across the lake in the building where he spends most of his time.

He surveys the room one last time. Photographs of him in high school stand solitary in their frames along the wall and the dresser. Photographs of him wearing his letterman jacket. Photographs of him with friends, laughing. Smiling. A photograph of him in a tuxedo standing next to a beautiful brunette in a long, flowing red gown.

He pauses as he sees this photo. He reaches out and takes the picture off of the dresser and looks closely at the girl in the photograph next to him. His first love. His one. He can still remember how nervous he was that night. How beautiful she was in her red prom dress. How he drove the long trip up to Shelton and visited three different flower boutiques before finding the perfect corsage of roses and dried sunflowers. How he had almost been grounded from even going to the prom because of how late he got home that night.

The young, beautiful brunette in the photo was only his date that night out of courtesy. Or maybe it was pity. Or maybe it was a joke all along. It didn't matter to him at the time, he was just happy he was able to imagine they were together as a couple and she loved him as much as he loved her. The love for her still burns strong in his heart, even after all this time.

He continues to reminisce. Fate had other plans that night, and those plans did not mean the beautiful young woman in the photo confessed her undying love to him while slow dancing under the multicolored disco balls above. Those plans were not the storybook ending he had daydreamed about for so long. No, those plans changed him from the stranger in the photos to who he is now.

He sets the photo back down on its spot on the dresser and looks at the photo to the left of it. A photograph of him, his arm casually draped around the shoulders of his best friend at the time. Both of the young men in the photo were laughing at something and pointing at the camera when the shutter had gone off, capturing their moment in time forever. His eyes narrow as he looks at the face of the other young man in the photo. The laughing face and happy eyes stare back. Mocking him. Not laughing with him, but laughing at him. The man knows this now.

The rage begins to bubble up inside again. He takes a deep breath and tries to ease the anger and hatred that is quickly racing to the surface. *Soon.* He takes one last look at the photo of the two young men. The figure, young and happy and oblivious to what was to come, and Colin, clearly laughing at how stupid he thought his friend was. He reaches out and picks up the photo, taking a moment to wipe his thumb across the face of the young Colin in the photo, leaving a light smear of blood it. He wipes his thumb the other direction, creating a bloody *x* over Colin's face. A slight smile comes to the man's face. *I'm not so stupid now, am I, Colin?* he thinks. *Do you still feel like laughing? Do you still feel like the joke is on me?*

The thought of setting the restaurant on fire briefly crosses his mind. A fire that would erase any proof of his existence. Erase any proof of his ties to Colin. To Karen. To everyone. But a second fire within only a few days might draw a large amount of unwanted attention.

He turns from the room and walks back down the stairs. He continues across the restaurant floor and stops at the entrance, bolting the front door and turning off all the neon signs. The only thing worse than a fire would be some unwitting patron wandering into the restaurant and finding Karen behind the bar. That would only lead to unwanted law enforcement attention. Better to make everyone think the restaurant is closed for the time being and avoid the extra interference.

He turns and walks back to the bar and around to the back counter. Karen's body is still lying in the same position as it was when he went upstairs. He takes a couple steps and stops at the lead edge of the bar. A pen and pad of paper are lying next to the register perched at the end of the bar. He grabs both items and quickly writes a note.

You won't find your daughter here. You won't find any answers here, either, at least not now since a certain someone is unable to speak ever again. Penny's life is in your hands. It's time for the last part of the game, Colin. You broke the rules, you were shown the consequences, and now it is time for you to face the final outcome. Time for you to atone for what you have done. To pay for what you have done. If anyone besides you shows up, Penny will die. Haven't enough people died recently because of your inability to play the game properly? Come visit us at the old logging camp. We'll be waiting.

P.S.: Don't mind the deputy. He's just hanging out.

He reads the note, proud of his wit at the last part. Smiling, he places the note on a part of Karen that isn't completely covered in blood. He doesn't need her blood to stain the letter to the point where Colin cannot read it. Content the letter will still be legible by the time Colin gets here, he reaches over and picks up the phone from the bar. Dialing Colin's number, he waits patiently as the line rings. After the sixth ring, Colin picks up the line.

"Hello?" The voice on the other end of the line seems haggard.

The man forces his voice to sound calm. Colin's voice sounds more angry than scared. Time to change that.

"The next step to find Penny is at Ellie's," he says. Before Colin has a chance to respond, he sets the phone back down on the receiver and hangs up the line. Moments later, the line rings. He watches the phone sitting on the cradle, ringing. Colin must be calling back the line that just called him.

After several rings, the answering machine picks up and Karen's voice echoes through the empty restaurant, causing a brief ephemeral feeling within him. "Thank you for calling Ellie's. No one is available to take—" Her voice abruptly cuts off as the caller hangs up the line. If he knows Colin at all, he knows Colin is going to be on his way here as fast as he can. It's time to go.

He carefully navigates his way around Karen's body and

walks into the back where the restaurant is. As he reaches the back door, he takes one final moment to look back at the restaurant. The restaurant in which he grew up. The restaurant where the lifeless body of his mother now resides.

The restaurant he will never see again.

He opens the door and steps outside, reaching back and pulling the door closed. He tries the handle, making sure it's not locked. He needs to make sure Colin is able to get inside. Get inside and see Karen's body. Get inside and find the note that will lead Colin to the final spot he needs to be.

The man quickly crosses the distance from the restaurant to the squad car and Karen's truck. He pauses at the driver's side door of the cruiser and looks in the passenger side window of the truck. True to her nature, Karen has left the keys to her truck in the ignition and the doors unlocked. She always was a little too trusting, living under the assumption no one would want to steal her old truck. The smile on his face grows slightly bigger. He knows someone who is going to want to use her truck without her permission when they finally get done walking here.

A muffled voice comes from inside the squad car, looking for car number twelve. He turns from the truck and gets into the cruiser, starting up the engine and putting it in reverse. The radio squawks again. The dispatcher is wondering where Deputy Gates is. The man smiles. *He's not available for your call at the moment,* he thinks. *Leave a message and I'll make sure he gets it.* A short laugh fills the car.

The man turns the car around and heads up the road away from the restaurant. Heading back to where Penny is patiently waiting for his return. It's time for her to get ready for the final part of the game.

He is lost in thought for the quick drive. Thinking about how long it will take to get Penny ready and if she will cooperate willingly or will need to be sedated again. Thinking about how long it might take Colin to actually show up. How long it might take him to find his way to the room the figure has spent years making perfect for the game. Recreating every detail to the best of his memory from that night. Thinking about the look on Colin's face when everything finally culminates and the finale is executed.

Then, finally, the man will have his own storybook ending. Only this time, he is the hero of the story.

Breaking out of his thoughts, he pulls the squad car into the spot he initially turned around in and shuts off the car. The squawking radio continues to chirp about Deputy Gates and why the hell he won't answer his mic. The man reaches forward and turns off the radio. Silence envelops the car.

He waits a moment and just sits in the cruiser, taking in the quiet. Smiling. So soon. So very soon. Years and years of planning. Of waiting. And now the time is finally here.

He opens the door and gets out of the car. He walks up the road and to the pathway, carefully avoiding the bear trap still armed on the ground. He pauses a moment and then turns back to the trap, carefully removing all of the brush from the edges, making it obvious there is a trap lying on the ground. The last thing he needs is for Colin to step in this trap and bleed to death right here.

He steps back and admires his handiwork once again. Only a blind person would miss seeing this now. He leaves the trap lying on the ground, still ready to clamp shut on the first thing that triggers the pressure plate. Although he doesn't want Colin to step on the trap, he still wants him to be scared and cautious. He doesn't need Colin rushing blindly and without regard into the final game.

Although, if Colin does end up bleeding out here, it means the man will be able to take his time with Penny. For as long as he wants. Doing whatever he wants. Exploring whatever he wants. Tasting whatever he wants. Just like he did with the one, until she died.

His pulse begins to slightly quicken at the last thought. The familiar stirrings from earlier once again begin to make themselves known. He forces the thoughts from his mind, turns from the trap, and begins to proceed down the pathway. In a short amount of time, he reaches the deputy's body. "Hi, Steve," he casually says as he passes him.

No response from the deputy.

The man laughs a little bit. "Have a good day, Steve, if it's OK I call you that."

Still no response. A few flies have begun to buzz around the deputy's head.

The man, still laughing, crosses the clearing and opens large sliding door to the building. He closes the door behind him, leaving it unlocked.

He repeats this process again and again until he reaches the room at the bottom of the stairs. He walks over to the table where he left the water bottles and the two remaining sandwiches. He picks it all up and sticks it back in the empty bag still on the table. Penny will need her strength for what is about to happen. He heads to the large metal door. The familiar screeching sound as the door slides open is like music to his ears. He steps into the hallway and pulls the door closed behind him, leaving it unlocked. That familiar sound will soon be the man's cue that Colin has arrived and the final game is about to start.

He traverses the length of the hallway and reaches the colorfully decorated door at the end. Silence greets him from the other side of the door.

Smiling, he unlocks the last door and opens it up.

He steps into the darkness beyond and closes the door behind him. It's finally time to get ready.

CHAPTER 13

THE INVITATION

When her captor finally closes the door at the other end of the room, the blackness becomes all-consuming. Penny continues to scream until she is unable to scream anymore. Soon, the only sound in the room is her ragged breathing.

The stench is overpowering. Fear races up and down every one of her nerve endings. She struggles to make sense of what she has recently seen. The multitude of people all sitting at tables around the room. Staring. Unmoving. Dressed up in formal wear. The decorations scattered all over, depicting what would appear to be a happy occasion. And the cage she now resides in, center stage, as if she is the main attraction.

The main show.

She grips the bars and tries to steady herself. Afraid to let go, she stands still, waiting. Trying to listen for any noise besides her beating heart.

The thumping in her chest seems to echo throughout the

cage. Bouncing off the bars. Growing in volume with each thump until the pounding is all that remains, crushing her against the cold steel, filling every available portion of empty space until it begins to squeeze itself out of the cage.

Outside the cage, only silence greets her.

She forces herself to move. She lets go of the bar that her left hand is tightly wrapped around and reaches out around her, cautiously feeling around in the utter darkness. Finding nothing nearby, she extends her left arm out a little bit farther and slowly waves it around. Still nothing. She can't remember everything she saw in the cage when she came to, right before her captor closed the door on her.

She slowly shuffles her feet a few steps from her original position at the door of the cage. Refusing to let go of the bar still clasped in her right hand, Penny continues to outstretch her left arm until it is fully extended. Feeling for anything that might give her some sense of bearings. She remembers the bed, somewhere behind her. There is something placed in the corner opposite of the bed, but she can't remember what it is.

She continues to find nothing but emptiness. She continues to shuffle away from the cage door. Both of her arms are now fully extended.

Her left hand waving up and down, back and forth in the air. Her right hand still tightly clasped to the bar.

Nothing.

Penny pauses in her search and takes a deep breath. She lets go of the bar in her right hand and begins to shuffle her feet slowly away from the side of the cage. She moves her right arm out in front of her and begins to pan it around with her left. Looking for anything to help give an idea of where things are. She continues to move farther into the cage, unsure what direction she is headed. The scraping sound of her feet, one after the other, is the only other noise she can hear beyond the rasp of her breathing.

Scrape. Scrape. Scrape. One slow, sliding step after another. Time seems to suspend while she scuffles along. Inch after agonizing inch. Panic begins to creep back in to her thoughts. What if, after she let go, the cage and her surroundings faded away, leaving her to wander the void of blackness. Of emptiness. Of nothing. Forever.

Scrape. Scrape. Her breathing begins to quicken again. The panic begins to escalate, her outstretched arms now moving around quickly, trying to connect with anything. Her shuffling picks up pace. Her body is screaming to run. At the very moment she almost gives into that feeling, the overwhelming despair begging her to flee, her left foot strikes something solid. The thud resounds throughout the large room.

Penny freezes in place.

Her hands are motionless, suspended in front of her. She listens for any additional sounds. Silence once again envelops her in its embrace.

Cautiously, she moves her left foot around, exploring the edges of the object she made contact with. Small, square, solid. She slowly resumes motion with her hands, moving them to the left and pawing her hands downward, straining to find what her foot made contact with. After surveying the area while standing up and finding nothing, she crouches down and repeats the process, pawing her hands through the air from the right to the left. It doesn't take her long to finally touch what her left foot had found. A silky soft, but firm, flat surface. The bed.

She recognizes the texture of the sheet draped over the mattress when she initially woke up, lying on it. An audible sigh of relief escapes her lips. She straightens her legs and stands up, still partially bent over, maintaining the contact with the bed. Shuffling along again, she follows the edge of the bed to the next corner, and then across a shorter distance where she finally once again meets the solid bars that have her imprisoned.

She strains to remember how many small steps she may have taken from the front of the cage to the bed. *Damn it, Penny*, she thinks, chastising herself for not being more careful. Not being more attentive. She makes a mental note to try to keep track of her steps, so she can get a better idea on the available room within her prison. She takes a deep breath and continues on her exploration, staying along the bars this time.

She counts the steps it takes from the bed to the corner of the cage. Turning to follow the new wall of bars, she again counts the steps, trying to focus and make sure each step is the same distance as the last. She finally reaches the next corner of the cage. Her confidence is returning with each step and she is beginning to move a bit faster. As she turns to the right to continue her trip down the new length of bars, her right foot strikes an object on the ground and sends it tumbling away. A loud noise, a hollow thumping that seems to reverberate on its own accord, indicates the object on its own journey across the wooden floor.

The noise is deafening in the confines of her prison.

A flash of panic once again races across her body. The hairs on her arms and the back of her neck stand up and her left hand tightly grips the bar. Penny's mind races as she tries to figure out what could have made that kind of noise. She can't remember what else was in the cell with her when she initially came to. The noise finally abates. The darkness is once again void of all sound with the exception of her heart quickly beating in her chest.

Taking a deep breath, she steadies herself and vows to make sure the rest of her exploration is done with a lot more care. She tries to calm her nerves, remembers where she left off on her step count, and continues her journey down the bars.

If it wasn't for the constant thought of the unknown, Penny's trip would quickly become monotonous. One cold metal bar after another. The steady shuffling of her feet across the wood floor. The all too familiar pounding of her heart. After rounding another corner and traveling down the next length of bars a bit, Penny finds herself back where she began. At the door of the prison.

She carefully explores the door, checking the hinges and the lock, making sure there isn't any key or latch within her reach outside the bars that may offer her the freedom she is beginning to think will never come. The door is solidly closed. Her hands continue to explore, taking the place of her eyes in this vacuum of light. The lock is a large, cold metal square with a single keyhole in the center. It reminds Penny of the locks she would see on the prison cells in the various movies she likes to watch with her dad.

She pauses in her exploration of the cell door when that thought crosses her mind and corrects herself. Used to. Used to watch with her dad.

A deep sadness begins to well up inside her and Penny forces herself to fight the feeling away. *Get ahold of yourself, Penny*, she tells herself. *You will see Dad again. You will get to watch more of those horrible movies he loves so much with him again.*

You will get out of here alive.

She wills herself back into movement. She finishes her inspection of the lock on the cell door and then continues her journey along the bars. Step after step. Bar after bar. She shortly reaches the next corner. The fourth one, per her count. Penny tries to think about how many steps it may have taken her to go from the bed to the first corner, before she started counting them. Five? Ten? She can't remember.

Scrape. Scrape. The sound of her shoes sliding along the floor is now a comforting sound, a familiarity piercing the darkness that has swallowed her completely. One slow step after another. Another bar, another step. Just when Penny thinks she should be reaching where the bed is located, a different noise echoes through the darkness. A noise Penny did not make.

From across the room, the sound of a lock sliding free dances through the darkness, across the tables and space, finding its way quickly across the room and right to Penny's ears. She freezes and turns her head in the general direction where the noise came from.

Silence once again greets her.

A wave of terror rushes over her body. What if whoever unlocked the door is already in the room? Already walking toward her? Already standing outside the cage, inches away from in front of where she is at and watching her, slowly reaching out to grab her? Penny quickly lets go of the bars and takes a few hasty steps back, hopefully far enough away from any arms that could reach in and grab her. She stands there, in the pitch-black, barely breathing. Straining to hear anything at all. See anything at all. A muted creaking noise echoes through the room and a brilliant beam of light begins to grow on the far wall away from Penny until it is blinding to look at. She averts her eyes away, unable to focus with the sudden incursion of light into the room. The beam of light apexes and then soon begins to decrease until it is no more. The darkness once again rules over all.

Seconds tick by while Penny anxiously imagines what will happen next. Another click is heard and another blinding eruption of light explodes from all the overhead lights as they turn on. Penny closes her eyes tightly, covers her face with her hands, and tries to dull the harshness of the artificial sun that has taken over the room and chased the darkness away.

Colin finishes his meal, gets up from the table, and puts the dishes in the sink. He stands at the sink and looks out the window into the woods outside. He spent the meal in silence, wondering if Steve has found anything and if Karen has her own set of rules she has to follow. The more he thinks about it, the more it makes sense Karen is also getting packages. For as long as he can remember, she has been like family to him. He knows how much she liked Alicia, even before she and he were together. If Karen is also being told what to do by this monster, it would explain her behavior. It would explain why she has been acting the way she has the last couple days. He nods, still staring into the woods outside. He knows what he needs to do next.

Colin turns from the sink and walks from the kitchen into his bedroom. He stops at his dresser and opens up one of the lower drawers, pulling out a pair of jeans. He puts them on and changes into a clean shirt, checking the bandages on his side to make sure they are still secure. The pain has graduated to a dull ache but is still present enough to remind him that, just a few days ago, a wrecked truck and his little girl leaving for college were the biggest of his worries.

He takes a deep breath, fighting back the wince that follows the quick jolt in his side when he does so. He needs to get over to Ellie's so he can speak with Karen and see if she will let him borrow her truck. Then he is going to go out to the old logging camp road and find Steve. Who hopefully has found Alicia's car and the driver. And Penny.

As he is getting ready to head out the door, the phone rings. Colin pauses and looks at the receiver. It rings again. Colin continues to stare at the phone. Another ring. What if it's Penny? What if she was able to get away and get to a phone and needs him?

His hand reaches for the receiver but pauses. Another ring. What if it's Steve, and he has found Alicia's car? What if he has bad news? Ring. What if he has good news? Ring.

Colin, breaking away from his thoughts, finishes his reach and picks up the receiver, putting it to his ear. "Hello?" he asks, almost hesitantly.

The voice from the other end says one single sentence. The only two words that stick with Colin are *Penny* and *Ellie's*. The other end of the line goes dead before Colin can think of any kind of response. He sets the receiver back down on the cradle and picks it right back up again, dialing back the number displayed on the caller id. The line rings a few times and then the recording for Ellie's machine picks up. Colin hangs the receiver back up before the recording has a chance to finish its message. Of course, he knew it was the number for Ellie's the moment it flashed on the screen. He has seen the number hundreds of times before. Dialed it hundreds of times before.

Then the reality of what just occurred registers with him. That piece of shit, who has his little hummingbird, is at Ellie's. Right now.

Colin steps outside onto his porch and quickly goes down

the steps, taking a right and going to the side of the house where his bicycle is sitting. On a normal day, Colin would take the bike out around the town and up into some mountain trails, stretching his legs out and getting in a few hours of exercise. On exceptionally nice days, he would take the bike to work and leave the truck for Penny to drive.

Today, it serves a different purpose.

He grabs the bike from where it is parked and takes off down the road, pedaling as fast as the pain in his side will allow.

Colin takes the shortest route he knows to get to Ellie's, cutting through a couple yards and corners along the way. His trip is greeted by two or three various horn honks and waves, as the normal day to day life in Orchard Lake continues on, oblivious to the evil lying underneath the happy small town facade. Colin waves back the best he can, making sure the facade continues on.

It's only a small amount of time before he reaches Sam's. He cuts across the main road and through Sam's parking lot, dodging a couple parked cars before he is across the parking lot and pedaling through the grassy median that separates the corner store from the road leading to Ellie's. He clears the median and begins to pedal up the road toward the restaurant.

He passes the post office on the right and continues on, only about a mile or so away from his destination. A white minivan passes him on the left and honks as it goes by. Colin nods his head and forces a smile for the driver, who is waving at him in their rearview mirror. The minivan speeds off up the road and disappears around the next turn. Colin continues his trek, finally reaching the turn off for Ellie's.

As he makes the turn, the dull pain in his side becomes a hot ember of anger, stretching its searing tendrils up his side and down his thigh. He forces his way through the pain and continues pedaling until he reaches the peak of the hill and begins the short downhill ride to the bottom of the road where the restaurant is set off to the side. The road continues on past the restaurant a bit, to a nice little fishing and camping spot on the edge of the lake that mostly only the locals know about. Colin used to take Alicia out there on dates after her shift ended at Ellie's.

He closes in on the restaurant but he slows the bike and brings it to a stop in the parking lot, still in the front of the building.

Something is wrong.

Karen's myriad of neon lights, which announce everything from open to cold beer to good eats, are turned off. Those lights are as much a part of the restaurant as Karen's smiling face is. They are almost never turned off, with the exception of the open sign, which is merely switched to closed. Colin narrows his eyes, straining to see if there are any lights on inside the restaurant. The afternoon light reflecting off the windows makes it difficult to see anything inside.

Colin gets off the bike and begins pushing it to the entrance. He leans the bike against the front wall and walks up to the door, reaching forward and giving it a solid pull. It doesn't move. He lets go of the handle and puts his face to the glass, cupping his hands on either side of his head to shield away the late morning sunshine. The interior of the restaurant is devoid of light with the exception of the various beams of light streaming in the windows. Everything looks in place from Colin's vantage point.

He steps back from the door and proceeds to walk around to the rear of the restaurant. He's only known Karen to lock the back door once in all the years he's known her, and that was the night Penny was born in Rockville. She had made a big display of it the night Alicia went into labor at the restaurant. A slight smile crosses his face at the memory. Alicia, leaning against the wall next to the bar with both her hands holding her big, beautiful belly. Colin had been enjoying a frosty beverage or two that night at the bar while he was waiting for her shift to end. Alicia insisted on continuing to work through her pregnancy, claiming she needed to teach their coming child the importance of dedication and hard work even before little Penny was born. Once she went into labor that night, Karen went into manic mode, trying to close everything up and lock the doors and usher everyone into the truck for the trip to the hospital. She fumbled with the keys six times before she was finally able to get the back door locked. Colin remembered how he was a chaotic mix of panic, excitement, fear, and laughter that entire night. The memory feels like it was a lifetime ago.

He rounds the corner and heads down the side of the building. Karen's truck is parked in the usual spot. Any smile he may have had from his reminiscing is gone by the time he reaches the back of the restaurant. Why would Karen's truck be here, yet the restaurant be dark and seemingly empty? An overwhelming sense of dread begins to creep through his body.

He slows his steps as he closes in on the back corner and cautiously makes the turn. The back door is closed. Colin pauses a moment in front of the door. He looks around, checking to see if anyone is watching. He frowns when it occurs to him what he was doing. He wonders if that bastard is watching him right now. He shakes his head in an attempt to shake off his paranoia.

He reaches out and grabs the knob, testing to see if the door is locked. The knob turns freely in his hand and the door swings free from the frame. He steps back and lets the door swing completely open. The back hallway of the restaurant lies before him, a place he has been a million times before, a place that now seems dark and foreign. He looks past where the light stops and down the hall into the restaurant. Again, nothing seems out of place.

Colin takes a deep breath and moves forward, stepping into the restaurant. "Hello? Karen? Karen, are you here?"

The only response he gets is the familiar beep of the answering machine from somewhere back in the bar. "Helllloooo?"

Colin's sense of dread increases. He raises his voice and almost shouts into the restaurant. "Karen! It's Colin! Are you here?!"

No response.

His voice seems to echo throughout the building. Another

solitary beep is his only response. Leaving the back door open, he slowly starts walking toward the bar, looking for anything that appears to be out of the ordinary. Cautiously taking one step after another, he continues to look all around him. Shelves line the sides of the hallway, filled with various pans and utensils, large cans of broth, loaves of bread. Everything seems normal. The way it always is. The way it should be.

Three feet. Six feet. Ten feet.

He finally clears the back hallway and steps into the kitchen area, staying close to the wall to his left, which has changed from shelves to a large dual sink. He stops and looks around. From the back hallway, the kitchen opens up to the right where the stoves and various prep tables are. The walk-in freezer is located at the far back right of the kitchen area, and stainless steel cabinetry runs along the back wall, around the kitchen to where the pass through is located. A small ticket turnstile and bell sit on either side of the shelf of the pass through. No chaos. No mess.

He looks forward into the bar area. "Karen? Are you here?" He hopes his voice sounds steady. Firm. Strong. Not laced with the apprehension and fear which is currently racing through his body. The beep from the answering machine once again penetrates the silence. He continues to move forward into the bar area.

As he steps from the kitchen into the walkway behind the bar, almost clearing the wall which separates the bar from the kitchen, something crunches underneath his right foot. He quickly pulls his foot back, looking down at the ground. A sparkle of light catches his eye and he bends down to inspect it. A couple of pieces of glass are lying in a thin trail of liquid, leading away into the bar.

Colin stands back up and takes the last step forward into the bar, his eyes following the trail of liquid along the floor of the bar as it gets wider and wider. More and more glass shards, scattered haphazardly, begin to appear. His eyes continue along their journey until they finally reach Karen's body.

It takes a moment for his mind to register what he is seeing. Karen is lying on her back, eyes open, staring at the ceiling. Blood covers a large portion of her chest and shoulders, with streams and splatters all across her face. Her neck is a jagged mess of skin. A mix of glass, blood, and liquid surround her. The reality of what he's seeing sets in. Karen's dead. The answering machine's beep cuts through the air again, almost as though it is agreeing with him.

He walks up to her body and falls to his knees next to her, oblivious to the glass and liquid. "No. Karen. No."

He reaches forward and grabs her left hand, holding it between both of his. Her hand is slightly cool to the touch. Tears begin to well up in his eyes. "I'm so sorry, Karen," he whispers, as if her ears could still hear him behind her dead, unseeing eyes.

He squeezes her hand tightly, as if that single act would bring her back to life. He forces the urge to cry deep down inside. He stares at the face of the woman he has known most of his life. A woman who was practically his mother while he was growing up. Who he helped when her son, his best friend, was killed while serving overseas. Who was there when Penny was born. Who was there when Alicia left. Who was there for him countless times over so many years when it seemed like no one else was. And who was now lying on the floor of her own home, her throat ripped open for the world to see. The tears in his eyes finally reach the overflow point and begin to fall down his face. He closes his eyes and lowers his head, his chin almost touching his chest. The sobs are quick to follow as he allows the memories and pain to flow over him like a waterfall.

The answering machine beeps once again as if it was trying to keep him on track. The voice inside his head finally speaks up. *Get a grip, Colin. You can't fall apart now. Your little hummingbird still needs you.*

He opens his eyes and lifts his head. He snorts, trying to clear his nose, and releases Karen's hand. He wipes his hands off on his jeans, trying to remove what blood he can, and then wipes the tears away from his eyes.

He gets ready to stand up, taking another look at Karen, as if he is apologizing for having to leave her this way. He isn't able to call the cops just yet. He has to find Penny. Which means he will have to leave Karen lying here, in the glass littered pool of her own blood. Just for now, though. Just until he can find and save his daughter.

As he pushes up off his knees and onto his feet, he sees a piece of paper lying on Karen's right shoulder. A few droplets of blood were smeared on the right side but it is otherwise clean. Colin bends forward and grabs the piece of paper, quickly reading what is written on it.

The words hastily scribbled on the paper confirm what Colin has already concluded. Karen was killed by the piece of shit who has his daughter. And that Penny is still alive. A jolt of elation races through Colin when he reads that part of the note. His little girl is still alive. The elation is short-lived though, and quickly switches to rage, matching the searing flame coming from his side.

"I'm coming for you, you fucking monster. I'm coming to save my little girl's life, and then I promise that I'm going to take yours." His words momentarily fight the silence away.

Colin surveys the area where he is standing, looking for anything he can use as a weapon. He notices a paring knife lying on the bar and steps over to it, grabbing it and tucking it into the back waistband of his belt, taking care not to angle the blade in a way where he will accidentally stab himself. He takes one last look at Karen, wishing he had time to do more for her than just leave her here. Right now, though, time is precious, and he turns to head out of the restaurant.

He walks down the back hallway and out the door, closing it behind him. He takes a couple steps toward the corner of the building, heading back to his bike when he glances over at Karen's truck. Every second counts now, he reminds himself. Especially now when he knows for sure where he needs to go. Riding the bike there might take too long. It may have already been too long riding it here. He turns his steps and crosses the gravel driveway. He reaches Karen's truck and opens the driver's side door, hopping into the driver's seat. The paring knife presses against his lower back, reminding him to be a little more careful.

Karen's keys are still in the ignition. Colin starts the truck up and pulls the door closed. He looks out the windshield and across the lake. On the other side of that lake is his little hummingbird. On the other side of that lake is the human shit than has caused this all. Colin puts the truck in reverse and backs the truck up to turn around. Putting it into drive, he steps on the gas a little too hard, leaving a shower of gravel raining upon the shed and trash cans behind him. The truck lurches forward and Colin is quickly on his way to the logging camp.

≈

As the truck pulls away from the restaurant, the answering machine issues another steady beep, as if trying to tell Colin that in his fervor of emotions, he missed seeing one important item: the now partially dried bloody steps. The steps leading out from behind the bar and up the stairs. Leading into a room long forgotten by Colin that has one specific photo that may have given Colin more clues into who is behind what is happening to him and his family. One specific photo that has a bloody x across the face, as though someone was trying to wipe the face from the photo.

Colin's face.

CHAPTER 14

THE STAGE

The man stands in the dark a few moments after closing the door to the large room where Penny and the rapt, adoring audience are waiting for him. The pitch-black of the room is comforting to him, as is the stench and the crushing silence. It was like finally coming home after being away for months, with all the things you love enclosing you with their familiarity. He takes a deep breath and sighs contently.

Satisfied, the man reaches over and hits the switch to turn on the overhead lights. The room is quickly bathed in light, the darkness retreating to the various nooks and corners from where it originally came. A smile graces his face when he sees Penny is still here, holding her face and standing near the left side of her cage. *Good girl*, he thinks, although it isn't like she would have been able to go anywhere. He quickly crosses the floor, navigating around a few tables and their occupants, until he reaches the stage. He walks up the stairs on the left side and continues on until he is standing in front of the cage, looking at the young girl who is still shielding her face.

"Hello again, Penny." The sound of his voice makes her jump and move back a bit. Still hiding her face. "I figured you might be hungry, so I brought you something to eat and drink."

He digs into the paper bag and brings out the water bottles and sandwiches from earlier. He hunches down and reaches through the bars of the cage, setting the two plastic bottles and cellophane-wrapped food down on the floor of the cage. "You need to eat. Your daddy will be here soon, and we need to get you ready for him."

The last few words make the impression he is hoping they would. Penny's hands drop from her face and she slowly opens her eyes, quickly blinking to get used to the light. She looks over at him and then down at the floor where the meal is sitting.

"I'm sorry it isn't better," he says, nodding toward the water and crushed sandwiches. "But then, this isn't Ellie's." He begins to chuckle at the last part. Penny clearly doesn't get joke as her face remains expressionless. She doesn't move.

He steps back a few paces and continues to chuckle at his joke. He watches as Penny looks around the cage. Watches as she pauses when she sees the bucket, which she must have run into while he was away since it is now lying on its side near the corner on the left side. He continues to watch the young girl finish her survey of the cage and then cautiously move forward, stopping just far enough away from the bars of the cage where someone reaching in could not grab her, but still close enough for her to reach the water and sandwiches. She reaches forward and quickly grabs one of the bottles of water, twisting the cap off and gulping down the entire bottle. Tossing the empty plastic container to the side, she reaches forward and grabs one of the sandwiches. Removing the cellophane, she cautiously takes a few bites before finally devouring the remaining portion.

He watches her intently. Watches her as she finishes the sandwich and, after tossing the crumpled cellophane aside, reaches forward and grabs the second water bottle. The ball of cellophane continues to roll along the floor of the stage until it comes to a rest near the empty water bottle.

Penny takes her time with the second water and sandwich. When she is done, she sits down on the floor of the cage and looks at him. "What do you want with me?" she asks.

Still smiling from his previous joke, her captor remains silent. She will find out soon enough what her purpose is in all of this.

"Please just let me go," the young girl pleads. "Please. I won't tell anyone. Just let me go. Let me go home." Her pleading begins to intensify.

His smile gets wider and he finally speaks.

"No."

The pretty young woman falls silent and quickly averts her eyes away from him, choosing to instead stare at the floor. She begins to softly cry. He finds a certain satisfaction with this and watches quietly. She wipes her tears away and soon quits sobbing completely, sitting there on the floor in silence, her head down and eyes still closed.

He finally speaks again. "We need to clean you up and get you ready. Daddy will be here soon, and everything needs to be perfect for when he arrives."

She doesn't react, which is fine. He knows she is listening. "I am going to open the door, and you are going to come with me so we can clean you up. I don't need you alive for what is to come, so keep that in mind if you are thinking about trying anything stupid like you did the last time. Do you understand?"

Her head nods up and down in acknowledgement.

The man reaches into a pocket and fishes out the keys to the cell. He steps up to the cage door and inserts the key, slowly unlocking it, watching as the sound of the click makes the pretty girl flinch. He grasps the bars of the door and pulls it open.

Penny continues to sit stoically on the floor. Suddenly unmoving. He narrows his eyes and knocks the keys against the door. The girl doesn't flinch this time.

He pauses before walking into the cage, looking closely at Penny. At her posture. At how tense she suddenly is. Like a cornered animal about to spring into action.

He reaches into his pocket and exchanges the keys for the white rag from earlier and a small bottle. The girl continues to keep her head down and eyes closed. Like a rock.

He quietly puts a small amount of the liquid on the rag and puts the bottle back into his pocket. "Don't even think about trying anything stupid," he says, mostly for effect. He already knows she is going to try something. She already knows she is going to try something.

He holds the rag ready with his right hand and steps into the cage, calmly walking toward the spot where Penny is sitting. When he is about two steps away from the pretty brunette, her hands quickly move to the floor and she begins to push herself up and at him, trying to explode up from the floor and into him. Possibly in a surprise attempt to knock him off balance and down while she runs for the exit.

Unfortunately for her, he expects this and instead of moving back in alarm, leaps forward and tackles her before she can get fully onto her feet. His weight easily overpowers Penny's petite frame and his forward momentum propels Penny backward. They both land on the floor of the cage, with the back of Penny's head slamming down onto the hard wood of the stage, effectively knocking most of the fight out of her.

He quickly clamps the rag over her face and holds it down while she feebly struggles to get out from underneath him. The feeling of Penny struggling underneath him brings back memories and causes a familiar stirring, causing his pulse to quicken. Soon, the girl stops struggling and goes limp, lying motionless on the floor underneath the figure.

He takes a few deep breaths, inhaling the scent of her while they are tangled together. She smells of blood and sweat and urine. Her smell, coupled with their contact, causes him to get fully aroused, the bulge in his pants pressing against the young girl's right leg.

Her sweat has a familiar scent to it. A scent he hasn't smelled in such a long time. A scent he hasn't experienced since the one. *Like mother, like daughter*, he thinks. He can feel the bulge in his pants throbbing. He can almost imagine what taking Penny would feel like. Making her his own, entering her at will.

Just like he did with her mother.

Not yet, he tells himself. Not yet. This is not why she is here. He scolds himself and releases the rag from her face, letting it fall to the floor next to her good ear. He pushes up and away from Penny and gets on his feet, standing over her.

Several things need to happen before he can allow himself the pleasure of taking the pretty young brunette. First, Colin has to pay. Then, Penny has to live through what is about to happen, which isn't a guarantee. Maybe then, and only then, will he give in to the carnal desires her body and her presence invokes.

He takes a few moments, breathing deeply, slowing his pulse and allowing his obvious excitement to soften. Feeling in control once again, he reaches down and picks up the rag, placing it back into his pocket. He then bends down and picks up Penny, lifts her over his right shoulder, and carries her out of the cage.

He carefully navigates down the stairs and to a door at the far end of the stage, partially obscured by the large curtains hanging down from the ceiling. He opens the door and steps inside, still carrying the unconscious girl over his shoulder. The room is compact, tiled from floor to ceiling, with an open row of three showers on one side and the same number of toilets on the other. A couple of sinks line the back wall. A series of metal hangers adorn the wall near the sinks and hanging from these are two clean garment bags. A large paper bag is sitting on the tile under the garment bags.

The man walks over to the center shower and gently lays Penny down on the floor. He then goes over to the paper bag sitting on the floor and digs into it, pulling out toiletries. He walks back over to his captive and sets down a washcloth, a bottle of a shampoo and conditioner mix, and a bottle of liquid body wash. He stands back up and looks down on the unconscious girl. He was planning on letting her do this alone, without his presence. That plan is clearly changed now and he will have to do this personally.

He takes a deep breath and kneels down next to her. He reaches forward and grabs the bottom of her dirty, blood-stained shirt, working it, careful not to touch the damaged side of her head, extracting her arms one at a time until the shirt is free of her body. He tosses the shirt into the corner. Turning back to Penny, he takes a moment to look over the soft curves of her skin around her shoulders. The flatness of her stomach. The swell of the top of her small breasts, still mostly concealed by her bra. He closes his eyes and pushes the thoughts away.

A few minutes pass until he finally reopens his eyes. Back in control. Resuming the task at hand, he leans over and removes Penny's sneakers, one at a time. First her left sneaker and her left sock. Then he removes her right sneaker and sock. All of them join her shirt in the corner, one at a time. Methodically.

He then reaches forward and unbuttons her jeans. He opens the front and grabs the sides, tugging them downward, pulling them down over her hips and her rear end, continuing the downward tug over her thighs and her calves, until he has to free the legs one at a time. He tosses the pretty brunette's jeans onto the ever-growing pile of her clothing in the corner of the room.

His pulse is beginning to race.

He takes a deep breath. Penny lies motionless before him, exposed in just her stained bra and panties, her chest moving ever so slightly as she breathes in and out. Focus. He needs to focus. There will be time at a later date.

Another deep breath. He leans forward and slides his arms around the almost naked young woman, unclasping her bra. He leans back and carefully slides the straps off her shoulders and down each of her arms until the bra is free. A quick flip of the wrist and the bra finds a new home among the other discarded clothes in the corner. Deep breath. He fights to focus on what he needs to do. He needs to clean up Penny so she is ready for the final part of the game. he tries not to notice the firm roundness of her breasts. The curvature of her areola. The pink color of her nipples.

He can hear his heartbeat now. Another deep breath. Another few minutes with closed eyes, trying to focus. Trying to keep control. This needs to be done. She needs to be perfect for Colin. He grinds his teeth together and resumes the task.

He reaches forward and grabs Penny's panties by either side and roughly forces them down to her ankles and then off her body. He tosses the panties in the direction of the corner, too focused on what it is supposed to be doing to notice where they land.

He stands up and aims the showerhead away from the naked young woman at his feet. He turns on the shower and tests the water coming out until it feels warm. A blast of cold water might wake Penny up, and that would only make matters more difficult at this point.

Once the water is an acceptable temperature, he turns the water on the motionless young girl and bends down to grab the washcloth and soap. He pours some soap on the washcloth and works up a good lather. He kneels back down on the tile, next to her, and begins to meticulously clean her, starting with her fingers and hands. Focused, he is oblivious to the fact he is getting soaking wet in the process.

He continues to methodically clean the young woman, moving down her arms to her shoulders. Across her breasts, her stomach. The small swell of her mons pubis and between her legs. Her thighs, her calves, and each of her feet. Lifting her slightly on one side, he cleans her back and her buttocks. The water swirling the drain constantly runs a soapy pink and brown mix, as the dried blood and dirt is washed away from Penny's body.

He then turns his attention to her head, where he carefully cleans the dried blood away from her mangled ear and hair.

Wiping the tear tracks and dirt away from her face. He carefully gathers all her hair together and reaches over for the shampoo and conditioner mix, applying a liberal amount and massaging it throughout her hair, allowing the cascading water to rinse the frothy mixture away.

Content the job is complete; he leans back and surveys his work. Almost all of the dried blood and dirt is washed away. Her skin is pink from the temperature of the water and the scrubbing of the washcloth. His focus begins to fade once again as his eyes allow his thoughts to wander, his pulse racing, and in an effort to appease the sudden want burning in his body, he reaches out and touches Penny's stomach with his left hand. This touch isn't like before. This touch is to feel, not to clean. Her skin is soft and silky, warm to the touch. He lets his hand slide down her stomach, gently brushing over her small patch of pubic hair, and slipping between her legs.

His pulse is racing and his heart is pounding heavily in his chest. The bulge in his pants is now so hard it's painful. Every inch of his body is screaming at him to take the young woman in front of him. To enter her and make her his own. To feel the daughter of the one and in a way, to be back with the one again.

He finally gives in to the want. The want which has become a need.

"You will belong to me," he says heavily, standing up and quickly stripping off his wet clothes, tossing them into the corner with Penny's existing pile. He puts his left foot between Penny's legs and bends over, pulling her right leg away from her left. Spreading her. Getting her ready for him.

After pulling her legs apart a sufficient distance, he steps fully between them and gets down on his knees. The pounding of his heart is the only thing he can feel. The need is in control now. His eyes glance over every inch of her exposed skin as he reaches over and soaps up his hands, which in turn are used to soap up the hard, demanding need between his legs.

Unable to control the need anymore, unwilling to even try to stop, his hands find a spot to support himself as he leans over and onto her. In one swift, smooth motion, he pushes his hips against the unconscious young woman, pushing her legs slightly farther apart and sliding his need fully inside her.

Finally making her his own. Finally feeling like he is back with the one. Finally making both of Colin's women his own.

The warm water continues to cascade down, minute after minute after minute, until the hot water finally runs out and the water begins to slowly turn cold. Another fifteen minutes pass before the water, now fully cold, is finally turned off.

≈

Groggily finding her way back to reality, Penny regains consciousness. Not possessing the ability to open her eyes just yet, she can tell she's lying on her back somewhere. Her arms and legs feel excessively heavy, like they did the time she woke up tied to the chair. Finally, she is able to open her eyes.

Bright lights greet her, making her squint. When her eyes are able to focus, she sees the bars of her prison above her. She tries to sit up, every muscle screaming as though it has not moved in weeks. She's finally able to sit up and look around. She's once again on the bed in the cage. Only this time, she's dressed in a red formal gown and heels.

She slowly swings her legs off the bed and onto the floor. Confusion quickly sets in. An unfamiliar soreness greets her from between her legs as she moves. The last thing she can remember is trying to leap up and get away from the dead-eyed monster who has been keeping her captive. She remembers that instead of her racing to her freedom, he tackled her and her head hit the floor. The rest is a blur mixed with nothing.

Penny inspects her surroundings. Her prison is now decorated in streamers and balloons, with confetti spread all over the floor, both inside and outside her cage. The empty plastic water bottles and cellophane wrappers from before are gone. As is the bucket. She can smell a type of vanilla perfume around her, similar to the bottle sitting in her dad's bathroom. The bottle he refused to get rid of because it was the scent her mother used to wear. A rose and strawflower corsage adorns her left wrist.

She attempts to stand up, but the strength hasn't fully returned to her legs and she sits back down again. The ever-constant throbbing from the left side of her head seems even more present than it did before. She grimaces in frustration. Is this what that monster meant by she needed to get ready? And ready for what? She is dressed like she is going to some sort of formal dance. In a metal prison. Her confusion with the situation only adds to her anger and fear of what might be next.

She looks around outside her cage at the bleachers on either side of the room, and the multitude of tables scattered across the floor. A single candle burns in a colored vase at the center of each table, and more confetti spread on the tablecloths. At each table, and at seemingly random places in the bleachers on each side, sit unmoving people. Each person is also wearing formal clothes, giving the room a festive feel with a variety of blues, golds, purples, reds, and greens. Only none of them are moving and each has the same blank stare as the next. Unblinking.

Penny tries to stand up again, succeeding this time but still unstable on her legs. The heels she is now wearing aren't helping. She wobbles slightly in the heels and slowly bends down to take them off.

"Don't do that."

The voice comes from behind her and she fights back a scream. She quickly turns around, almost falling over in the process, and sees her captor standing there at the side of the cage. He is staring at her with the same dead eyes as before. The same eyes that every other person in the room has. He, is now also dressed in formal wear. And smiling at her.

"The game isn't over yet," he continues. "Until then, you will stay where you are at. And you will continue wearing exactly what you are wearing now. If you choose otherwise, and remove anything, I will kill your father in front of you. Then I will kill you. Do you understand me, this time? Because clearly you did not the last time."

Penny nods her head in agreement.

"You know, you look beautiful. You look just like she did."

She looks down at the dress. It's a burgundy asymmetrical chiffon dress, with a sweetheart neckline and ruffle beading sequins. Although dated, it's pretty. In any other setting, it would be a beautiful dress to wear out. In here, in this place, it seems ridiculous. The entire situation seems ridiculous. It's like some horrible B-rated movie on television. Is she being held hostage merely to play in some lunatic's weird formal dance fantasy? The frustration of not knowing only makes Penny angrier.

She finally speaks again, only this time she lashes out due to frustration and anger, tired of being silent. "What the fuck is going on? What do you want with me?" She motions toward all the people in the crowd. "Who are these people? What is wrong with them?" Penny turns toward the people at the tables and yells, "Can you hear me? What the fuck is wrong with you? Why won't you help me? Why wouldn't you help me before?"

Her voice echoes throughout the room. The man continues to stand there, smiling.

"You have her same fire, too. This will be even better than I expected it to be." He turns and walks away from the stage, toward the back. "Daddy should be here any moment."

Penny watches him walk away. He stops right before he reaches the back curtains and turns once again to look at her. Stares into her. "You really do look beautiful."

He then turns back to the rear of the stage and disappears through the curtains. Leaving Penny standing there, feeling uneasy about the way he said that last sentence.

She turns and looks back to the front of the room. The door leading out of the room is closed. Various colored streamers are now hanging from two poles extending from the wall above the door, almost like a streamer hallway. The broom she remembers seeing against the wall is also gone now. She slowly walks over to the door of the cage, teetering a bit in the heels she is wearing as she tests the door. It's locked. Penny shakes her head. Not like she would have been able to run very far in these heels anyway.

She walks back to the bed and sits down. The sore ache between her legs scares her. She tries not to think about the possible reason behind it. The very real fear she could have been abused while she was unconscious crosses her mind. She quickly pushes the thought away. She can't think about that now. She just needs to do what that monster says and make sure nothing happens to her dad. To play along with this madman's game until the opportunity to get away presents itself. There will be time to figure out what else may have happened after she is free.

A loud hum fills the room, as if several large speakers have suddenly been turned on. Penny looks around, trying to locate the source of the sound. She spies several large speakers on stands she hadn't noticed previously, located in each corner of the room. The hum changes to a piercing screech, and then a voice fills the room.

"Ladies and gentlemen, our guest of honor should be here

very shortly. Thank you so much for your patience. I know many of you have been waiting here a very, very long time. Feel free to help yourself to the punch and snacks, just no spiking it, and you can get your pictures taken in the back whenever you are ready."

The last part inspires laughter from the voice over the speakers and the sound of it makes Penny cringe.

After the laughter dies off, another slight screech from the speakers is heard and then music begins to play, filling the room. Penny recognizes the song, although at the moment she is unable to place exactly where she has heard it before. The man reappears from behind the curtain in the back of the room and walks past Penny's prison, pausing to look at her once again and smile before continuing on down the stairs and across the floor. She watches him walk, with an air of confidence, as if he already knows exactly how all this will end. She narrows her eyes, wishing the pure hatred she feels could drill holes in the back of his head and hoping that, no matter happens, the satisfaction this monster is looking for is never found.

She continues to watch as the man finally stops at the far end of the room, next to the door leading to the hallway. He reaches out and flips a few switches, causing the overhead lights to turn off. The room plunges back into semidarkness, with the only light in the room coming from the candles placed on each one of the tables. The flickering lights from the candles dance on the audience's faces, partially lighting their festive apparel and giving their frozen visages a dark, almost evil appearance.

In contrast to the multitude of expressionless faces, the room takes on an oddly romantic appeal due to the music and decor.

Penny strains to still see where the man is at. She can barely see him as he moves away from the light switch panel and to the back right of the room, where he finally is swallowed by darkness as he walks outside the range of the candles. Penny glances around, her eyes slowly adjusting to the low amount of light in the room, making sure no one is standing next to her cage.

The song playing over the speakers comes to an end and after just a few seconds of silence, begins to play again, as if on a loop. Seemingly on cue with the music, several disco balls hanging from the ceiling spring to life. Multicolored facets of light fall upon every portion of the room, lazily rotating around on their set orbit, dancing across the tables and floor, carving long sweeping pathways across the walls. Penny watches as the droplets of light dance around the room, occasionally being eaten by the flame of a candle, only to come back to life on the candle's other side. In another life, in different circumstances, she would have loved this.

Only now, it's some perverse trip down memory lane with a monster who is using her to get her father here for some reason or another. She wishes she knew why.

A noise to the right side of the stage breaks Penny from her thoughts and she quickly looks in the direction of the sound. The man is standing on the main floor, within a foot or two of the edge of the stage. He walks across the floor and stops in front of Penny, putting both hands down on the stage and leaning forward a bit. "Make sure you smile real big when your daddy gets here and the curtain opens. His life is now in your hands," he states. She doesn't answer.

The man pushes away from where he was leaning and walks to the left end of the stage where it meets the wall. He reaches out and pushes a button on wall. The large curtains hanging on either side of the stage begin to close, slowly blocking Penny's view of the rest of the room, inch by inch. The colorful dabs of light dancing across her and her prison get fewer and fewer until the curtains close completely, plunging her world once again into darkness. The song playing over the speakers fades to silence and then once again starts back up.

CHAPTER 15

THE REALIZATION

Colin closes the distance between the restaurant and the old logging camp road in a hurry. He reaches the turn off and pauses a moment before making the turn. He takes a deep breath, turns the wheel, and steps on the gas. The truck bounces along the unpaved road, low hanging branches occasionally scraping the roof.

He navigates a couple turns and as he clears a small ridge, a flash of color catches his eye. To the right, parked partially in the bushes, is an Orchard Lake police cruiser. Colin slows the truck to a stop at the back end of the cruiser and looks around. The road, which at this point is more like two ruts with compacted underbrush in the middle, ends about sixty feet in front of him. Two more cars are parked in the brush on the right side close to the end of the road and a path leads off into the woods on the left side. He looks back at the other two cars, his breath catching in his throat.

Alicia's car is parked there. Colin knows it. He recognizes it. He feels it.

He puts the truck in park and turns off the engine, leaving the keys hanging in the ignition. He gets out, still staring at the farthest car down the road. He closes the door to the truck a little too hard, and the noise seems to reverberate off the nearby trees. The sound is foreign among the normal noises of the forest and snaps Colin out of his concentrated focus on the car he is convinced is Alicia's. He looks down at his feet and takes a deep breath, his ribs shooting a couple jabs of pain up his side. *Be smart about this, Colin*, he tells himself. *You can look at the car in a moment. The first thing you need to do is check the police car.*

He walks around the front of the truck and to the back of the police car, keeping a wary eye on the forest around him. He reaches the cruiser's driver's side door and pulls it open. The inside of the car is clean. Quiet. Colin looks around the interior for anything he could use as a weapon. Finding nothing, he closes the cruiser's door and turns toward the two other vehicles parked along the road. He cautiously walks to the nearest one. It looks like Dr. Elyse's car and as Colin gets closer, he becomes confident it is her car. He walks up to the passenger side and looks inside. On the floor of the back seat is an overturned purse. Penny's purse. Colin would recognize that purse anywhere. He walks around the back of the car and pauses before heading to the driver's side door. His attention is held by the car parked next to Dr.

Elyse's car, only a couple feet away from him.

It has to be Alicia's car.

Colin forces his gaze away and turns his attention back to what he is doing. He clears the last few steps and tries the driver's side rear door of Dr. Elyse's car. The door swings open, and Colin quickly inspects the contents of the purse, confirming it belongs to Penny. Making a note to grab everything after he finds and saves his little girl, he finally turns to the other car.

The car that looks so much like the one he has spent countless years looking for.

He approaches it cautiously, as though it might disappear if he gets too close to it. He steps up to the passenger side door and reaches out, testing the handle. The door opens before him, almost like an invitation from a long-lost friend. He closes his eyes for a moment, picturing the last time he saw Alicia. The last time he held her in his arms. The last time he tasted her kiss and buried his face in her hair. The last time he saw her car.

This car.

He opens his eyes and gets in the passenger side, leaving the door open behind him. He looks around the interior, looking for anything familiar. Anything to confirm what he believes in his heart to be true. He checks the glove compartment and the visors. He looks around the seat and in the center console. Nothing. The car is clean, devoid of personal items. He takes a deep breath and for a second he thinks he can smell her perfume in the air. He shakes his head, as if to shake away all the old memories that have been hidden away for so long. *You are imagining things, Colin. Even if this is her car, why would it still smell like her after all these years?*

He finishes searching the interior and stares out the windshield into the lush forest for a moment. There really is only one way to find out if this is her car or not. Colin reaches over to the driver's side and hits the button to pop the trunk. The solid click of the trunk latch releasing is heard from behind him. He gets up out of the car, wincing at the spike of pain from his side and closes the passenger door behind him, turning and walking to the rear of the car. He slows as he rounds the back end and grabs the trunk lid with both hands. He takes a deep breath, grimacing slightly, and lifts the lid all the way up.

Underneath the trunk lid, scraped into the metal, are the letters and misshapen heart he hoped he would find. Maybe hoped he wouldn't find. A hand-carved design made by the woman who has never been far from his mind for as long as he can remember. The woman who disappeared on him so many years ago. The woman who his beautiful hummingbird is beginning to look more and more like every single day.

Colin drops to his knees, the letters hitting him like a spear straight through his heart. It is her car. Alicia's car. A multitude of questions race through his head while an equal number of emotions race through his body. He lowers his head and looks at the ground. One question continues to surface above the rest: Why does this piece of shit have her car? He needs to know why. He asks the question over and over again in his head until his emotional roller coaster begins to slow and finally settles on one emotion. Anger. He punches the ground in front of him. This bastard, this monster, has his little girl. He has Alicia's car. He punches the ground again, drawing blood from his knuckles.

This bastard must have answers as well.

Answers Colin is going to get. Answers he will pry out of this monster in any way necessary after he has saved his little girl from whatever twisted fate this fucking piece of shit is planning.

He takes a deep breath and pushes himself up off the ground, getting to his feet. He ignores the hitch of pain in his side and takes one more look at Alicia's car parked before him. Reaching forward, he grabs the trunk lid and pushes it down hard, slamming it shut. The noise causes a few nearby birds to take flight through the trees. Colin turns from the car and looks at the pathway that leads away into the forest. He takes a few slow initial steps away from the car, almost hesitant to leave it behind, but then begins to increase his pace, crossing over the road and to the edge of the path.

A quick flash of light from something on the ground in front of him catches his attention. At the beginning of the path, barely covered at all, is a large metal trap. The trap is set to spring, with rusty and jagged teeth hungry for a meal of flesh and bone. He pauses a moment, looking at the trap. It looks as though it had been covered at one point, as the surrounding leaves and foliage clearly have been disturbed and lie in small piles near either edge of the pathway. Although he can go around it, he doesn't know what condition his little girl might be in when he has to come back this way. Colin nods as if in agreement with his thoughts. It would be better to disarm it now instead of a possible accident later.

He continues his inspection of the area, spying a rock about the size of his hand lying near the edge of the road, halfway between where he is currently standing and where Alicia's car is parked. He walks over and picks up the rock, hefting it in his right hand and judging the weight. *It should do the trick*, Colin thinks. He takes a few steps toward the trap, making sure there is still a good distance between it and where he is standing. Colin estimates the distance and tosses the rock at pressure plate on the trap.

The rock sails past the trap and lands with a thud about four feet down the pathway, rolling a little bit farther before coming to a stop on the right edge of the path. *Easy there, Hercules*, he thinks to himself. He shakes his head and looks around for another rock, finding one lying just a few feet away from the first. He picks it up and once again repeats the process. This time, the rock lands about a foot short of the trap but the momentum causes it to roll forward and connect with the edge of the pressure plate. The jaws of the trap slam shut with a hungry ferocity, the resulting metallic clang echoing through the forest like a gunshot.

Colin waits a moment longer to make sure the trap stays closed and then begins to move forward again. He carefully navigates around the now closed trap and stops to pick up the first rock he had thrown. He needs to be prepared if there are any more traps like this one waiting for him. Gripping the rock tightly, he continues onward.

The path is relatively straightforward, although small, with the occasional turn and dip. The ground underneath is well trampled, with little to no underbrush growing on it. The tree branches and brush are a different story. With his focus on the ground and looking for more traps, rogue branches scrape across the side of his head more often than not. In certain spots, the brush is so thick it is almost like walking through a tunnel to get through it. He continues to pick his way down the pathway when he finally starts catching glimpses of a large building through the trees.

As he gets closer, Colin can see the building is set back in a clearing but any other details are obscured by the woods. He pushes forward until something on the pathway in front of him causes him to stop. Through the myriad of greens and browns, a shade of tan can be seen. The same shade of tan that is found on the uniforms of the officers who serve in the Orchard Lake sheriff's department. He watches the patch of color through the underbrush, craning his neck while trying to get a better view without making any noise.

The patch of color is motionless.

Colin takes a few cautionary steps farther down the path, trying to remain silent. The outline of a person can now be seen in contrast to the clearing beyond the woods. Still mostly obscured, they appear to be squatting slightly, although at an awkward angle. A branch cracks under his left foot and he stops his forward progress, staring at the outline and looking for any movement. The figure remains still. Multiple scenarios run through his mind. It could be the deputy staking out the area from the tree line and he just hasn't heard Colin approaching yet. It could be a different deputy who is posted as a guard in case his little girl's captor tries to get away. Another, darker, thought crosses his mind. It could actually be the monster, lying in disguise and waiting for Colin to approach the abandoned camp.

Colin takes a breath and gets ready. In a moment, he will either be raising his hands and hoping he doesn't get shot for startling an officer, or he will be charging some monster down with the intention to connect the rock in his right hand with the side of their head.

"Pssssst." Colin tries to keep his voice down and attempts to get the figure's attention again. "Hey! Psssst!"

The outline remains motionless.

Colin frowns. Unless they are completely deaf, there was no way they didn't hear Colin's loud whispering attempt to get their attention. Holding the rock at the ready, he begins to move forward again.

The foliage between Colin and the outline begins to thin out and after he rounds a final curve in the overgrown pathway, he can see there is something terribly wrong. The officer, about twenty feet away from Colin, is suspended by a chain hanging from the branch of a tree above the pathway. Their arms hang motionless down at their sides. A deputy's hat lies on the pathway a little behind them, seemingly forgotten.

Colin continues to move forward, one step at a time, trying to take in everything he is seeing. Ten feet away and Colin knows the officer is dead. Five feet away and Colin is able to clearly see why. The jaws of a steel trap, similar to the one on the ground at the start of the pathway, are closed around the officer's head, and the pressure of those jaws has caused a side of the officer's face to collapse inward. A large pool of blood has gathered under the officer's body. He doesn't need to look at the remnants of the officer's face to know it's Deputy Gates body hanging in front of him.

Colin's grip on the rock loosens and it falls to the ground next to him. The noise pulls him out of his transfixion on the suspended body and he looks down to see where the rock landed, intending to pick it back up. He locates the rock, but at the same time he spots something else lying on the dirt of the pathway. A service pistol is lying on the ground next to the deputy's lifeless right foot.

Colin crouches down and moves forward until he is able to reach the gun, taking care not to disturb the deputy's body. There will be time for mourning later. After Colin has saved his little hummingbird. After he has gotten answers about Alicia's car.

He picks up the gun and looks it over. Colin isn't an expert marksman by any means, but he is familiar with the workings of a firearm. He releases the magazine and looks at the number of bullets remaining. Three. The deputy must have gotten a few shots off before his demise. Colin racks the slide and a bullet in the chamber is ejected, falling to the ground. He crouches down and picks the fourth bullet up off the ground and pushes it into the magazine with the other three. He slides the magazine back into the pistol, clicking it into place, and thumbs the slide release. The slide lunges forward, loading the round back into the chamber.

Standing back up, he makes sure the safety is on and tucks the gun in the front waistband of his pants. As he secures the gun, he feels a solid object press against his back and reminds him he still has the paring knife from the bar. He had forgotten about the small knife. He wonders if any of the shots the deputy fired found their target. He looks at the deputy's body one last time before stepping around it and walking the last couple steps between the pathway and the clearing. Dr. Elyse, Karen, Steve. Too many people have died because of this piece of shit. Colin is going to make sure there are no more deaths at this monster's hands. Going to make sure his little girl is around to live a long and happy life. Going to find out why they have Alicia's car.

Colin steps from the tree line and into the clearing. The midafternoon sunlight streams across the ground, chasing the shadows from the trees away, and the sounds of the forest seem to amplify as though the clearing is allowing the sounds to fill the open space from tree line to tree line. The building in front of him appears to have been long abandoned. The windows near the top of the building are all blacked out. Interestingly enough, none of them are broken as Colin would have expected to see on a building in this state of disarray. Wild grass and weeds have overtaken most of the immediate ground along the edges of the building. An old truck, well-rusted and partially buried by the foliage, sits at the far end of the building near a loading dock. Colin begins to head toward a set of stairs leading to a large sliding door set in the middle of the building.

He navigates around several dead stumps and shortly finds himself at the base of the steps. He walks up the steps and grabs the handle of the large metal door in front of him. He pulls to the right, ignoring the pain in his side, fully expecting the door to either be locked or rusted shut, but to his surprise the door begins to slide open, the metal on metal contact screeching throughout the cavernous room inside the building and outside across the clearing. Although not well greased, the large door slides open without much difficulty.

The room beyond is dark, the smell of dust and wood permeating the air. The light pours in from the open door, chasing the immediate darkness away and giving Colin a glimpse into the large room. A pathway of footprints is visible in the dust of the floor, disappearing out of sight around some old metal tables. The room is quiet and appears to be vacant. He takes a few hesitant steps into the room, measuring his surroundings, determining his best options if someone or something is to suddenly spring out at him from behind one of the various dust-covered machines that are scattered around the floor of the large room. He checks to make sure the gun tucked into his waistband is easy to get to. The feel of the cool steel against his hand reassures him, more so than the small knife still tucked into the back of his waistband does.

Channeling whatever bravado he has left, Colin starts to follow the path of footsteps deeper into the room. He bypasses one metal table, then a second. One foot after another, deeper into the room he goes. The reach of the light from the open doorway begins to fade with each step he takes and the darkness slowly starts to seep in. The path of footsteps gets darker, harder to see.

Just when the pathway is almost completely lost to Colin's vision, the outline of a door appears. Colin stops and looks around, blinking his eyes, still trying to adjust to the limited light available to him. A mix of gray tones and shadows seamlessly blend with the encroaching darkness, leaving little visible to the unassisted eye. He can make out only vague outlines of what looms before him. The door appears to be part of a small enclosed room within the large processing hall of the abandoned mill. He reaches for the doorknob and grabs it, almost surprised it turns easily in his hand. The door pulls free from the frame and swings quietly toward Colin, revealing a gaping maw leading into complete darkness. He again puts his right hand on the butt of the gun in his waistband, ready to pull it and start firing if he has to.

He steps forward to the entrance of the door, reaching his left hand out and into the darkness beyond the door frame. He feels along the edges of the wall around the doorway, hoping to find a light switch. Hoping that if he does, it will work. And hoping if a light turns on, there won't be anything standing directly in front of him.

Colin wasn't looking forward to stumbling into whatever may be in that room, or what may be waiting where the footprints come to an end, without any light.

As if in answer to his brief prayer, his left hand finds the smooth surface of a switch. He flips the small toggle up and a dim, solitary light bulb about six feet in front of him illuminates. He quickly squints, the sudden intrusion of the light harsh but a relief. The light is a welcome sight, as is the fact there isn't anything standing directly in front of him. A short hallway extends away from him for about eight feet before it turns to the right. He takes one final look over his shoulder at the outside world. A variety of lush, green trees against a strikingly blue sky, all outlined by the dark rectangle of the open door. Colin feels as though he is looking at a painting on a black wall. A painting of a different world he is no longer a part of. A world of color and life he can barely remember. Even the sounds of the forest seem to dull and fade away the farther he gets into the building, allowing the silence to continue its reign. It is as if the darkness of this place, as if the overall sense of evil, is so strong that life itself cannot exist here for long before it is smothered away.

Colin looks forward again. The end of the hallway seems to beckon to him. Inviting him into the darkness. His little girl has to be this way. His hummingbird. And his answers. He takes one step forward, pausing hesitantly, and then starts to steadily walk forward.

The turn of the hallway is fast upon him, and Colin is able to see the corner is also the beginning of a set of steps descending downward and making yet another turn to the right. He can't see all the way down to the bottom of the stairs, but the glow of another lightbulb can be seen shining from farther below. Colin cautiously takes the steps one at a time, still prepared for something to jump out at him from the corner as he approaches. He reaches the turn of the steps and rounds the corner, now able to see the bottom of the staircase. Another lonely lightbulb hangs from the ceiling, similar to the light at the top of the stairs. Just in front of the light, a closed wooden door stands stoically against the gray and white wash of the floor and walls. The path of footsteps carved through the dust on the floor disappears under the door and into whatever may lie beyond. He approaches the wooden barrier, pausing before grabbing the handle, and listens for any sounds on the other side. Silence once again greets him. He continues to listen, his head turned a little to the right and tilted slightly forward, as though he thought having an ear closer to the door would give him a better chance at hearing through it.

Just as his right hand closes on the doorknob, a faint sound reaches him. A fleeting hint of a melody being played from a long way away. The tune is gone before Colin can place it, but for a quick moment, a memory of his prom surfaces in his mind. The night a young Colin learned a young Alicia was pregnant with his child and was convinced his life was over. The same night that, after Penny was born many months later, became one of his most cherished memories.

He focuses, hoping to hear something else, but there is nothing else there. Nothing else besides the crescendo of his heartbeat that seems to have found a home reverberating inside his head in an effort to combat the complete silence absorbing him. He closes his hand around the knob, which is cool to the touch, and turns the handle. It turns freely, another unlocked door, and the latch is soon free from the plate. Colin is slightly surprised at how cool the doorknob is. He was almost expecting the knob to be hot, since he has been fighting the sinking feeling he was descending into the depths of hell, or what might turn into a hell, as he was coming down the stairs.

The wooden door swings open revealing a medium-size room with two overhead florescent lights already illuminated. Before he has a chance to look around, his eyes immediately fall upon the chair in the back of the room with small piles of rope lying around it. There is a varying amount of a maroon-colored splatter around the chair. Colin's eyes widen and it feels as though his heart stops beating in his chest.

Is this where Penny was being kept? Is that stain around the chair from her blood? Or does it belong to someone else? As questions flood his mind, Colin fights the urge to run into the room and begin to yell Penny's name. Still standing in the doorway, he forces himself to look away from the metal chair and instead look around the rest of the room.

A metal chest is sitting a little distance from the chair, with what appears to be a sander on it, covered in a thick layer of dust. An empty can of soda lies on its side next to the sander. A large table is on the far right side of the room from where Colin is standing. Papers, various metal tools, and a butane torch are scattered across the surface. To the left of the room, a broken wooden chair sets near the base of a water cooler. A large metal door, closed, takes up a sizeable portion of the wall on that side of the room. Colin directs his attention back to the table and the paper scattered on it.

Crumpled pink tissue paper. Just like the paper Colin found in the box with the ear.

He still refuses to accept that the ear which was in the box may actually belong to Penny. The hair on the back of his neck stands up. She must have been here, though.

He finally steps from the doorway and into the room, walking over to the table and inspecting the rest of the objects scattered about the table's surface. A rag covered in dried blood lies next to the small torch. He cringes at the thought that those items may have been used on his little girl. Colin turns from the table and walks over toward the chair.

As he gets closer to the chair, the slight hint of music dances through the silence again. Only this time, it remains. Colin listens closely. The faint, muffled music appears to be coming from beyond the metal door on the far wall. He takes a few steps closer to the door and the muted sound gets just slightly louder. After a few bars, he recognizes the song. He frowns, slightly confused. At least now he knows why the thought of his prom night crossed his mind a moment ago. The song playing beyond the metal door is the same song that was playing when Alicia broke the news to him that night. It is also the same song they played at their wedding. "Truly Madly Deeply" by Savage Garden.

But why here? First it was Alicia's car, now this song. It's just too many coincidences.

Question after question races through his thoughts, although he is beginning to think he may not want to know the answers. He again checks to make sure the deputy's gun and the small knife are both still tucked away in his waistband. Content they are still there, he closes the remaining distance to the metal door and grabs the handle, pulling the door toward him. He needs to find his little girl.

A metal on metal screech from the hinges loudly echoes throughout the room as the door swings open. Colin cringes. So much for keeping the element of surprise. He lets go of the metal door and looks down yet another hallway. Unlike the last one, he can see the end of this one from where he is standing, and this one ends at yet another door.

A door covered in brightly colored balloons and what appear to be streamers.

Colin blinks a few times to make sure he isn't imaging what he is seeing. The festively decorated door is still there.

He takes a deep breath, ignoring the pain from his side, and proceeds down the long hallway to the next door. With each step, the music coming from behind the door gets a little louder. With each step, more questions form on top of the multitude of questions already there. Thoughts continually cross his mind, mingled with anger and fear. Is Penny still alive? What does any of this have to do with her? With him? With Alicia?

Alicia.

He finally reaches the jubilantly decorated door.

An even darker thought crosses his mind. What if the person who is orchestrating all of this actually isn't a monster at all? What if it's someone who he has loved for as long as he can remember?

What if it's Alicia? It can't be Alicia, could it? The voice on the phone was male, wasn't it?

A new fear surfaces in Colin's mind as he grabs the knob of the door and turns it, opening the door and allowing the music to finally reach him, free from the room it is being kept hostage in, wrapping around him and filling the hallway, as though it's trying to provide a sheltered blanket from what is about to happen.

As Colin takes in the scene before him, as he tries to process what he is seeing, he realizes no amount of blankets could shelter him from what is coming.

The song playing fades to silence and begins to play once again.

CHAPTER 16

THE GRAND FINALE

Colin's first thought is that he has somehow been transported back in time to his senior prom. The room before him is a large gymnasium, filled with candlelit tables and people, and multicolored, sparkling disco balls. A colorful streamer archway, just like the one he remembered, welcomes him into the room. The overhead lights are turned off, leaving the far corners of the room wrapped in the darkness this place seems to exude.

Colin's second thought is of the stench which accompanies the music, now unfiltered by the door. A smell of earth and decay, mixed with a contrasting hint of lavender. The lavender must be coming from the candles on the tables, he thinks. It would be appropriate if he really was transported back to his senior prom. It was a lavender candle that he accidentally spilled all over his best friend's jacket that night. His best friend, Nick, who left suddenly for the military shortly after prom that year and then did not make it home. Mrs. Ellie, Nick's mom, never spoke about him much after he left, beyond telling Colin and Alicia that he left and then the unfortunate news of his death while he was deployed.

Colin always believed it was because she refused to believe Nick was truly gone. Colin made sure he never asked too many questions or brought up Nick at all when she was around. He never understood it himself. Nick never mentioned anything about the military to Colin, and Nick was not the military type of guy. Yet, after he heard about Alicia being pregnant that night, and then Colin proposing to her shortly afterward, Nick just up and left. Colin never heard from him again. A tinge of sadness races through him. At least Karen is with her boy now.

Thanks to this bastard. This monster, who has his little girl. This monster, who may be his missing wife. Colin tries to force that possibility from his mind but it persists. Who else could have done this, known all these details? And why?

He looks around at all the people sitting at the tables. Unmoving. Like a sea of lifeless dolls, sitting in the chairs around each table as though they are merely part of the décor. Colin finally speaks, raising his voice to be heard over the music.

"Hello?" He isn't sure what else to say.

No one moves. No one turns in their chair to look at him. The effect is unnerving.

"Hello!?" Colin practically shouts at the large group of people.

No one acknowledges him. Just as he is about to yell one more time, he hears a reply from the far back of the room, somewhere behind the closed curtains.

"Daddy?"

The sound of Penny's voice erases any other thoughts from Colin's mind. His little girl is here and alive. He quickly begins to move toward the curtains, paying no attention to the other people sitting at the tables. Paying no attention to anything else other than getting to his daughter and saving her from this sick nightmare.

"I'm here hummingbird, I'm coming to get you." He skirts around one table after another, until he is passing the last table and heading straight for the curtain.

"Daddy, hurry, I don't know where he is." Her words reach him just as he is about to reach the curtain.

Where he is? He? Colin attempts to process what he just heard. He hesitates at the curtain, internally fighting what he has almost convinced himself as the truth. It might not be Alicia after all. Momentarily lost in his thoughts, he doesn't notice anything going on around him. What he does notice, a moment too late, is a heavy impact to the back of his head and how quickly all the colors and sounds around him fade to nothing.

≈

The man, after closing the curtain to the stage, walks over to the table closest to the stage and sits down. He reaches forward and picks up a large pipe sitting on the table and rests both the pipe and his hands in his lap. He waits patiently. The head table, specially prepared for tonight and the guest of honor. The man smiles, content everything is in place. Months, years of planning. Of preparing. Of playing this very day over and over in his head.

He's ready. Ready to play the final game. He looks across the table at the only other figure sitting there. The one. She is still beautiful to him, even now, even with so many months of decay visible underneath the makeup he has put on her. She is even wearing the same dress as she did that night. *Not that Colin will even notice*, he thinks.

The man, during one of the days he was following her, watched her pawn the dress at a consignment shop in Shelton. He was quick to get into the store and buy it before anyone else could. He kept it safe for her because he knew one day she would want to wear it again. He remembers she had left the store in tears after selling it. The smile on the man's face fades and his thoughts once again turn back to Colin.

You caused her that pain, Colin, he thinks, *and tonight you will pay for it. You will pay for all the times you caused her pain and you will pay for what you did to me.* He continues to look at the one. Penny really does look so much like her. Feel so much like her. And like he did with her mother, the man has made Penny his own. The smile returns to his face.

You may have taken everything from me that night, Colin, but now I have taken everything back. This thought plays on repeat through the man's head, as though in unison with the song playing over the speakers, until the entrance door on the far wall opens and the light from the hallway beyond outlines the guest of honor. The man takes a deep breath and sits motionless.

He listens as Colin brazenly announces his arrival. He listens as Penny responds. He listens as Colin daringly soothes his daughter and reassures her that he will save the day. The man is surprised the weakness he had become used to hearing in Colin's voice is now gone. At least, it seems like it is gone. Colin was always good with the false bravado when he had his image to uphold. The man remembers those days very well.

He continues to remain motionless as Colin rushes past him, lightly brushing the man's back with his arm. Penny's voice speaks up once again and he watches as Colin comes to a stop in front of the curtain.

The man slowly, and quietly, slides his chair back from the table and stands up. The slight scraping noise of the chair legs on the floor is inaudible over the music playing. He slowly walks toward Colin, holding the pipe tightly in his left hand.

Five feet away. Four feet away.

The man stops once he is within arm's length and swings the pipe at the back of Colin's head. Hard enough to incapacitate but not hard enough to kill him. The solid connection of metal on skull reverberates down the pipe and through his arm. That feeling, long dreamt of, is almost orgasmic. He watches as Colin stumbles forward and then crumples to the floor. He continues to watch Colin a moment longer, watching for movement, until he is satisfied Colin isn't going to be waking up any time soon. He turns and walks back to the table, setting the pipe back down.

"Daddy?!? Where are you??!" Penny's voice, with more than just a tinge of panic, escapes from behind the curtain. The man's smile grows larger.

He turns back to the curtains and finally speaks. "He will see you soon. He needs to get ready first."

Penny's lack of a response confirms she heard him. He isn't expecting her to respond. She will understand soon. And like her mother did, she will learn to love him. No matter how long it takes.

He walks over to the unconscious Colin and grabs him by his arms, dragging his body over to the head table. He reaches under the table, pulls out a large plastic bag, and begins unpacking the contents. He has to work fast to get Colin ready and in position.

≈

Penny stares at the direction she last heard her captor, waiting to see if any of the light from the other side of the curtains pierces the utter darkness on her side. Her elation at finally hearing her daddy's voice left her quickly after hearing the monster's voice telling her that her dad needs to get ready. Ready for what, she wonders. How can it get any worse than it is now? She strains to identify any other sounds beyond the music coming in over the speakers, but the song is all she can hear. The song comes to an end and then restarts. She waits.

Another end and restart. And another.

Just when she begins to think the rest of her life will be spent here in the dark, listening to the song over and over again, light finds a way on the far right side of the stage to cut through the darkness which has enveloped her. Although faint, candlelight and little flashes of multicolored light illuminates a portion of the stage. A shadowy figure stands in the spot where the curtain is parted. For a second, Penny's hope returns and the image of her father standing there floods her mind. Standing there, telling her everything will be all right and she has nothing to worry about anymore.

A voice reaches her from the person standing at the curtains. "Make sure you smile your best smile for your daddy when the curtain opens."

Penny's mouth opens but no words come out. Instead of her daddy's voice saving her, the monster's voice ends her momentary hope she would finally be free of this nightmare. She closes her mouth and just stares at the dark outline until it lets the curtain go and the pitch-black is once again all-consuming. The song stops and then once again starts, diligently continuing on its permanent repeat cycle.

Penny loses count of how many times the song stops and restarts before a whirr of machinery above her kicks on and the curtain begins to slide open once again, inch by inch, until they are fully retracted. The first thing she is able to focus on is her father, sitting at the table closest to the stage, and he is staring right back at her. She begins to open her mouth and stops when he slightly shakes his head no. Her captor is sitting next to him, looking at her as well. Smiling. The remainder of the audience continues to sit in the same positions as before. Stoic. Unresponsive. The man finally begins to speak. Even after all she has been through so far, Penny is not prepared for the events of the next hour.

≈

The first thing Colin can recognize, as he groggily comes back to reality, is the music. The song that was the theme to the love he shared with Alicia. He head is throbbing. He forces his eyes open and tries to focus on the blurry, flickering light in front of him. After a few blinks, the flame of a candle resting in an elegantly etched glass housing comes into view.

The deputy's service revolver sits next to the candle, as does the paring knife. Colin tries to move his arms but they are secured to the arms of his chair. His legs are securely fastened as well. He looks down at his restraints and sees he is now dressed in a dark gray tuxedo. The feeling of nostalgia races through him again.

Raising his head, he looks around. Sitting at the table, to his left, is a figure with its head down, also formally dressed. The figure is unmoving. Colin wonders if this figure is just another prop for whatever is going on here. He looks to his right and what he sees drives an ice pick into his heart.

Alicia.

His beautiful Alicia. His missing wife. The mother of his amazing daughter. She looks older now, at least what remains of her does, but there is no mistaking it is her. He looks into a younger version of that face every single day.

There is also no mistaking she is dead.

Years spent wondering. Spent searching. Spent wishing. Years of pain and frustration and unanswered questions. All of them come crashing down upon him at once. Here she finally is, sitting less than four feet away from him. Torn between screaming in rage and breaking down into tears, Colin forces himself to look away from his dead wife. Only this time, when he looks to the left, the previously slumped over figure is now looking at him. And smiling. Colin opens his mouth to speak but stops. The eyes staring at him are unblinking. Hollow. Dead. The man sets his hands on the table, clasped together, and leans forward toward Colin.

"Hello, Colin." The voice is almost a whisper and nearly lost under the music. "I have been waiting for this moment for so long. It's good to be able to talk to you again."

Colin stares at the man, this monster sitting near him, his thoughts a confused mixture of anger, sadness, and questions.

As though he is reading Colin's mind, the man speaks. "You have questions, I'm sure. I'll answer them in time. Just keep in mind, everything that has happened, everything that is about to happen, is entirely your fault."

The man goes quiet a moment, still smiling, as though he expects Colin to respond. Expects Colin to apologize for whatever he is referring to. Maybe even expects Colin to know what he is talking about.

Colin remains silent. Waiting. As long as this fucking bastard is talking, he's not hurting Penny, wherever she is at. The man's constant smile, coupled with his empty eyes, is unnerving. Colin hopes he will have a chance to rip the smile off his face, permanently, before this is over.

"First, say hello to your little girl."

The man reaches forward to the table and picks up a small black box, pushing the bottom button and setting the box back down. They both turn to watch as a whirring noise starts somewhere near the ceiling.

The curtain in front of Colin begins to open and he watches as a large cage is slowly revealed in the center of the stage. Standing near the front of the cage, wearing a dark red gown, is his little hummingbird. Her eyes meet his and before she can say anything, he quickly and subtly shakes his head. He needs this bastard to continue talking. To give Colin some answers, anything, to help explain what is going on. The ball of anger in his chest is back.

He averts his eyes from Penny's and once again looks at the man sitting next to him, fighting the urge to look over at his deceased wife. The man continues to smile, staring at Penny.

Unblinking. Colin takes a deep breath, the pain in his side forgotten. The ball of anger in his chest growing in size, as if the additional oxygen is pouring more fuel on it.

The man is motionless. Still smiling. The ball of anger inside Colin feels as though it is about to explode out of his chest and consume everything it touches once it is free.

The persistent, unending smile on the man's face finally gets to Colin. "What do you want from us, you fucking piece of shit?"

The man's smile falters just a moment, as though the harshness in Colin's voice is unexpected. He turns and looks at Colin. The smile disappears, and the man's eyes harden, his gaze now filled with an evil Colin instantly wishes could be unseen.

A wave of fear races through Colin's body, and the meteor of fight in his chest rapidly cools down as though an ocean of water was just dumped on it.

"It's not us, Colin. It hasn't been us in a very long time. You made sure of that." The man motions to Alicia. "On the other hand, it was us for years, once I had finally gotten her back. All those years you spent looking for her and here she was merely just a few miles away, with me. She still is, of course, and always will be." The man looks from Colin to Alicia. "Isn't she beautiful, Colin? Isn't she just as amazing as the day you last saw her? Just as amazing as she looked the night you had to claim her as yours and betray my trust. The night you chose yourself over my friendship. The night you went and took the love of my life away from me merely because you could."

The man pauses and looks back at Colin, his dead eyes seething with hatred. "But she came back to me. Not willingly at first, but she did finally come back to me. It became clear to me the only way she would ever be mine again was to get her away from you. Away from the toxic control you seemed to have over her."

The song playing over the speakers comes to an end and starts back up again. As the music once again begins to fill the large room, it all becomes clear to Colin. This whole scenario really is his prom. The night he found out Alicia was pregnant and the night he vowed he would make her his wife. Colin's eyes widen once the realization sets in and a single word escapes his mouth.

"Nick?"

The man's eyes soften a bit and the smile returns.

"I thought you were dead. We all thought you were…" Colin's voice trails off as he realizes that if this is really Nick he is looking at, then this same man killed his own mother. And this monster looks nothing like the Nick from Colin's past.

Nick waits a moment to see if Colin says anything else before speaking again. "Being dead is easy when everything you had to live for was ripped away from you in one single night. I found a new strength in not existing anymore. Strength to take back what I lost. Strength to go back to the night it was all taken away and rewrite history. Tonight, Colin, I will get the girl. Tonight, your life will be the one that gets shattered."

Memories flood Colin's mind. Memories of Nick and Alicia and himself. He looks away from Nick and at Penny, who is still standing at the bars of the cage, wide-eyed and pale. Colin wonders if she can hear what Nick is saying. He wonders if she knows the corpse to Colin's right is the corpse of her mother. The meteor inside him begins to burn again.

Alicia never left him. His presumed dead friend, his fucking best friend whom he mourned over, had kidnapped her and killed her. His best friend who has also taken his little hummingbird. Who has also hurt his little girl. The inferno inside Colin continues to grow.

Colin turns his eyes from Penny and back to Nick, who is sitting there smugly with that smile on his face. The blaze finally hits meltdown.

"You let the people who cared about you think you were dead so you could kidnap Alicia and kill her? And then what, Nick? After she was dead did you decide you wanted to kill innocent people and call it some fucked up game to get revenge against me? To hurt my daughter? Alicia's daughter? For what, Nick? Because you are too fucking weak? Because you lacked the balls to open your mouth and talk to anyone years ago? Or was it because you had to fuck up everyone else's life as much as yours was? You killed your own mother, you spineless fucking weakling." The words flow out of Colin, laced with as much poison as he can muster. He wants Nick to be angry. To overreact, to do something stupid which will give Colin a chance to rip every ounce of life away from him.

Nick's eyes once again harden while Colin is yelling at him.

Colin chooses his next words carefully, hoping it will cause a tipping point in Nick's demeanor. "Alicia could have never loved you because she thought you were a joke. She wanted the man who will always be better than you."

The smile on Nick's face is gone. Colin watches, waiting for him to say something in response. Instead of speaking, Nick quickly reaches forward with his right hand across the table and grabs the paring knife. In that same fluid motion, he leans to his right and stabs the knife down through Colin's left wrist with enough force to bury part of the hilt into his skin. Unable to pull away, Colin watches the knife blade disappear into his flesh.

A searing explosion of pain rips up his arm and down to each of his fingertips. He involuntarily screams out, and in that instant he can hear his own scream mingle with Penny's as she reacts to what just happened. Nick stands up from the table and steps over to Colin, grabbing his hair and jerking his head back hard enough to cause Colin to rock back on the hind legs of the chair.

Nick's face is only inches away from his own. "Who's too fucking weak now, Colin?" Nick forcefully screams, tiny droplets of spittle spraying Colin's face. "Who's the fucking better man now? Looks like the fucking joke is on you because after tonight you will be dead and Penny will belong to me. Just like her mother does."

Nick lets go of Colin's hair and takes a step back. Before Colin is able to make himself focus through the searing pain in his arm and the tingling in the back of his head, Nick kicks out with his right foot and connects with Colin's left shoulder, sending the chair off balance to the right and crashing down to the floor on his side.

The impact causes a renewed eruption of pain from Colin's

right side where the stitches are. He looks around to locate Nick and sees him walking away from the table, toward the stage. He can hear Penny screaming for him over the ringing in his head and the music. Something else also catches his eye.

His left arm is lying across his body instead of tied to the arm of the chair. Nick must have hit the rope with the knife.

Colin lifts his left arm, noticing how weak it now is, and looks at it. The knife is buried to the hilt in the top of his arm, with almost an inch of the blade sticking out the other side. Blood is pouring from the wound and Colin can see it dripping at a rapid pace from the tip of the knife blade. A mild dizziness sets in as Colin watches his blood droplets fall onto the suit jacket he is wearing.

"Daddy, please. Please daddy, help me! Get away from me, you bastard!" Penny's voice brings Colin back to the present.

He focuses his eyes and looks around. At his angle, he is unable to see Penny or where Nick is at. Forcing himself into movement, Colin realizes he needs to get the knife free from his arm so he can cut himself loose. He flexes his fingers on both the left and the right. His left hand barely closes and his right hand has gone numb from being pinched by the ropes that bind it to the arm of the chair. He wouldn't be able to reach the rope if the knife is in his mouth so he does the only thing he has left to do. Taking his left arm, he positions it over the rope on the right and begins to saw the rope with the blade of the knife sticking out of his arm.

The pain in his left arm is excruciating, shooting lightning bolts up his entire arm each time the knife moves. Blood is now everywhere. Only seconds pass, but the pain makes them feel like hours, until finally the rope securing Colin's right arm falls loosely away.

"Daddy! Please help!"

Colin flexes the fingers of his right hand, trying to get feeling back in them. Within seconds, the familiar tingling sensation in his fingertips appears. He blinks the lightheadedness away, grits his teeth, and grabs the hilt of the knife with his right hand. He takes a deep breath and yanks the blade free from his left arm.

The pain causes Colin's world to begin to spin again. He forces himself to focus and quickly works to cut the ropes around his chest and legs, finally freeing himself from the chair. His little girl needs him.

He lets go of the knife, using his right hand for leverage on the slick, blood-covered floor, so he can stand up. Now on his feet, Colin stands all the way up, wobbly from how lightheaded he is feeling. The first thing he sees is Nick, standing at the base of the steps, holding Penny in front of him with both of his arms wrapped around her.

"Pay attention, Penny. Your daddy, the hero, has gotten free. Sadly, he is also going to be saying good-bye very soon. How 'bout it Colin, how are you feeling? You don't look so good. There is an awful lot of blood on the floor where you are standing."

Even through the fog which is forming on the edges of

Colin's vision, he can see the smile is back on Nick's face. A large wave of dizziness hits him and he stumbles forward a step, instinctively putting both hands down on the table in front of him to keep himself from falling over. The music playing seems to be getting more and more muted by the minute and the excruciating pain in his left arm seems to be subsiding.

Penny is still screaming for him. *I will save you, Penny*, the voice in Colin's head yells back to her. His eyes glance across the table and for a moment Colin thinks he sees the deputy's service pistol on the table still. Almost right in front of him. Colin blinks his eyes a couple times to make sure he's not imagining things and his knees almost give out in the process. The dizziness is trying to take over. The blinking isn't helping.

Penny screams for him again and this time he can hear Nick scream for him as well, in a mocking, high-pitched voice. Colin grits his teeth and fights to regain control. The pistol is there. Right there. Not even six inches away from his right hand. It's not his imagination. *It's now or never, Colin*, he tells himself. *Time to save your little girl and avenge your wife.* He forces his head up, makes eye contact with his little girl, and nods his head. *Please let this be the right decision*, he begs.

≈

Penny watches as her daddy stumbles to the table and wobbles back and forth while he tries to stay on his feet. His entire left side is glistening with blood. Nick has both of his arms wrapped around her tightly and despite her struggling; she is unable to squirm free. She keeps yelling at her dad, trying to keep him awake.

The man holding her starts to mock her when she cries out, laughing while he does it, his voice unwelcome from behind her right ear. Penny knows she has to get free somehow and when her father finally looks at her again and nods, she knows what she needs to do. Whipping her head back as hard as she can, Penny makes contact squarely with the man's face, a crunching sensation on the back of her head a confirmation of the connection.

Nick screams in pain and momentarily releases his grip, allowing Penny to break free. With the heels she is wearing and the polished wood floor, she only makes it a step or two away from him before she slips and falls. As she is falling, she can see several fireballs explode from the barrel of the gun now in her daddy's hands. And aimed at her captor.

≈

The moment Penny breaks free from Nick, Colin steadies his balance the best he can and reaches forward with his right hand, scooping up the pistol. He uses his remaining strength to raise the gun and aim it at Nick, narrowing his eyes so he can try to focus. Repeatedly pulling the trigger as fast as he can, he fires off the four bullets still remaining in the gun, hoping he hits his target. He continues to pull the trigger, even though the magazine is now empty and the slide is locked back, as his strength finally gives out completely and the dizziness takes him to the floor.

He doesn't feel the impact. He opens his eyes and stares at

the ceiling, not wondering how he ended up lying on his back on the floor. He knows why. He has lost too much blood, but then he always sort of knew in the back of his mind this might be a one way trip. He knew it would be when he saw how the knife had exited out of his wrist.

He hopes his little hummingbird is OK.

The lights overhead begin merging with the foggy ones hazing his vision. Spinning around and around. The music is barely audible now, as though he is trying to listen to it through several walls.

He doesn't see Penny scramble over to him on her hands and knees. He just knows that suddenly his little girl is there, next to his side, looking down on him.

"Are you OK?" he asks. He smiles weakly when she nods. "Did I get him?" She nods again, taking a quick glance behind her to the left.

"He isn't moving, Daddy," she says. "I am going to go get help."

Colin slowly shakes his head, stopping her from leaving his side, her eyes wide with fear. He raises his right hand and brushes the tears away from the side of her face he can reach. "Don't cry, hummingbird. Everything is going to be all right now. I'm so proud of you, of the amazing young woman you have become. Your mother and I will always be watching over you, OK?" Colin isn't sure if he's even talking out loud anymore. Penny's face, his beautiful little girl's face, seems to be getting farther away as everything starts to fade. "I love you so much, sweetheart."

Her voice reaches him one last time, "I love you too, Daddy." His little girl, his world, is finally safe. His thoughts turn to Alicia. *Alicia, my love, I'm coming home to you. I've missed you every second of every day we have been apart.* He tries to smile one last time before it all finally turns to black.

≈

Penny holds her daddy's hand as he passes and cries until she is unable to cry anymore. The song playing over the speakers stops and starts again multiple times before she finally moves.

She takes off the heels she's wearing and tosses them to the side before she stands up. She looks back over at the bastard who caused all this, still lying on the floor, a pool of dark red blood around him. She walks cautiously towards her captor's body, getting close enough to look him over. Her dad found his mark with three of the four bullets. Two bullets had struck the man in the chest and a third bullet struck the man in the face, just under his right eye. The dead eyes that will haunt her dreams for an eternity are now closed, never to open again.

Penny spits on the man, an act of retaliation more for her benefit than anything else. She turns and looks at the body of the dead woman still posed at the table where her father was sitting. The mother she didn't could barely remember anymore. She looks a lot like the photos her dad used to show her. Penny could see her resemblance to the woman, although she her memories are fleeting of their time together when she was a small child. She wonders how long the woman has been dead. She looks around at the rest of the audience and wonders the same thing. All merely bodies, decorated and posed, so this lunatic who killed her mother could play out some sadistic fantasy to get revenge on her father.

Penny takes one more look at her father, now forever motionless, and begins her walk to the exit. To finally escape this nightmare.

Penny reaches the door, opens it, and steps into the light of the hallway. She takes one final look back, momentarily frozen with the thought the figure was right behind her. His body, however, is still lying on the floor near the stage. Lifeless, to finally match his eyes. Penny shivers and pulls the door to the room closed behind her.

The light reflecting off the disco balls once again takes over the room. The small, multicolored squares continue their circular dance with each other as if nothing has happened.

One by one, the candles burn low, finally reaching the end of their journey and flicker out for good.

EPILOGUE

"Pen, get your fat ass over here!" Laura yells from across the quad.

Penny flips off her friend and then waves, walking over to where Laura is standing. "Congratulations on graduating college," she says.

Laura giggles and strikes a pose. "As if there was ever any doubt," Laura states with confidence.

Penny shakes her head and laughs.

"You did it, Pen, you really did," Laura continues. "Your dad would be so proud of you today."

Penny nods at her friend and looks down at the ground briefly. What happened in Orchard Lake seems so long ago to her now, even though it has only been five years. She still occasionally has nightmares about the events of those few days. Mostly about her captor's eyes. She shivers and tries to push the thoughts away.

Laura's voice penetrates her thoughts. "Pen, you all right?"

Penny nods. "Just miss him, Laura. I wish he could have been here to see me graduate."

Laura smiles. "I agree, I never did get that chance to seduce—"

Another voice interrupts Laura's before she is able to finish. "Mommy!"

Both of the ladies turn toward the sound. "I also wish he could be here to have met this amazing little man." Penny kneels down in her graduation gown and outstretches her arms. "C'mere, you handsome little devil."

The little boy tugs to get away from Laura's mom, who is holding his hand as they approach, and finally frees himself, racing toward his mommy.

Penny scoops up the little boy as he reaches her and stands up. "Did you have fun watching mommy walk across the big stage, Colin?" she asks.

The little boy nods with enthusiasm. Penny looks at her son, who is still a little flushed from his dash over to her, his eyes full of love and life and innocence, and she again reminds herself how happy she is that little Colin's eyes look nothing like the hollow, dead eyes of the man who was his father.

ACKNOWLEDGEMENTS

A large thank you goes out to all the contributors who helped me make this novel possible:

Danielle Phillips

Matt LaFave

Ben Keener & Hunter Hall

Cindy Tucker Blangeard

Wilson Garcia

Ray Lane

Paula Prinzi

Jeff Macolino

Kristina Alderman

Walker Gibson

Adam Porter

Toni Turocy

Linda Wade/Wade Palmer Shoemaker

Tim and Jaimee Johnson

ABOUT THE
AUTHOR

RJ Sundean was born in upstate New York but currently resides in central Florida, along with his cat. (Cat as in one cat, not four, so no crazy cat guy tendencies). He has bachelor degrees in both clinical psychology and business administration, as well as served two enlistment terms in the Army as a paratrooper. In his spare time, RJ enjoys restoring classic cars, running ultramarathons, and spending time in his kitchen cooking.

You can find out more about the author and his upcoming works at RJSundean.com.